You Picked the Wrong Stagecoach

and Other Short Stories from the Arizona Territory

BY

Rik Danielsen

(AKA Prescott Parson, SASS# 104764)

WITH A BONUS STORY BY

Carolyn Danielsen

AND

Two bonus Cowboy Church Sermons

Warner House Press

1325 Lane Switch Road

Albertville, AL 35951

USA

Published 2021

Printed in the United States of America

Scripture quotations from The Authorized (King James) Version. Rights in the Authorized Version in the United Kingdom are vested in the Crown. Reproduced by permission of the Crown's patentee, Cambridge University Press

26 25 24 23 22 21 1 2 3 4 5

ISBN: 978-1-951890-27-8

This book is dedicated to three men who were real Cowboys.

Each one impacted my life in a positive way and have gone home to be with the Lord:

*My pastor—Brother Bob McLeroy,
a great deacon—Jack Carlisle,
and a wonderful friend—Wade Carlisle.*

These men lived the cowboy life and lived it for the Lord.

Praise for

You Picked the Wrong Stagecoach

"Prescott Parson, Rik Danielsen, writes in a way that kinda grabs ya and hangs on. Not since Jack Sheafer has a writer captured the essence of the west as well as the Parson. His ability to reach into the soul of a hero leads his stories right to the action. His stories will keep you awake even after you finish reading, saying, "What would I have done in these situations?" He brings out the real life of the old and new west, with a Christian flavor.

"His characters live. Victoria, the strong woman. The preacher with the power of prayer to change the lives of many. A brother coming home. The sorrow filled drunk sheriff. The Deputy that is just ordinary and becomes extra-ordinary. All are as real as life and given challenges that go above the routine but are there daily in one way or another.

"What would you do in these situations?"

—Doug Ball, Author

"Arizona is a mixture of incredible beauty and harsh reality. Rik's stories give both extremes. There's the beauty of the goodness in people and the astonishing power of redemption on a broken heart. I cheered for the women, especially. They knew the painful reality of being female among the hardened culture of male dominance and the extreme skills needed just to survive. Rik's characters stick deep within your heart. His historical knowledge educates you on a life of guns, saloons, pioneer churches, and the rugged trails through our favorite places like Prescott, Wickenburg, and Bisbee."

—Sheila Jones, Arizonan and Author of *In the Garden*

TABLE OF CONTENTS

Chapter 1:
The Sheriff Faced Two Killers

Day One

It was midmorning when Jim Appleton woke with a start. He was jolted from his sleep by someone shouting his name. As the fog began to clear from his mind he could see that he was once again waking up in a jail cell. There was a small pool of vomit on the floor next to the cot he'd passed out on and, sadly, some of that smelly mess was on the cot itself. Jim had slept in his clothes and woke up with his boots on. "What? What is all of this commotion?" he wondered. There it was again: someone shouting.

"Sheriff! Sheriff! Wake up! The bank's been robbed and young Charles has been shot! Sheriff, wake up!"

As Jim looked around he could see Fred Malone, owner of the General Store, standing in the open door of the jail cell. Fred had his shopkeeper's apron on and his hands were on his hips. He leaned forward as he looked directly into Jim's bloodshot eyes.

"What? What are you saying, Fred?" Jim asked as he shielded his eyes from the sunlight coming through the office window.

"Tarnation, Jim! It's 9:00 in the morning and you're still asleep in this jail cell! Sleeping it off again, are you? Well, sometime during the night, someone robbed the bank, shot Charles Smith and got clean away! Jim, your town's in trouble and you're sleeping off yet another drunk!" declared Fred. "Get up, Sheriff, and do your job!"

As Jim pushed himself up from the cot, he felt kind of woozy. He wasn't sure he'd make it across the cell much less out into the street to deal with this problem. As he steadied himself against the jail bars, he looked down and realized he didn't have his guns on. Then he reached up to feel his head to see if he had his hat on. "Guns and hat? Where would they be?" he wondered. Then he looked at the coat rack on the wall and saw his gun belt hanging there. "Good, now where's that hat?" Before he could find it, Fred was picking his hat off the floor below the coat rack. "Hmm, musta dropped it when I took it off last night," he thought.

The sunlight hit Jim's eyes like the flash of a dynamite explosion. He actually stumbled, it was so bright. He pulled his hat lower and raised his left hand to shield them in an attempt to see what was going on around him. As he walked toward the bank and the crowd of people that had already gathered outside, he rolled his tongue inside his mouth. "Wow! That's nasty," he thought to himself. "Tastes like a polecat died in my mouth. Hope it don't smell as bad as it tastes."

People were staring at Jim as he made his way through the crowd. His disheveled clothes, his crumpled hat, his unshaven face and that smell. Some thought the fact that he hadn't bathed in a month of Sundays was the overwhelming odor. Others thought the stench of stale whiskey mixed with vomit was worse. Either way, their sheriff looked like a mess and smelled even worse.

As Jim and Fred stepped up onto the boardwalk in front of the bank, they could see another crowd milling about inside. The center of attention in the bank was Liam Smith, the president of the bank and father of the deceased. Mr. Smith was wearing one of his fine suits, and his boots were spit and polished as always, but his grey hair was a mess. He must have grabbed his head in disbelief when he saw his son lying dead in a pool of blood. Liam Smith was a gentle man, not just a gentle-man. No one could remember him ever raising his voice. He was able to deal with irate customers with such kindness that they settled down and a reasoned solution for their problem was developed. But the moment he saw Jim Appleton step into his bank he rose from his chair with his teeth and his fists clenched. His fists were clenched so tightly they were shaking. It was painfully obvious that Jim was the immediate target of the rage that was rising in Mr. Smith's heart.

As Mr. Smith took a few steps toward Jim he asked, "Where were you while my son was being murdered, Sheriff?" He didn't shout or scream. The volume of his voice was low. People out on the boardwalk could not have heard what he said, but every word dripped with venom.

Even in his hungover condition Jim had sense enough to try to redirect Mr. Smith's anger. "Liam, I am truly sorry for what has happened to your son. Please, tell me what happened." Then he looked around the crowd and saw Elizabeth, one of the young women who worked at the cafe next door. "Elizabeth," he said, "could you bring Mr. Smith and me a cup of coffee? Thanks." Elizabeth immediately turned to go to the cafe to fetch two cups of coffee.

Mr. Smith straightened his vest a little and sat back down in the chair he had just gotten out of. He thought for just a second and said, "My son, Charles, was working on a very important account late last night. This morning his wife came to the house to tell us he never came home. So I dressed and came in to the bank to find Charles lying on the floor dead. You can see the pool of blood he was lying in and the blood that splattered the wall over there." Mr. Smith's voice began to quiver so he hesitated for a moment and swallowed hard.

"Liam, I know how difficult this is for you, but can you tell me anything else about what you saw when you came into the bank?" asked Jim.

Mr. Smith coughed into his hand and said, "Well, the safe door was wide open and I could see that the back door was slightly ajar."

"Do you know if money was taken from the safe and if it was, do you have any idea how much?" Jim asked.

Mr. Smith looked at the Sheriff with mournful eyes. "Yes, all of the cash was taken from the safe, but we won't know how much until my bookkeeper, Mr. Fitzsimmons, has had a chance to do a quick audit of the books."

At that moment Elizabeth reentered the bank with two coffee cups in one hand and a coffee pot in the other. She handed each man a cup and proceeded to fill them with hot coffee. "Freshly brewed," she said softly. The Sheriff thanked her immediately while it took Mr. Smith a moment to recognize what she was doing. Finally, he looked up and softly said, "Thank you, Miss."

"You are more than welcome, Mr. Smith," she said as she turned away and set the pot down on one of the desks. "There's plenty more if you need it." Then she walked quietly out of the bank and went back to the diner to serve her customers, if there were any.

Turning his attention back to the task at hand, the Sheriff looked at the crowd of people in the bank and asked, "Does anyone remember seeing any suspicious people in town yesterday? Maybe just a stranger?"

The folks in the room began to consider the question and in just a moment one of the men said, "Now that you mention it, Jim, there was a feller hanging out at the Lucky Diamond Saloon yesterday. Big guy, kinda, you know, burly looking. Looked like one of them fellers that would have to shave twice a day, if he ever actually shaved."

Jim perked up a bit, might have been the coffee, but more than likely it was this bit of information. "Did you talk to him?"

"No, sir. Didn't have need to, but I think he spent most of the day in the Lucky Diamond. You probably ought to talk to the barkeep."

"Thanks," Jim said, "I'll do that. Anyone else? Anyone see this man or anything else unusual yesterday?"

Fred Malone spoke up and said, "As a matter of fact I didn't see anything unusual yesterday, but I heard something unusual in the night."

The Sheriff's attention snapped to Fred. "What was it, Fred?"

"Well, last night I got up to go to use the, you know, the thunder pot about one or two in the morning. Just about the time I was finishing, I heard a horse racing down the street. I looked out the window, but it was mighty dark out and I couldn't see anyone or anything out there."

"Good. That's good information, Fred," Jim said. "Could you tell which way the horse was heading?"

Looking thoughtful, Fred scratched his head for a second then said, "That horse was heading east, Jim. Yes, sir, it was heading east and in a big hurry, too."

"If the killer was on that horse, he's got a 7 or 8 hour head start on us already. What about the horse? Did anyone see this feller's horse?" Jim asked.

Another man in the crowd, John Boling the town's butcher, spoke up, "Yesterday I noticed a roan, a blue roan, tied up outside the Lucky Diamond. Never saw it before and don't recall seeing it this morning."

"Again, that's good information," the Sheriff said. "Would someone run over to the livery and see if they have a blue roan there or if they saw one yesterday?" Another man said he would and ran off to check.

Jim looked at Mr. Smith and said, "Liam, you probably ought to go home. I promise you I'm going to do everything in my power to catch the man who did this. I'll bring him back for trial, Liam. He'll be brought to justice."

Mr. Smith listened intently to everything the Sheriff said. Then the fire came back into his eyes. He looked past the Sheriff and directly to the people standing in his bank and said, "I'm offering a $1000 reward to anyone who brings this killer in," he paused for one second, then went on "and I don't care if he's brought in alive or dead across the back of a horse." The man who robbed his bank and killed his son would fall over dead, if words could kill. No one ever spoke with more hatred than Liam Smith just had. At that, he rose from his chair and said, "I'm going home to my Martha now. She'll need me." And he walked out the door.

The Sheriff walked to the front door of the bank and looked at the people standing there, then at the people in the street, "I need every man who can ride and shoot to join the posse. Gather your things and meet me in front of my office about one o'clock. I'll deputize you and we'll hunt the sidewinder who done this thing and bring him in. Alive if possible." At that the Sheriff walked down the street to the Lucky Diamond Saloon.

As he got to the bat wing doors of the saloon, Jim Malone thought about the dozens, if not hundreds, of times he'd walked through those doors to start drinking and how many times he'd fallen out of them blasted out of his mind. "This last year sure has been hell," he thought. It all began when he and a posse were off chasing a band of rustlers who were headed toward Old Mexico. While he was gone his house burned down. The worst of it was that his wife and little boy burned to death in that house. Their bodies were so badly burned that no one would let him see them. He sank into a bottle and hadn't wanted to climb out ever since. The folks in town had been patient with him, but he could tell their patience was wearing as thin as a cigarette paper.

The Swede was tending bar, but since it wasn't even ten o'clock in the morning, there weren't any customers to serve. "Terrible thing, this bank robbery and murder," said the Swede. "Yes, sir, mighty terrible. You ready for something to drink, Jim?"

"I'll take a cup of coffee, Swede. Thanks." The Sheriff said as he slid up to his usual spot at the bar. "Say, some of the folks were telling me about a stranger who was in town yesterday. Said he might have been in here. Do you remember him?"

"Yes, I remember him," said the Swede. "He came in here in the early afternoon. Sat over there at that table in the corner and nursed two beers all day. Ordered a steak and some beans for supper and nursed one more beer. Didn't leave until I was ready to close."

Looking at the table in the corner, Jim asked, "Did you or anyone else talk to him? Find out his name or anything about him?"

"No, you know how it is. Folks don't bother strangers much. If they want to be left alone, they usually are," said the Swede.

Jim turned to look at the Swede, "What did he look like? Can you tell me anything about how he was dressed? Did he have any scars?"

"He was a big fella," Swede said. "He was wearing a pair of dark pants and had on a wool vest. Double breasted one, it was. Grey. His shirt was just dirty white and his hat was black. It was an old hat. Pretty dirty and sweaty, like a lot of the men around here."

"Any scars that stood out?" Jim asked again.

"Scars? Now wait a minute," Swede declared. "Now that you mention it, his left ear wasn't all there. It looked like someone had shot a chunk of it off. I remember thinking that it reminded me of a deer I'd shot once. It had a bullet hole in one ear. I thought that deer had gotten lucky one day, but his luck ran out the day I met him. Jim, I think that fella was lucky in a gun fight once."

"Lucky, huh? Well, I'm going to call this hombre 'Lucky' until I can find out his real name. Let's hope his luck runs out real soon," the Sheriff said as he walked out of the saloon. "Been a long time since I walked out of this saloon sober," Jim thought to himself as he pushed his way back out of the batwing doors.

Jim went back to the Sheriff's office to get his gear ready for the posse. First, he checked his guns. Jim checked each of his Colt Navy Revolvers. He used to carry a pair of Colt 1873 Single Action Army's in .45 caliber, but he sold them a few months back in order to buy more liquor. The Navy's were from the war and he got them pretty cheaply. They were well worn, but still shot. His Winchester had gone the same route as the .45's. Now he had an old Spencer that had survived the war, too. He could hit a deer at 75 yards with it when he was sober, but it certainly wasn't a Winchester.

He went on to fill two canteens with water and picked up a bed roll and placed it on the desk next to the canteens. Next he gathered together a few things he would need in his saddle bags: some jerky, some coffee, a small coffee pot and a cup, a handful of cigars and some matches, a box of shells for the Spencer and the possibles for the Navy's. Jim looked around to see if anyone was looking. When he was sure no one was, he slipped a bottle of whiskey into the saddle bags, too.

Jim took some of his gear out to his horse. The canteens were hung around the horn of his saddle and he slid the Spencer into the scabbard that hung on the left side of his saddle. The bed roll was tied on behind the saddle. He was going back into the office to get his saddle bags when he saw his good friend Robert McLeroy walking down the boardwalk toward him. He and Jim had been friends for more than ten years when they were both in their teens. They'd gotten into a few scrapes together and there had been days when their fathers wondered if these two would ever grow up, but they did. Robert got himself a small ranch south of town and Jim was hired to be the Sheriff's deputy. They both got married within a year of each other and started their families. Things were going pretty well for both of them until the day Jim's family died in that house fire. Like a true friend, Robert had stuck by his compadre through thick and thin.

"Jim, I heard about this business at the bank," Robert said as he approached the Sheriff's office.

"This is about as bad as it gets, amigo. I'm getting up a posse and we're leaving at one o'clock," Jim replied.

Robert put his hand on his friend's shoulder and said, "I've heard about the posse and I'm going with you. I'll have to go back to the house to get my things, but I'll be back by one o'clock."

Jim looked relieved and smiled, "I'll be glad to have you with me, Robert. Hopefully, we'll have this business over in the next day or two."

Robert McLeroy wasn't a big man. He only stood five foot eight or nine. He had a round face and when he took off his hat, you could see that his hair was starting to thin. But everyone who knew him knew he had a big heart. If you were his friend, you were his friend for life. He never picked a fight, not anymore at least, but he never backed down from one either. He worked hard, took care of his family, and helped his neighbors whenever they needed it. His reflexes were as fast as a bobcat's, which made him good with a gun. He'd only had to draw his gun in a fight once and he was so fast his opponent backed down immediately. He could shoot the wings off a horse fly at fifty yards with a Winchester, too. Robert McLeroy was a good man and he was Jim Malone's friend. He might have been Jim's last friend.

At one o'clock Jim was standing next to his horse in front of the Sheriff's office. Nine of the men from Prescott had gathered with their horses and gear ready to ride with the posse. Jim had a little box he normally kept in a drawer in his desk. It was filled with old, worn deputy's badges. Fortunately, only one had a dent in it from a bullet it had stopped and none were blood stained. Jim addressed the men, "Fellas, I want to thank you for coming out today. As you know the man we suspect of shooting Charles Smith and robbing the bank has an eleven or twelve hour head start on us. We believe he was heading east when he left town, so that's the direction we're going. Hopefully, we can find him and persuade him to surrender pretty quickly. If so, we should be home in a day or two. Now I want you to raise your right hand as I swear you in as deputies. Repeat after me: I, state your name, do swear that I will follow all of the laws of the Arizona Territory and will obey the orders of the Sheriff of Yavapai County."

All of the men took the oath and Jim passed out badges to the men, but before they could ride off, Mr. Smith walked up the boardwalk. He said, "Men, everyone in Prescott appreciates how you have volunteered to go after this, this person that robbed my bank and killed my son. No one appreciates it more than Martha and me. I want to remind you that I'm offering a $1000 reward to the man who brings in this murdering son of a…well, you know what I mean. Frankly, I'd be just as happy to see him come into town with a .45 slug in his head." Mr. Smith couldn't help but notice that upset the Sheriff, so he continued in a mocking voice, "But you boys do as your Sheriff tells you. We certainly want this murdering thief to get a fair trial before he's hung." With that he turned and walked back to the bank.

The Sheriff mounted his horse and looked at the men as he said, "Men, I want to remind you of the oath you just swore to. We are going to do everything we can to bring this man in for a fair trial. Everyone…deserves…a…fair…trial."

Town folks were lining the street as the posse rode out of town. Folks waved and shouted, "Good luck, men." Some of the men's wives were lining the street, too. They called out, "Stay safe" and "Come home soon." The men tipped their hats and felt their chests swell with pride. "We're doing something important," they thought. "Folks are proud of us."

The biggest settlement east of Prescott was Fort Verde, a US Army outpost about forty-two miles east. They wouldn't make the fort that day. They had to cross the mountains to get there. They'd have to make camp somewhere along the trail and get a fresh start in the morning. Along the way they came to the little settlement of Dewey. Dewey was about eighteen miles from Prescott and a good place to water the horses.

The men stopped at a small ranch house to water their horses. A large man came out of the house. His trousers rode high on his belly and he wore a dirty grey shirt. The pants were too short for him and revealed just how well worn his boots were. He had his thumbs in his suspenders and a big smile on his round, unshaven face. "Howdy, gents. What can I do for you this fine day?" He might not have been so happy to see eleven men ride up onto his place, but he could see the stars pinned to each man's shirt and recognized they were a posse. He was just glad they weren't looking for him.

Jim stepped down from his horse, took off his glove and extended his hand to the rancher, "I'm Jim Appleton, the Sheriff in Prescott. We're looking for a man that robbed the bank and killed a man. Just wondering if we could water our horses?"

The big man shook hands with the Sheriff and said, "Mighty glad to meet you, Sheriff. My name is Fred Fellars and my wife Sarah is in the cabin there. We'd be proud to have your men water their horses here. The pump is here close to the house and there's a trough you can fill up for the horses. Is there anything else we can get you? My Sarah makes some of the best biscuits in the territory. Could she make you and your men a batch of biscuits?"

"Would that be much trouble, Mr. Fellars?" the Sheriff asked.

"Trouble? No trouble at all. Sarah, she likes cooking. You can see I'm a mighty satisfied customer of her cooking, too," he said as he made a circular motion pointing to his big, round belly. He turned his head to the cabin and called out, "Sarah!"

In less than a second a short round woman stepped into the doorway. "What is it, Fred?"

"Sarah, this here's the Sheriff from over in Prescott. He and his posse are watering their horses and I told him you'd make them a batch of your heavenly biscuits. You wouldn't mind, would you?"

Sarah's round face turned into a huge toothless grin. "Mind? Why I'd be plumb proud to send these brave men off with a batch or two of my biscuits. By the time they've all watered their horses and rested for a minute they'll be ready." At that she turned back into the cabin and got busy making the biscuits for the men.

Fred turned to the Sheriff and asked, "Who is the man you all are looking for, Sheriff?"

"We don't know his name," Jim said. "We're looking for a big man with a heavy beard and a piece shot out of his left ear. We think he's riding a blue roan. Have you seen anyone that looks like that today? He might have ridden through here in the early morning hours."

Fred rubbed his chin for a short minute pondering the question. Then he said, "No, sir, I haven't seen anyone like that and I'll tell you the truth, I sleep pretty soundly so I didn't hear anyone either. But I will tell you that there were fresh hoof prints around my watering trough this morning. Someone watered a horse here before I got up this morning."

The Sheriff nodded and said, "That could have been our man, Fred. Thanks."

The men watered their horses, checked their cinches and rested in the shade of the barn for a few minutes when Sarah came out with two big pans of fresh biscuits. Each of the men were able to take two big, fluffy biscuits. Some of the men ate one and packed the other in their saddle bags, while others packed both of their biscuits.

Jim thanked the Fellars for their hospitality and the posse mounted up and rode off. Fred and Sarah stood in the yard of their cabin and waved to the men.

The posse headed north and east in order to cross the mountains into the Verde Valley. They came to a little stream in the mountains still running with water from the spring rains. The area was flat and had grass for the horses so they decided to camp for the night. A rope corral was put up and the horses were cared for. A couple of camp fires were lit and the men settled in for the evening. All of them enjoyed Sarah's fresh biscuits with their jerky and coffee for supper.

The men sat around their fires rolling smokes, drinking coffee and swapping stories about deer hunts and battles with hostile Indians. The later it got the bigger their stories got. Some of the deer were the size of a house and the Indians came by the hundreds. Evidently, there had never been as heroic a group of men as this posse. The Sheriff must have felt mighty proud to have them with him.

As the men were starting to head into their bedrolls for the night, Jim slipped over to the place he laid his saddle and saddle bags. Again, he looked around to see if anyone was watching and reached into his saddle bag to fetch his bottle. Robert McLeroy slipped up to Jim as silently as an Apache brave who was hunting deer or blue coats. Before he knew it Robert was right next to him. "Well, uh, hey there, Robert. I thought you'd turned in already," Jim said as he tried to hide the bottle behind his leg.

Robert looked at his old friend and asked, "What are you doing, man? You can't be drinking out here. These men have followed you and they trust you to stay sober while we hunt down this murdering thief."

Jim's face fell. Robert's words cut him like a knife. He dropped the bottle and sat down on his bedroll. His hands went to his face as he began to weep. Robert hadn't seen him weep like that since they day they buried his wife and son. "I know you're right. I know it. You know how it is with me. I haven't stopped drinking since the day of the funeral. I don't want to let these men or the folks back in town down, but I'm having a really tough time here. Robert, I'm starting to get the shakes and it's only going to get worse if I don't get a drink. Then I won't be any good to anyone. What am I going to do?"

Robert put his hand on his friend's shoulder and said, "Jim, I understand this is tough, but you can't be getting drunk out here. The men will leave you if you do. Here's what we'll do. You give me the bottle and I'll give you a drink or two at night so you can taper off of the booze. But you only get a drink when I say so, agreed?"

Jim's hands dropped from his face as he looked up at his friend. "Thanks, amigo. I need all the help I can get and you're the only one I trust to help me through this."

At that, Robert picked up Jim's coffee cup and poured two fingers of whiskey in it. He handed it to Jim as he said, "Here, take a little to steady your nerves. Get some sleep and I'll see you in the morning."

Day Two

The next morning the men rolled out of their bed rolls as the sun was coming up. Some of the men brought some bacon with them and were cooking it over their fires. Coffee was brewed and a breakfast of bacon and jerky was consumed. The horses were saddled and the posse was off again, heading for Fort Verde.

They reached the fort just before noon. It was different than the forts on the frontier in that it didn't have high walls all around it. It was an Army camp with several buildings on one side and rows of tents on the other side. There were corrals to hold the horses and barns to hold the hay and the tools used to care for the horses.

As the posse road up an officer stepped out of the largest building in the center of the camp. He walked up to the sheriff as he was dismounting and introduced himself, "Morning, I'm Captain Brookes, the commanding officer here at Fort Verde. How can I help you men?"

The sheriff took off his right glove and extended his hand to the Captain, "Good morning, Captain. I'm Sheriff Jim Appleton from Prescott. We're chasing an hombre that robbed our bank and killed the banker's son Charles Smith. He's a big man with a thick beard and a chunk missing from his left ear. One of the men in town said it looked like he'd had a piece of his ear shot off. We think he's riding a blue roan. Might have stopped here yesterday afternoon or evening. Have you seen anyone like that around?"

"Yes, he was here," said the Captain. "He rode in yesterday afternoon and ate with the men in the mess hall. And, yes, he was riding a blue roan." The Captain looked at the Sergeant standing near him, "Sergeant, did that man spend the night and, if he did, is he still around?"

"Yes, sir, he did spend the night," said the Sergeant. "He slept in the barn last night and ate with us for breakfast. As soon as he ate, he saddled his horse and headed out."

"Any idea where he was headed, Sergeant?" asked the Sheriff.

"Well, sir, I overhead him telling one of the men that he had a cabin somewhere between here and Strawberry. Could be going there. As a matter of fact, he was heading east when he left this morning and that'd be the right direction."

"Thank you, Sergeant. Sheriff, it's about time for chow. You and your men are welcome to eat with the troops. You can water your horses and fill your canteens before you leave, too. And if you'd like, I'll send one of my trackers with you to help you find your man," the Captain said.

"Well, sure, we'd be grateful for all the help, Captain," Jim said. Then he turned to his posse and said, "Men, the Captain has offered to let us eat with his troops, water our horses and use one of his trackers. Take care of your horses and we'll eat with these soldiers."

The Captain told the Sergeant to tell the mess staff to prepare for the extra men and to send one of their trackers to start looking for the bank robber's tracks. The Sergeant turned and carried out both orders immediately.

After the Sheriff and his men had eaten and cared for their horses they inquired about the tracker. The Sergeant told them the tracker would be back shortly, that he had been out searching for tracks while they were still fresh.

About a half hour later the tracker returned to the fort and reported to the Sergeant. The tracker was an Apache who stood about five foot six. He was wearing a Cavalry uniform except he had on moccasins that came up to his knees instead of boots and had a head band around his head instead of a hat. His raven black hair was pulled back behind his ears and hung down to his collar. He carried a Colt in his Army issued holster and belt, but he also had a large knife in a sheath tucked under his belt. He looked to be between eighteen and twenty years of age.

When the Sheriff saw that the tracker was an Apache he turned to the Sergeant and asked, "Does he speak English?"

The Sergeant looked at the Sheriff and said, "This here's Charlie and he's one of the best trackers we've got. Charlie's command of the Queen's English is probably about as good as mine, but my Ma said my grammar was 'atrocious,' whatever that means."

Charlie approached the men and said, "About half a mile outside of the fort I found a single set of tracks heading east. I believe that would be your man. He's a couple of hours ahead of us. We need to leave now."

"Thank you, Sergeant, we are ready. Please tell your Captain 'thanks' again for us. We hope to catch our man and come back this way in the next day or two." At that Charlie got on his horse and began to move out with the posse following closely behind him.

The "road" between Fort Verde and Strawberry was really just a trail that was wide enough for a freight wagon to travel. At times they were going up and down hills and at other times the road lead them through some flat meadows. Several of the men commented that those meadows would make good pasture for cattle. There were streams throughout the country and a small lake. "Water and grass," the men thought. "What more could a cattleman want?" Tall pines and boulders dotted the landscape. Some of the men began to think this was the prettiest country they'd ever seen in the Territory.

About two in the afternoon Charlie raised his hand in a signal for the men to stop. He got down off of his horse and began to look intently at the ground. Holding the reins of his horse he walked for twenty or thirty yards off of the road. He was moving north away from the road to Strawberry.

Charlie got back onto his horse and road back to the posse. "Sheriff, the man we've been following has left the road and is heading north."

"You're sure?" the Sheriff asked.

"Yes, sir. They pay me to be sure," Charlie said.

"Then we need to head north," the Sheriff said as he signaled his posse to move forward.

The tracker moved ahead of the posse. Each step of the way he was looking down to follow the trail and then ahead to make sure they weren't being lead into an ambush. The further north they went the more the trail climbed into the tall pines. This country was as pretty as any man could want to see, but every tree and every boulder held the potential for danger. Two legged predators could hide behind every tree and four legged predators could be waiting to spring on the men from atop every boulder.

As the posse approached the crest of a hill, Charlie road back to them and told the Sheriff to have the men wait there. Then he asked the Sheriff to dismount and follow him. The Sheriff handed his reins to Robert and the Tracker handed his to one of the other men. The posse all dismounted and the horses were allowed to graze on the grass in the little clearing they were standing in. The men began to roll smokes and talk in hushed tones while the Sheriff and Charlie walked on up the hill.

Before the two men got to the top of the hill, Charlie motioned for the Sheriff to get down. From there they crawled to the top of the hill. Soon they were looking over into a small meadow and there at the north end of the meadow was a cabin. There was no other sign of life in the area. There were no horses in the little corral to the east of the cabin and no smoke came from the chimney.

Silently Charlie motioned for Jim to follow him, then he moved slowly to the east just inside the tree line. The men were circling around the side of the cabin to see if there was any sign of life, anything that would give them a clue as to whether the man they were looking for was inside. They walked hunched down and did their best to stay behind the trees and bushes on the side of the hill overlooking the small cabin. They spooked a doe that was bedded down in the brush. The men froze in their tracks as they watched that deer bound out of sight. Fortunately for them she ran down the hill away from the cabin, not toward it. They didn't want to raise the suspicion of whoever might be in that cabin.

After several long minutes and probably a hundred yards of walking like an Apache, Jim could see the back of the cabin. There it was. A blue roan was tied up behind the cabin where no one could see it. Charlie and Jim looked at each other and nodded a knowing nod. They had found the man they were looking for.

The Sheriff made some hand signs to indicate he would go down to the posse and that Charlie should stay there and watch the cabin. As quietly as he had come up the hill, he returned to the men waiting for them. "Okay, men. Here's what we've found," the Sheriff started. "There's a cabin on the other side of this hill. It's at the far end of a meadow two or three hundred yards from the top of the hill."

"Who's in it, Sheriff?" one of the men asked.

"Is it the fellar that killed Charles?" asked another man as he took the thong off of the hammer of his Colt.

The Sheriff raised his hand to quiet the men and said, "Men we don't know who is in that cabin for sure, but it looks like the hombre we've been trailing could be there. There's a blue roan tied up behind the cabin, but there's no smoke in the chimney and no movement outside. Charlie is up there watching the cabin to make sure no one escapes while we are getting ready to move into position."

One of the men in the posse was Michael Flannery, a red headed Irishman. He too had a round face. His red hair was topped off by an old derby hat and his red mustache was so long you would swear it flowed in the wind. Michael looked at the Sheriff and asked, "What's our next move, Sheriff? How can we get the sidewinder that killed Charles?"

Jim snapped to face him and said, "Michael, we don't know if anyone is in the cabin. If the man we have been following is in that cabin, we certainly don't know if he is the one who killed Charles. We need to do everything in our power to take him alive and bring him back for trial. We will let a jury decide if he's guilty or not."

"Jim, you might be the High Sheriff and all, but we know this is the man who killed Charles in cold blood and we don't need no jury to tell us that," Michael said. "We're here to get us a murderer and get that reward Mr. Smith has offered." Several of the men began to respond in favor of Michael's proposal, almost cheering.

The Sheriff gave the men a hard look. His hands rested on his guns as he leaned forward from the waist. "Men, I want to remind you of the oath you took when you joined this posse. You swore to follow the law and my orders. We will do everything possible to take 'Lucky' alive, if we find him. We don't even know if he's in that cabin. We only know that a blue roan is tied up behind it. He might have swapped horses and lit out for all we know. You need to turn in your badges and head home if you can't follow my orders. Do you understand?"

"You old drunk, how dare you lecture us! You can't even stay sober long enough to catch this hombre." All heads turned to another of the men. Seth Burleson was a Texas transplant who had only come to Prescott in the last few months. He was a young man who had proved to be a good hand on one of the local ranches. He stood about six feet tall and had a full head of dark hair under his hat. His Winchester was in both hands as he looked directly at Jim. "I've seen you and your pard here drinking whiskey together late at night when you thought the rest of us were asleep. My daddy couldn't abide a drunk and neither can I. Why in the world should we listen to you?"

Robert McLeroy stepped next to Jim and said, "Men, it's true that Jim has had a drinking problem. But I assure you he hasn't been getting drunk since we've been on the trail. I gave him a drink last night to help steady his nerves right before he turned in, but that's all. I myself have not had one drink since we left town."

The other men couldn't believe what they were hearing. Their voices intermingled as they decried Robert's comments. "Are you kidding me?" "Do you expect us to believe that?" "You liar!"

Jim looked at Robert and said, "Pard, I don't blame them for not believing us. We can't argue with them, but I'm not going to let them take the law in their own hands either."

"Men, I know why you don't believe that I've been sober on this trip, but it's true whether you believe it or not. I am still the Sheriff and I'm in charge of this posse. I repeat, turn in your badges and head home if you can't follow orders. Do I make myself clear?"

Seth Burleson stepped up to Jim and gave him a quick shove with his rifle. "You're not in charge anymore, Sheriff."

As Jim took a step back he pulled one of his Navy revolvers and used the butt of the gun to hit Seth in the face. It was a hard blow that landed directly on Seth's nose. Blood squirted out as Seth fell backwards unconscious.

Jim took another step backwards and cocked the hammer of his Colt Navy and Robert McLeroy pulled his Colt at exactly the same moment. Both men stared down the other nine members of the posse. "You men decide right now if you are following me or quitting the posse. I'm as serious as an undertaker. What'll it be?"

To the man, the others took off their badges and threw them on the ground. Michael Flannery looked at Jim and said, "You won't have a job when you get back to town, Sheriff. So don't come back." At that Michael helped Seth back to his feet and the nine men mounted their horses and headed home.

Jim and Robert lowered the hammers on their guns and holstered them. Then Jim looked at his old friend and said, "Well, pard, thanks for backing my move. Are you still with me?"

Robert pulled a handkerchief from his back pocket, removed his hat and mopped what seemed like a bucket of sweat from his head and said, "Yes, sir, I'm still with you. Let's see if we can't get this fellar and take him back for trial."

As the two men stood there pondering their next move, Charlie the tracker came running down the hill. Jim and Robert turned to look at him, wondering what was happening. Charlie stopped in front of the men, he didn't seem winded at all, which amazed them, but then he spoke in his slow Apache manner, "Sheriff, there's movement at the cabin. A big man came out of the cabin and looked around before he took a bucket out to the well. He filled the bucket and went back into the cabin."

"What did he look like, Charlie?" asked Jim.

Charlie crouched down into a squat like he wasn't in any hurry to answer, "It was hard to see from the distance I was from the cabin, but he's a big man, white man with a heavy beard I'd say."

"Sounds like the man we've been looking for, Robert," Jim said. "Let's see if we can't get him."

The three men tied up their horses at the foot of the hill, grabbed their rifles and checked all of their guns to make sure they were loaded. Robert slipped a sixth round into his Colt Peacemaker and put the hammer on quarter cock. This was no time to play it safe. "A man might need every round in a fight," he thought. As they began their ascent they spoke in hushed tones. "Charlie, I want you to go around to the back of the cabin. Be as quiet as you know how. See if you can move his horse away from the cabin and be ready to set fire to it when I give the signal. Okay?" asked Jim.

Charlie looked at the Sheriff and gave him a look that communicated, "I'm an Apache. Of course I'll be quiet." But he didn't say anything. He simply nodded in agreement. Charlie had been working with the Army long enough to know these white men said things that were just plain stupid and there were times you had to just go along with them. But Charlie did have a question, "What's the signal?"

"I'm going to try to talk him out, but if you hear any shooting, I want you to set fire to the back of the cabin. We'll try to smoke him out."

Charlie nodded and turned to go back to the cabin to move the horse and gather some kindling to use for the fire.

Jim turned to Robert and said, "You cover the window on the west side of the cabin and I'll cover the door on the south side." Robert nodded in agreement, too.

Jim positioned himself behind a pile of boulders that lay about fifty yards from the front of the cabin and Robert took cover behind a tall pine tree about fifty yards from the west side of the cabin. From his vantage point Jim could see Charlie move the horse from behind the cabin. He took it about one hundred yards to the east and tied it to a smaller tree. He was picking up kindling as he silently moved back to the rear of the cabin.

When Jim was certain that Charlie was in position, he called out, "In the cabin. This is Sheriff Jim Appleton from Prescott. I want to talk to you. Come out with your hands up so we can talk."

The door of the cabin cracked open and a voice called back, "I ain't got no business with you, Sheriff. No reason for me to come out to talk to you."

Jim looked over at Robert and could see he was ready for a fight. His Winchester was aimed at the cabin and resting on a branch of the pine tree. He responded to "Lucky." "I don't mean you any harm, mister. I just need to talk to you. My posse and I need to question you regarding a recent incident in Prescott."

The voice from inside the cabin called back, "I was in Prescott a few days ago, but I don't know nothing about no bank robbery."

The Sheriff looked back at Robert. They both knew they had their man. Jim called back, "I didn't say anything about a bank robbery. You need to come out right now. No guns. Hands up."

"What if I refuse? What're you going to do then?" "Lucky" asked.

"I've got plenty of men here, mister. We've got grub and water to last for days. My guess is that we can out wait you," Jim replied.

"That's not happening," was the reply from the cabin. In an instance a Winchester rifle barrel poked out of the crack between the door and the door jam and two shots rang out. The bullets landed in the rocks near where Jim was hiding, but they were high and to the right. Both Jim and Robert returned fire hitting the heavy pine door.

Charlie had started a small fire close to the corner of the cabin. As soon as he heard the gun fire he picked up his burning twigs with a forked stick and placed them under the corner of the cabin and started adding more sticks. Soon he had a growing fire and the corner of the cabin was starting to catch. It wouldn't be long until "Lucky" realized his hideout was on fire. Hopefully he would be motivated to surrender.

On the other side of the cabin, Jim and Robert patiently watched to see what was going to happen next. They didn't have to wait long. Suddenly "Lucky's" rifle barrel broke through the glass in the window on the west side of the cabin and several shots rang out. He was shooting wildly out into the woods. He seemed to know someone was out there, but he didn't know where. Jim and Robert shifted their focus from the door to the window. Again, each of them responded with two or three shots. Jim's two shots hit the cabin wall right next to the corner of the window, but Robert's shots all crashed through the remaining glass in the window. Undoubtedly, shards of glass were flying through the window at "Lucky" as well as hunks of hot lead.

"Lucky" returned fire again, only this time he knew where Robert was and was shooting at the tree Robert was hiding behind. Robert tried to make himself as small as possible so he could hide behind the tree and Jim moved to the other side of the boulder pile and began to pepper the window area with shots from his Spencer. The Spencer was slower to shoot than a Winchester, but the fact that it threw a .56 caliber bullet made up for the lack of speed. Glass and wood splinters were flying everywhere as Jim shot until his gun was empty.

Inside the cabin "Lucky" shifted his weight to the left and sat down behind the heavy log wall. He pulled a bandana out of his back pocket and wiped blood from his forehead. Shards of glass had cut him in several places and the blood was flowing pretty freely into his left eye. He swore under his breath as he reached for a box of .44 caliber cartridges and reloaded his rifle. Suddenly his attention was drawn to the back corner of the cabin where smoke was starting to curl up from under the log wall. He swore again and knew what the posse had done. They were trying to smoke him out. He knew it wouldn't be long before those wafts of smoke were open flames and he would be in danger of burning to death.

Jim and Robert reloaded their carbines during that lull in the battle. Charlie quietly snuck up to the south side of the cabin and hid behind a tree. They were ready to take this hombre if he came out.

"Lucky" moved over by the door and called out, "Sheriff, I'm ready to come out. I surrender. Don't shoot."

At that the Sheriff called back, "Okay. Throw your gun out of the door and come out with your hands up."

A Winchester flew out of the door and crashed onto the ground. Then "Lucky" stepped out of the cabin with his hands up. Jim and Robert could see his holsters and both were empty so Jim began to step out from behind the boulders, his Colt Navy in his right hand. Robert had him covered and Charlie started to step out from behind the tree he was using for cover. In a split second "Lucky" lowered his right hand and reached behind his back where he had hidden a Colt Sheriff's revolver. It was smaller and easier to hide, but just as deadly as a full-sized Colt. In a flash a gun appeared where there had been none. The short barreled Colt boomed. Smoke and flame belched out of that gun, and then a .44 caliber chunk of hot lead ripped into Jim Appleton's right shoulder. Jim was spun around like a top and thrown to the ground.

Robert and Charlie responded instantaneously. Robert sent his own .44 caliber slug down range striking "Lucky" in his right hand. His short barreled Colt was sent flying and his hand was torn to pieces. This hombre would never use that hand to hold or shoot a gun again. Charlie ran to "Lucky" and launched himself into the air like a mountain lion, drawing his knife as he flew through the air. Charlie grabbed "Lucky" from behind and put his knife to the man's throat as he landed squarely on top of him.

Just as Charlie was about to slit "Lucky's" throat, he heard a voice call out, "Don't kill him! Stop! Don't kill him! We've got to take him alive!" Holding his prey closely Charlie looked to his left and saw the Sheriff raising himself on his left arm. Jim was insistent that the man be taken alive. Charlie had no expression on his face as he moved his knife from his prey's throat and used the butt of the knife to knock "Lucky" out.

Robert could see that Charlie had "Lucky" under control so he turned his attention to his best friend. The wound was a through and through gunshot, the bullet went into Jim's right shoulder and exited his back. Robert pulled the bandana from his own neck and used it to press against the entry wound, but realized he needed something else to press against the other side of the wound so he took Jim's bandana from his neck and used it to press against the other side of the wound. "Do your best to hold this against your wound. I'm going to get the horses and the supplies we need. The Tracker has that hombre 'Lucky' under control. I'll be back in a few minutes." The Sheriff didn't say anything, but nodded in agreement as he moved his hand to the bandana on the front of his chest. He lay down on the ground with hopes that would help hold the other bandana in place.

As Robert started to walk away, Jim sat straight up like a man frightened out of a sound sleep. "Robert, the cabin! It's on fire! We've got to see if there's any evidence inside." Jim tried to get up, but the pain in his shoulder went through him like the original shot. He fell back onto the ground unable to get back up. Robert looked at Jim and then at the cabin. The flames were leaping out of the roof like so many dancing demons and smoke was pouring out of the door. Robert knew the time was now or never to recover any evidence that was in that cabin. He threw his hat down, ducked his head and ran into the cabin. The smoke made visibility almost non-existent. Robert fell to the floor and began to search the small dwelling. Off to the side of the fireplace he saw two bank bags. One was already on fire, but the other was not. Robert crawled over to the fireplace and retrieved the bank bag. It was marked "Smith and Son's Bank, Prescott, Arizona." Along the way out of the inferno he found "Lucky's" Colt Peacemakers and picked them up. His eyes and lungs were burning because of the smoke, but he persevered and got out of the cabin. He crawled out of the door and collapsed, but he had what he needed, he had the evidence to convict "Lucky" of murder and bank robbery.

Charlie had tied "Lucky" to a nearby tree and came running up to help Robert away from the cabin. After several minutes the two men turned their attention back to the Sheriff. Jim's wounds were bleeding profusely and they needed to do something.

"Jim, we're going to have to cauterize your wounds. Let me get that bottle of whiskey. You're going to need a good stiff belt," Robert said as he started to go fetch the horses and supplies.

Jim looked at his old pard and said, "No! No, whiskey, Robert! I'm done with that. If you have to cauterize these wounds, I'm going to have to do it stone sober. No more whiskey, pard."

After Robert fetched the horses, he and Charlie built a fire. Robert pulled the bullets from two of his .44 caliber cartridges and poured the powder into the wound in Jim's chest. Charlie gave Jim a piece of rope to bite on and used an ember from the fire to light the powder. The pain was excruciating and Jim passed out.

Day Ten

It was about eleven in the morning when folks noticed three men riding into town, Sheriff Jim Appleton, Robert McLeroy and a big man who looked familiar to some, but whose name they didn't know. The Sheriff and the big man were both bandaged up. The Sheriff's right arm was in a sling and the big man had a bandage on his right arm where a hand used to be. Robert McLeroy was holding the reins of the big man's horse as the big man had his left hand handcuffed to the horn of his saddle.

A crowd started to gather as the men stopped in front of the Sheriff's office. Jim and Robert dismounted and started tying their horses to the hitching rail when Mr. Smith came walking over from the bank. "Is this the man that killed my son, Sheriff?" he asked.

"All of the evidence seems to point to him," the Sheriff said as he finished tying his horse's reins to the rail. "Let me get this hombre into the jail and I'll be glad to talk to you about the evidence we have against him, Mr. Smith."

"Jail? Why bother putting him in jail if you have the evidence to convict him? Let's just hang him now!" Mr. Smith shouted. At this some of the men in the crowd began to support Mr. Smith's plan with shouts of, "Yeah!" and "Come on. Let's hang the murdering thief!"

The Sheriff raised his left hand and called out, "Men. Men. Quiet down now." The men quieted themselves in order to hear what the Sheriff had to say. "Men, this has been a pretty rough week and a half…"

A voice from the back of the crowd asked, "What's the matter Sheriff, run out of whiskey?"

As the Sheriff tried to scan the crowd to see who might have said that he replied, "I understand why you would ask that, but I haven't had a single drink in over a week. This here hombre shot me back there on the trail and as you can see he got shot, too. We've been at Fort Verde where the Army doctor treated my wound and amputated his hand. It was so badly shot up that it couldn't be saved. Both of us rested up at the fort. Me, I was in the infirmary and he was in the stockade. We brought him back to face trial. I've taken an oath to uphold the law and that's what I'm going to do."

"Sheriff, you let us have this man and we'll see that justice is done," said Mr. Smith. "You can give him to us or we'll take him from you."

Jim turned his attention to the banker. These men couldn't be much more different. There stood the banker who was wearing his fine suit and polished boots and there stood the Sheriff in his trail clothes that were covered in dust and stained with his own blood. "Mr. Smith, you and I have both lost sons, so when I say 'I know how you feel,' you know I really do. But I will not let you lynch this man without a fair trial. Please go back to your business and let me do my job," the Sheriff pleaded.

Mr. Smith's eyes were ablaze with anger and hatred as he shouted, "Men, you know what to do!"

The men in the crowd began to move forward and press against Jim and Robert. They seemed intent on pushing them aside and taking the prisoner from them. Jim pushed the men back and reached for one of his Navy revolvers with his left hand. As he pointed it in the air and fired once, the crowd shrank back a couple of steps.

"Stop, please stop," the Sheriff begged. "We can't do this today. We're all neighbors. You know me and I know each and every one of you. In the last week and a half I've had to fight the greatest battle of my life. You all know how I crawled into a bottle after my family was killed in that house fire. You all know I've been a drunk for over a year. Well, with the help of Almighty God and my friend Robert McLeroy I've been able to get free of the booze. I'm sober today and I intend to stay sober. In the midst of fighting off the hold the devil's whiskey had on my life, I also had to track this hombre down. Again, it was with God's help and the help of my friend Robert and Charlie the Apache Scout that we captured him and have brought him in for trial. In the process we were able to return with his guns and a bag that appears to have come from Mr. Smith's bank. At least one other bag was destroyed in a cabin fire, but we do have this one bag. All of this evidence will be presented to the judge when he gets here in three days. Listen, you all elected me as your Sheriff and I took an oath to uphold the laws of the Arizona Territory and those laws guarantee this man a fair trial, just as they guarantee all of you a fair trial if you are ever accused of a crime. I serve as your elected Sheriff and if you decide to vote me out of office, well, I'll accept that. But you need to know what you would be firing me for. You would be firing me for upholding the law. I'm confident that justice will be served when this man goes to trial. Let's do the right thing. All of us will sleep better at night knowing we did the right thing."

The men had listened to Jim's plea and, when he finished, they looked at one another and one by one began to walk away. The crowd dispersed and three men were left standing there: Jim Appleton, Robert McLeroy and Liam Smith. Jim stepped down from the boardwalk in front of the Sheriff's office and went over to Mr. Smith. Mr. Smith was looking at the ground and when he brought his gaze up to look at Jim, tears were streaming down his cheeks. He looked at the Sheriff and softly said, "I miss my son."

Jim embraced the banker and quit fighting back his own tears. As the two men stood in the middle of the street, Jim turned his face to Mr. Smith's ear and said, "I know. I miss mine, too."

CHAPTER 2:
SAMUEL AND SHARPS TO THE RESCUE

The sun was high in the sky as Samuel Holt rode across the desert. It was a hot day, but then again, it was mid-July in the Arizona Territory and days are always hot that time of year. Samuel was heading home. He hadn't seen his folks in five years and wondered how things had changed. He was certain the biggest change would be with his kid sister Sarah. She was only eleven years old when he left home. She'd be sixteen now, a grown woman. "Wonder if she's married. She could have kids by now!" That was a lot to think about but traveling by horse gives a man a lot of time to think. As Samuel squinted to see the next ridge he realized there was a column of smoke rising somewhere on the other side of that ridge. Thick black smoke signaled trouble ahead. That smoke was coming from the direction of his folks' place. Samuel and his painted pony, Chief, would have to go another mile before they got to the base of the hill that hid whatever it was that was burning. The closer they got the more they could smell the smoke, and the more they could smell, Samuel and his pony could tell that it was not just wood that was burning. They could both smell flesh burning, too. Chief turned his head to look at Samuel and Samuel nodded in agreement with him. The closer they got the more they could hear sounds from the other side of the hill. There was the sound of a large fire crackling, but there were human sounds, too. Samuel could hear voices that sounded like war cries. When he had traveled through the Dakotas he heard the Sioux Indians' war cries. This was similar, but it definitely was not the same. Didn't sound quite right to Samuel's ears. He swung down from his saddle and ground tied the pony before pulling his Sharps rifle from its scabbard. He ran up the hill until he got to about ten yards from the crest. Then he crouched down and crawled behind the few bushes and rocks that lay between him and the top of the hill. As he crawled those last few yards he pulled four .45-110 cartridges from his cartridge pouch, one he slid into the rifle's chamber while the other three were held between the fingers of his left hand. His Sharps was accurate and the .45-110 round was powerful enough to take many a buffalo, but he knew he needed to be ready to load one round at a time quickly if there was trouble on the other side of the hill.

He lay down on the ground as he got to the top of the hill; there he saw the small ranch house he'd helped his Pa build burning not more than three hundred yards from where he lay. He could see a couple of horses in the corral near the burning house, but he also saw some other horses tied to the corral fence. These horses had blankets on their backs, but they didn't really look like Indian ponies. Then Samuel realized why they didn't look like Indian ponies. The blankets were draped over saddles. These horses were disguised as Indian ponies and they might have fooled a few people from a distance, but they didn't fool him.

One by one, three men emerged from behind the burning ranch house and the out-buildings, all dressed in loin clothes and wearing knee high moccasins. Their hair was long and black with a head band around their foreheads, but none of them looked like any Indians Samuel had ever seen. They were all too tall, too fat and far too white to be Indian braves. Two of the men had on vests with no shirts and the third was wearing the blue uniform shirt of the US Cavalry.

One of the men was busy shooting arrows into the sides of the buildings. Another of the men was going through the belongings in a trunk that looked like it had been drug from the house. He would hold different items in the air to get a better look at them and whoop and holler like the Indian imposter he was when he found something he really liked.

But it was the third man, the one with the blue Cavalry shirt on, who really caught Samuel's attention. The third man was dragging a young woman, who was kicking and screaming for all she was worth, into the open. It was Sarah! Old Blue Shirt would try to love up on her, but when she resisted and fought him, he would slap her and scream that she was going to learn to love him before the day was over.

Samuel had heard reports of some ranches in the territory being burned and robbed by a band of renegade Indians in the last few months. The Army hadn't been able to find them yet, but they were in hot pursuit every time a new incident was reported. Samuel knew he was looking at the renegade "Indians" who had been burning ranches and killing the ranchers. He knew he had to do something before Sarah was their next victim.

Samuel knew his Sharps was up to the task. He popped the Vernier sight up off of the tang, and estimated the distance to the first "Indian" and adjusted his sights. He wanted to save Sarah first, but she was directly behind Old Blue Shirt and he couldn't risk the bullet going clean through him and hitting her. So, he pulled the hammer to full cock and set the trigger. He drew a deep breath and slowly let it out, taking aim on the fella looking through the trunk. When the breath was completely expelled he touched the trigger on his Sharps and it roared. A cloud of black powder smoke came from the rifle and a half a second later he heard a thud as the 500 grain lead bullet found its target. That thieving "Indian" was thrown back onto the ground never to move again. The others looked at their compadre and began to look around to see where the shooter might be. Samuel busied himself reloading the Sharps for the next shot. He pulled the hammer to half cock, moved the lever forward and pulled the first cartridge from the chamber of the rifle. He quickly slid a fresh cartridge from between his fingers into the chamber and closed the breech by pulling the lever back into place. As he took aim on the arrow shooting renegade he cocked the hammer and set the trigger again. With his next breath expelled, he touched the trigger. Again the cartridge fired, with a cloud of black powder smoke. Again the bullet found its mark. The second renegade was thrown to the ground. He would not bother anyone again.

Old Blue Shirt grabbed the girl and threw her across the saddle of his own horse, with another phony war cry he put his foot into the stirrup of his saddle and swung up onto the horse. He, the girl, and the horse were galloping off headed due north. Samuel wished he could shoot the man who'd killed his folks and was kidnapping his sister, but again he knew he might hit her.

Samuel ran down the hill, jammed his Sharps into the scabbard, snatched up Chief's reins, and practically flew into the saddle. He and Chief would have to go around the hill to catch up with the renegade and Sarah. They had a lot of practice dodging brush and boulders when they were pursuing game or being pursued by someone wanting to do them harm. Today Chief seemed to instinctively know how important this chase was and was doing an exceptional job of making his way through the desert.

It was only a few minutes into the chase when Samuel saw Old Blue Shirt and Sarah. Samuel knew he and Chief had the advantage because Blue Shirt's horse was larger and not as fast as Chief and that horse had two riders instead of one.

Chief had slowly closed the distance between them and Blue Shirt to twenty or twenty-five yards. Samuel wanted to pull his Colt and start throwing lead at Blue Shirt, but he knew it was difficult to shoot from the back of a galloping horse and he knew Sarah would be in greater danger if he did try to shoot.

Unfortunately, Blue Shirt didn't seem to care about any of those problems. He drew his .45 and started slinging lead back at Samuel. Samuel ducked down behind Chief's head and neck as best he could. He didn't want his horse to get shot, but he really didn't want to get shot himself. After four rounds, Samuel wondered if Blue Shirt had five rounds loaded or six. Very few men would load six unless they were anticipating a gun fight. Almost everyone let the hammer rest on an empty chamber for the sake of safety.

The question of five versus six rounds seemed of little importance when the fifth round was fired because that bullet hit Chief right in the neck. Chief went down head first. All that momentum caused him to plow a pretty fair furrow when he hit the ground. Samuel was thrown off into the brush and he tumbled several times before he slid to a stop. He was knocked out and woke up wondering where he was and what had happened. It only took him a second to get his bearings, but it took several seconds to get up off the ground because he was hurting all over. He found his hat several feet away and had to search for a few minutes before he found his

Colt. As his mind cleared he turned his attention to his pony. Chief was piled up next to a mesquite and was covered in blood. Samuel could see Chief's eyes were wide open when he approached him. He looked terrified. Samuel assessed the situation and realized his old friend was mortally wounded. Chief was suffering from the gunshot wound and had broken a leg in the tumble he had taken. He was never going to recover from this. Samuel knew he didn't have a choice. He knelt down next to Chief's face and stroked his nose. He thanked him for all the years he had been his friend and apologized for what he would have to do next. Samuel pulled a bandana from his saddle bag and used it to cover Chief's eyes. After stroking his mane one last time, Samuel stood over Chief, drew his Colt from the holster that hung on his side and fired a round into Chief's skull. He and Chief jumped when the Colt went off, but Chief didn't get up. He lay motionless.

"That stinking renegade is going to die for what he's done today," Samuel said out loud.

Samuel struggled to get the saddle and tack off of Chief, but when he did he laid them neatly under the mesquite near where Chief lay dead. He hoped he would be able to come back for his tack, but knew if things went wrong the critters would likely eat it up like they would Chief's lifeless body. He sat down next to the saddle for a few minutes to draw up a plan. Samuel thought to himself, "That renegade thinks he's stopped me because he shot my horse out from under me. He may think I'm dead or that I won't try to follow him, but he's wrong. The last time I saw them, they were still heading north. I'll grab what I can and head north to see if I can find them."

Later that afternoon Blue Shirt rode right into a campsite like he knew it was there all along. He threw Sarah onto the ground next to the fire pit and swung down from the saddle. He walked his horse over to a bucket of water and let him get a good drink before taking the saddle off him and tying him to a nearby tree. The girl looked around and wondered for a minute whose camp this was, but quickly realized this was the camp of the renegades who had killed her Ma and Pa and burned their cabin to the ground. There were three bedrolls laid out on the ground, pots and pans near the fire pit, and another horse tied up nearby, a pack horse she imagined. Before she could get up and run off Old Blue Shirt was back warning her against trying.

Blue Shirt held out a dirty, smelly hand and cupped the girl's chin with it. "My name's David," he said, "What's yours?"

The girl shook her face out of his hand and refused to speak. "You ain't being too friendly," snarled David. "Let's try this again. My name's David! What's yours?" he said with a growl.

The girl tightened her lips and turned her face from this animal. She was not going to give him the satisfaction of knowing her name or anything else about her.

This time David raised his dirty, smelly hand and hit the girl so hard that she was slammed against the ground. When she came to she was sitting up next to a boulder, with her hands tied behind her back. David stepped over to her, leaned down and said, "Tonight we are going to get to know one another real good. You, you're going to fix me my supper and after I've 'et, I'm going to enjoy the full pleasure of your company. Do you understand what I mean, girl?" The girl stared off into space as though he wasn't there and as though she didn't understand what he meant, but she and the horses and God all knew what he meant. David drew back and slapped her again, not as hard as the last time, but certainly hard enough to get her attention. "Do you understand what I mean?" he shouted. This time she nodded her head, which satisfied him for the moment. "I've shot us a rabbit for supper; you can cook it and some biscuits. All the fixins is over there by the fire. I'm going to untie you now; don't make me do anything we will both regret."

The girl found the rabbit and all the ingredients for biscuits in a wooden box near the fire pit. She gathered kindling and started a fire adding dry wood as it was needed. David had already skinned and cleaned the rabbit so she put salt and pepper on it and put it on a spit over the fire. The biscuit dough was mixed and placed in a greased Dutch oven. The Dutch oven was placed over some hot coals and more hot coals were placed on top of the lid. The young girl went about fixing coffee like this was a normal day, even though it was the worst day of her young life. Dinner wouldn't take long now.

Samuel had gathered up a few things he was sure to need whether he found Old Blue Shirt and Sarah or not. He had his saddle bags, which had a little food and two boxes of ammunition, one for his Colt and the other for his Sharps, his one and only canteen half full of water and his Sharps rifle. Even though it was the hottest part of the day, he began his journey north, hoping Blue Shirt assumed no one was following him and hadn't gone too far. He didn't much like walking across the desert, he figured that's why God invented horses, but on he went. He knew how to follow a trail and that trail told him they were still heading north.

Late in the afternoon, just as he was beginning to wonder if he could possibly find that good-for-nothin' renegade and his sister, Samuel caught the faint smell of a camp fire. He wasn't too close to that fire, but it could be the folks he was looking for. He moved on. In a little while, the smell of the fire was stronger and something was added to it—the smell of meat cooking and coffee brewing. He was getting closer. In just a little while he could see the smoke rising up in a clump of trees about a quarter of a mile away. If this was the renegade's camp, he would have to be very careful not to let them know he was coming.

Samuel carefully picked his way through the scrub brush and rocks, doing his best not to make a sound. As he approached the trees that hid the folks who were cooking supper, he moved to the east side of the trees. He slid another round into the chamber of his rifle and loaded a round into the sixth chamber of his Colt knowing he could need every shot if he was going to win this fight.

Samuel began to move into the trees. Slowly and silently he moved from one tree to another hoping to keep his presence a surprise. After a few minutes he came to a point where he could see the girl near the fire and Old Blue Shirt sitting up against a fallen log a few yards from the fire. Just as Samuel was about to jump out to engage Old Blue Shirt, Sarah moved over next to him. She looked down at him and said, "Supper will be ready in a few minutes, but we could begin to get better acquainted now, if you'd like." Old Blue Shirt stood up as quickly as he could, he looked at the girl and said, "Well, uh, sure. That'd be just fine." Samuel could see something Blue Shirt couldn't. Sarah was holding a knife behind her blue and white checked skirt. She reached up to touch Blue Shirt's face with her left hand. When he moved forward, she plunged the knife into his gut. The look of shock that came over Blue Shirt's face was priceless. How many folks had that same look of shock on their faces when he shot them for no good reason? Sarah let go of the knife and stepped back. Blue Shirt grabbed the handle of the knife and pulled it from his gut with a scream of pain. He looked at the blood stained knife then at the girl who had stabbed him. His look changed from shock to anger as he threw the knife down and pulled his Colt from its holster. "You, you stupid girl, you've killed me! Well, I'm going to finish you off before I die!" Blue Shirt cocked the hammer of his Colt and pointed it at the girl, she screamed, and a gunshot shattered the afternoon silence.

Samuel was probably fifteen yards away from the couple when he fired his gun. The lead slug from his Sharps found its mark in a split second. Blue Shirt went flying back onto the ground. He landed with a crash into the brush. His Colt flew from his hand and landed on the ground. Sarah walked over to where Blue Shirt lay mortally wounded. His eyes were still open and looking around to see what would happen next. The girl bent down and whispered into his ear, "Oh, yeah, my name is Sarah and I'd hate to be you. I don't think you are going to wake up in heaven." At that Blue Shirt took a deep breath and died. In fact, he didn't wake up in heaven.

Sarah looked around to see her big brother standing behind her with his Sharps rifle in his hand. She ran to him and collapsed into his arms. Sarah had not had time to mourn the loss of her parents, but when she got into Samuel's arms the weight of all that had happened that day hit her.

"Ma and Pa are gone, Samuel. They're gone," she said as she began to sob uncontrollably.

"I know, honey, but I'm here now and we'll make it through this together."

The next morning they packed what they needed on the renegades' horses and headed south to start life over on their folks' place.

Vivian Barret
AKA Victoria Foreman

CHAPTER 3:
YOU PICKED THE WRONG STAGE TO ROB

On a bluff overlooking the nearly deserted town of Gillette, three highwaymen sat on their horses discussing their plans to rob the stagecoach when it stopped in a few hours. This little gang was quite a sight. Two skinny white men, and a portly Mexican who couldn't button his waist coat, sat there making plans like generals overlooking a battle field. The two white men, Lefty and Wesley, spent more time drinking than eating in recent months and looked like a stiff breeze would carry them away. They thought they were clever when they nicknamed the Mexican "Gordo". None of them had bathed in a month of Sundays and their clothes hadn't been washed in at least that long. Wesley was the self-appointed leader of this band of geniuses. He'd done time in the Yuma Territorial Prison for bank robbery, and during that time he'd learned about a "sure thing" from one of his cell mates.

Lefty looked at Wesley and said, "Tell us again about how you know we're going to be rich after this job, Wesley."

With an audible sigh and a roll of his eyes, Wesley looked at this sad looking gang of his and said, "Okay, one more time. I was in the cell for a year and half with a fella I only knew as Smithy. He'd been the black smith in Gillette and successfully robbed the stage four times. He says the payroll for Fort Whipple comes through on the stage the last Friday of every month. That's today. We can't miss, fellas, and hopefully we won't have to kill no one doing it neither."

"How come he was in prison, if it was such a sure thing," Gordo asked while adjusting his sombrero.

"Look," said Wesley, "he was in prison because he was stupid. He stayed in town one job too long and was gambling with the loot he'd gotten. Someone figured out what he'd done and he got caught. We aren't going to get caught because I'm, er, I mean, we're not that stupid." The insult seemed to pass right over the other men's heads.

"We're a good two hours early for the stage carrying the payroll. Let's go on and get ready before the stage rolls in," said Lefty.

"Wait a minute. We need to go over the plan one more time before we go down there," Wesley said. "Lefty, what are you going to do when the stage pulls into the stop?"

Lefty wasn't too happy at being quizzed like that. It made him feel like he was back in school and in trouble with the teacher. He lowered his head and said, "I'm supposed to wait until the passengers are all off the stage and inside the cantina and the driver has taken the horses over to the watering trough. I'll watch to see that Gordo has snuck up behind the guard. When he has, we'll hit both of the men in the head and take their guns from them."

"Good. That's exactly right," said Wesley.

"Wait a stinking minute," Gordo exclaimed. "What are you going to be doing while we're doing the dangerous work?"

"One more time, Gordo. I'm going to be inside the cantina robbing the bartender and the passengers. I'll come out when I hear your signal and we'll get the payroll and head out. That's what I'll be doing. Is that alright with you?" Wesley asked, not caring if Gordo agreed or not.

"Won't everyone see us, if we go down now?" asked Lefty.

"I reckon they will," Wesley admitted, "but I'm not sticking around after we do the job. We'll hightail it out of the area as soon as we do the job and stop north of Prescott like we planned. We'll split the loot and all go our separate ways. Me, I'm heading over to California to buy a saloon somewhere. No one knows me in California and I can use the loot to get a new start. Now come on. Let's head down there and get ready for the stage to arrive."

Gillette was once one of the fastest growing towns in the Arizona Territory. It was nine miles from the silver mine at Tip Top. Tip Top didn't have a mill to process the ore but Gillette did. All of the ore from Tip Top was shipped to Gillette. As a result a town grew up around the mill. At its zenith there were four taverns, a large hotel, and a post office. Unfortunately for the community of Gillette, the mine owners at Tip Top built their own mill, which ultimately killed the town of Gillette. The only business that survived was the stage stop which consisted of a livery stable to take care of the horses and a small cantina to take care of the passengers.

Charles Adams ran the cantina and supervised the stable hands at the livery and his wife Kathleen cooked the food for the passengers. They were both the children of Irish immigrants. Their families met in Boston and it was just assumed they would marry. They moved west a few months after their wedding, but life in the west wasn't easy. Charles moved from place to place and job to job until late in life they were running a rundown stage stop in an all but dead town.

The three of them road down the hill and made their way to the back of the old hotel where Lefty and Gordo tied up their horses. "Gordo," Wesley said, "you hide across the street from the cantina, by the old black smith's shop. And, Lefty, you hide between the old general store and the cantina. Both of you be ready when that stage rolls in."

The men took their positions, each one thinking about how he would spend his share of the loot.

Wesley looked around the cantina to get the lay of the land as he strolled in. The bar was directly across from the door and there were four tables to the left. Charles stood behind the bar. He was reading a newspaper while chewing a cigar. You could pretty well tell what kind of food the cantina served by the stains on his apron. He hadn't shaved since his last bath and that bath wasn't recent. A pretty young woman was the only other person sitting in the cantina. She sat at the table in the corner furthest from the door playing solitaire, but she always had one eye on the door. She wore a ribbon to hold her light brown hair back and her face was lightly tanned because of the time she'd spent working outside. Her dress was light blue and freshly pressed. As soon as Wesley came into the room her attention shifted from the cards to him. She didn't take her eyes off of him as he strode over to the bar.

Wesley walked over and stood with his right side against the bar. He faced the girl and looked her and the little cantina over. "Give me a whiskey," he said to the bartender. Charles picked up the bottle and a glass like he had a thousand times before. He sat the glass down in front of the stranger and poured him a drink.

"What else can I get you?" he asked as he placed the cork back into the bottle.

"Tell me about the girl over there," Wesley demanded.

"Her? Oh, not much to tell. She came in on the stage to Phoenix about three weeks ago and just seemed to stay. She asked if we needed any help serving food and drinks here and Ma and I decided to give her a chance. Been here ever since," Charles said.

"What's her name?" asked Wesley.

"I asked her what we should call her," Charles said. "She said we could just call her Victoria. She never said that was her name and she never gave us a last name. So we just call her Victoria. Reckon that's good enough for now."

Wesley continued to stare right at the girl and said, "She looks pretty clean for a whore."

"Now just a minute, mister," Charles said sternly. "She's no whore. We pay her fifty cents a day plus room and board. She makes a little in tips, too. We made up a cot for her in the back room but she's no whore. Seems like a real nice young woman, a Christian young woman."

"They're all whores," Wesley said as he picked up the bottle and glass and started over to the table where the young woman sat.

"Mister, you're asking for trouble," Charles said angrily.

Wesley didn't look back as he said, "Mind your own business or I'll show you what trouble looks like, old man."

The girl's eyes were fixed on Wesley as he walked across the room to her table. "May I help you?" she asked coldly.

Wesley pulled out a chair, sat down and poured himself another drink as he addressed this pretty young thing, "You don't sound too friendly. I just wanted to come over and get friendly with you, miss. Could I buy you a drink?"

Victoria looked back at the cards on the table and said, "I don't drink. Thanks." With that she laid down the next three cards from her hand.

"Come on. You working girls always drink with your customers," Wesley insisted.

"Mister, I'm a waitress, not a whore! You need to leave my table right now," Victoria said as she looked Wesley directly in the eye.

"You're all whores in the end. Sister, you and me, well, we're going to have some fun. How much for a poke? I've got a ten dollar gold coin. Will that be enough?"

Victoria gritted her teeth and narrowed her eyes as she said, "You are making a huge mistake. For both of our sakes, get up and walk away. Please."

Charles overheard their conversation and reached under the bar where he kept his scatter gun. Faster than anyone could have imagined Wesley drew his Colt. The hammer was cocked so quickly that no one heard the four tell tale clicks of a Colt Single Action Army. Now Charles was staring down the barrel of a .45.

"Charles! Mr. Charles!" Victoria screamed at the bartender. "Please, don't do anything crazy. It's going to be alright."

Charles, slowly raised his empty hands and Wesley turned his head toward the front door and yelled, "Lefty, Lefty, come in here." Victoria and Charles looked at one another and then at Wesley. They both wondered who Lefty was and where he would be coming from. In just a minute they could hear the sound of boots running up the boardwalk in front of the cantina. Then a skinny man skidded to a stop in front of the door.

"What? What's wrong, Wesley?" Lefty asked as he strained to catch his breath.

"I need you to keep Charles here company. Me and Miss Victoria are going into the back room and have a good time. I need you to make sure Charles stays here until we come back. Understand?"

"Yes, I understand, but we don't have time for this nonsense. We've got something to do, remember?" Lefty asked as he nodded his head toward the street.

"Don't worry, hoss. We've got plenty of time. Victoria and I need to see this back room over here," he said as he pointed to a door at the back of the cantina. "Watch that feller. I'm pretty sure he's got a gun or something under that bar."

At that, Lefty pulled his Schofield revolver and cocked the hammer all in one smooth movement. Once again, Charles was staring down the barrel of a gun. "You got a gun under that bar, Charlie?" Lefty asked.

Charles looked exasperated and said, "Yeah, a double barreled twelve gauge."

"Reckon you can take it out real careful like and put it on the bar? No funny business now," Lefty said.

Charles sighed heavily and reached under the bar with both hands. When he pulled the shotgun from under the bar, his left hand was on the barrels of the gun and his right hand on the stock. Lefty gave Charles a very stern look, shook his revolver at him and said, "Careful there, Charlie. Put it down real gentle like and step back. Okay?"

Charles put the gun down on the bar very gingerly. Then he lifted both hands shoulder high to show he was not touching the gun. As Lefty was stepping forward to get the gun, Charles stepped back, as he had been ordered to. Lefty picked up the shotgun with his right hand and placed it on the nearest table. After Lefty had stepped back to the bar he said, "Let's have a drink together, Charlie. On the house, of course."

In the meantime, Wesley was leading Victoria to the back room. His left hand held her hand tightly while his right hand was still holding his Colt. Wesley became even more aggressive as soon as they stepped into the back room. He drug Victoria into the room and kicked the door closed. As they approached the cot in the back corner he swung Victoria onto it. She screamed, "Alright! Alright! Stop! Don't tear my dress! This is the best dress I've got and I don't want it torn. Let's do this the right way. A girl wants to be wooed properly."

Wesley was shocked. He'd never heard a woman say anything like that before. This was going to be different from all the other times. He wouldn't have to gag this girl or knock her unconscious. "Okay, fine," he said.

Victoria softly brushed her hair back from her face and said, "Take off your gun and pants and things. I'll get undressed and be ready for you. But turn around, I want everything to be really nice."

Again, Wesley was dumbfounded, all he get out was, "Um, okay."

"Well, turn around then," Victoria said with a little smile. At that Wesley did the nicest about face you've ever seen and began to undress. He laid his gun belt on a small table near the bed, but his clothes and boots were simply thrown onto the floor. Soon Wesley and Victoria were down to their undergarments. He was quite the sight in his stained, red long johns, but she was a vision in her chemise and corset. He turned around slowly, but before she turned around she felt around in her corset until she found what she was rummaging for. Whatever it was, it was small enough to fit in the palm of her hand and conceal behind her back when she did turn to face Wesley.

He was trembling when she touched his cheek with her left hand. Then she moved closer to him as if she was going to kiss him. Suddenly, Victoria's right hand came up from behind her back and Wesley felt something cold under his chin. Victoria was holding a Remington double derringer under Wesley's chin. The next thing he heard was her cocking the hammer. Suddenly he was very still.

Her eyes narrowed and her teeth were clenched as she said, "I told you I'm not a whore." Those would be the last words Wesley would hear on this earth. The next sound he heard was that .41 caliber derringer go off. For one split second Wesley had a look of pure shock on his face, then he dropped in a heap on the floor. Victoria cocked the hammer and fired the second round into Wesley's skull. She leaned toward Wesley's lifeless body and softly said, "I'm not a whore."

She didn't hesitate for even one second as she jumped into action. She grabbed Wesley's Colt and ducked down behind some crates of Tequila. She knew Wesley's confederate would be bursting through the door any second and she had to be ready.

Out in the cantina, Lefty heard those two shots and the thud of Wesley's body falling to the floor. He just stood there staring at the back room door for a full second, then he launched himself at the door to see what was going on in there. Lefty threw the door open as hard as Wesley had kicked it shut. As Lefty looked around the room he could see Wesley lying on the floor, dressed only in his long johns and lying in a pool of blood. "Where is that girl?" he wondered.

Victoria knew she couldn't hesitate if she was going to survive. The Colt was the largest gun she had ever held, but she jumped up, holding the gun with both hands, cocked the hammer and pointed it straight at Lefty who stood a mere five yards away. She really didn't remember pulling the trigger, she didn't hear the gun go off or feel the recoil, but she did see the look on Lefty's face when the .45 slug slammed into his body. It was a look of disbelief.

Lefty's body was thrown through the open doorway. He looked like a pile of dirty laundry when he landed in the cantina.

Victoria didn't know if she could relax or not. She had seen these two hombres, but didn't know if there were any more out there so she ducked back behind the tequila cases.

Gordo had been patiently waiting by the old blacksmith's shop until he heard those three shots. He ran across the street and up onto the boardwalk in front of the cantina. He slowed down as he approached the bat wing doors and peeked into the cantina. He could see two important things: first, he saw Lefty's lifeless body lying on the floor with a large bullet hole in his chest. Then he saw the bartender pointing a double barreled shotgun at him. Gordo wisely decided this wasn't a fight he had to join. He tipped his sombrero and turned to leave. He and his palomino turned toward his mama's casita in California.

It was almost two hours later when the stage coach with the payroll finally arrived at Gillette. When the driver brought the stage to a stop, he and the guard saw the bodies of two men lying in the street in front of the cantina. The two bodies were bloody and lifeless. He looked at Charles and asked, "What have we here?"

"Got a couple of passengers for you. I think they were planning to rob you, but they won't be giving you any trouble now," he said.

"Okay, but that don't explain how they ended up dead," the driver said as he pointed to the bodies.

"Yeah, well, that one with the top of his head blowed off tried to attack my waitress and the other one made the mistake of coming to his pard's aid," Charles explained. Then he asked, "Can you take them to the Sheriff's office in Prescott and see if there's a reward for either of them?"

"Yeah, help me get them into the boot. Reckon they won't mind riding back there, will they?"

A week later Sheriff's Deputy Willy Howell rode up to the cantina in Gillette with some new wanted posters. He went into the cantina and said, "Hey, Charles I need to ask you about that gal who was working for you. You said she killed them two highwaymen last week, right?"

Charles started pouring the deputy a drink and said, "Yes, sir. She did. She was defending herself against them two."

Willy held out one of the wanted posters and said, "Take a look at this and see if this is the same gal."

Charles looked at the poster and there he saw a drawing of a woman who was wanted for murder. The name listed was Vivian Barret. Charles handed the poster back to Willy and said, "No, sir, I don't believe that's the gal that worked for us. It says here this woman is wanted for murder. That's the first time I've ever seen a poster for a woman wanted for murder. That's kinda unusual, ain't it?"

"Reckon it is," said the deputy as he wiped the whiskey from his mustache. "They say she killed her husband. Shot him with a derringer. Stuck it right under his chin and pulled the trigger," he said as he pretended to put a gun under his own chin and pulled the trigger. "Does that sound familiar?"

"Well, yeah it sounds like a similar situation. But it's not the same girl. Any explanation as to why a pretty thing like this would kill her husband?" Charles asked, while trying to act nonchalant.

Willy gave Charles a quizzical look, "You know this here gal, do you?"

"No. No, I don't know her," Charles protested. "Why would you think I know her?"

"You said she was a 'pretty thing'. How would you know if she was pretty?" the deputy replied.

"Oh, well, uh, the picture here on the poster. You can tell she's pretty looking from the picture. That's all," Charles said as he laid the poster down and started wiping the bar with a damp cloth.

"Oh," the deputy said. "Well, folks said her husband beat her pretty regular. I reckon she couldn't take it anymore. Kinda snapped I guess."

Charles stopped wiping the bar for a minute as he considered that. "Sounds like self-defense to me," he said.

"Self-defense!" Willy exclaimed. "He wasn't killing her, just beating her once in a while. She could have left at anytime. Ain't a court in the land that would say she was defending herself. It's murder, plain and simple," Willy said as he finished his drink. "Have you seen this gal or not?"

"Me? No, I ain't seed that gal. But if I had, I'd wish her luck in getting away," Charles said as he resumed wiping the bar.

CHAPTER 4:
VIVIAN'S LIBERATION

It was about ten o'clock in the morning and Vivian's morning chores were all done. The bed was made and the breakfast dishes were washed and dried. She had bread for the evening meal baking in the oven. The little cabin she and her husband, Lincoln, shared on the outskirts of Prescott in the Arizona Territory was as quiet as a church on Saturday night. This was Vivian's favorite time of day. Her husband was out working his claim in the hills and wouldn't be home until the sun went down. She had the cabin all to herself with no interruptions to her thoughts and work.

In that quiet moment Vivian slipped to the steamer trunk that sat at the foot of the bed. Even though she knew she was alone, she looked over her shoulder before she opened the trunk and reached under the bed linens and found her diary in the bottom corner. No one could know she had a diary or what she wrote in it almost every day. She got up and placed the diary, a bottle of ink and a pen on the dining table that sat in the northeast corner of the cabin. She smoothed her simple cotton dress and apron then she sat down and with a sigh, picked up the pen, dipped it in the ink and began to write.

"Friday, October 21, 1881

"Dear father, I miss you and mother so very much. This is one of those days I wish I could come home to St. Louis, walk in the front door of our home and rest in the knowledge that you would not let anything bad happen to me, but I know you are in heaven looking down on me, father. You gave Lincoln permission to marry me and at the time I was thrilled that you did, but today I would say we both made a mistake in judging his character. Everything was fine while we lived in St. Louis, but it all changed when he and I set out for the west to make our fortune. Nothing worked the way Lincoln imagined it would, which drove him to drink and when he had too much to drink he took his frustrations out on me. It all began when we lost our little ranch outside of Tucson. We had worked so hard to build a house and corral. Our little herd of cattle was beginning to pay off when the Apache attacked, burning down the house and taking the cattle. I wouldn't be writing this today if Lincoln and I hadn't hidden in the hills. But watching our house burn and the Indians take our herd was more than Lincoln could stand. That weekend was the first time he hurt me, father. He was so remorseful and promised it would never happen again, but alas, he hasn't been able to keep that promise. He heard men were doing well in mining near Prescott, so we set out once again to make a new start. For Lincoln moderate success is as bad as outright failure, especially when he hears of others striking it rich. He finds enough gold in his claim to support us. We want for very little, but we are not getting rich and that drives poor Lincoln to drink. Recently, I had to resign my position as school teacher because I didn't know how to explain my black eye and swollen lip to the children or their parents. I hated to resign that position, father. The children and I enjoyed being together so much.

"One of the things I remember about growing up with you and mother is the way you taught us the wonderful stories of the Bible. Somehow mother always seemed to find the stories of strong women in the Bible to read me. I loved the stories about women like Mary the mother of our Lord and Ruth and Naomi. Today I am thinking about the story she read to me about a woman named Jael who killed Sisera when she drove a tent peg through his head. I wonder, father, if I might have the courage to kill a man who is so oppressive to me? You needn't worry, I still have the little gift you gave me before we left St. Louis. I have it very close in case I need it.

"Many would tell me to leave the brute, but that isn't an option. One day after one of Lincoln's 'unfortunate episodes' Lincoln told me I'd better never try leaving him. He said he would just hunt me down and kill me. He said no one would ever know what happened to me. Father, I believe he would do it.

"I'll go for now, father. I'm fixing a nice stew for supper from a deer Lincoln shot the other day. It will need to simmer much of the afternoon so I'll need to get to work on it soon. Do not worry about me. God will give me the strength to do what I need to do. Tell mother I love her. Until the next time. Love, Vivian."

Vivian Barret put down her pen and blew on the pages of her diary to make sure the ink was dry. She sighed as she closed and latched the cover of the book then returned it to the back corner of the trunk.

Vivian went out the door of the cabin and turned to the right. She and Lincoln had worn a little path around the corner of the cabin to the entry to the root cellar. Lincoln had put hand hewn planks down for steps and the door was very short, so short that even Vivian had to duck her head when she entered. It was much cooler in the cellar. Vivian enjoyed going down there during the summer months, but even in late October it could be a nice break since the weather in the woods outside of Prescott wasn't terribly cold. Some days were even warm. The walls of the cellar were lined with shelves which were filled with fruits and vegetables Vivian had canned. These foods would be necessary to see them through the winter. Even though Lincoln made a decent living from his claim, there wasn't a lot of money to spare.

Vivian had a small basket in the cellar to put her groceries in. A few potatoes from one basket, an onion, some canned corn and carrots, "Yes," she thought, "that'll be enough." Then she turned to the deer hanging from the ceiling. Picking up a butcher knife from the little table that sat in the middle of the floor, she cut a small roast from the rump of the deer and placed it and the knife into the basket. Vivian took a quick look around the cellar to see if she'd forgotten anything before she started for the door. Satisfied that she had everything for a tasty stew, Vivian went back up the steps closing the door behind her.

Just after sundown Vivian heard the sound of her husband's horse coming up the path to the cabin. She looked out the window and confirmed that he was the one coming. He looked to have worked hard, the dirt from the dig covering his hat, face and hands. She gave a sigh of relief; that meant he hadn't had time to go to the saloon in town to get a drink. He got off of his horse and took his hat off and used it to brush the dirt from his clothes. He took his rifle from the scabbard and leaned it against the cabin wall as he prepared to put his horse in the barn and put away his saddle and tack. He came back to the cabin and commenced to wash his hands and face in the basin of water Vivian had put on a stand outside the door. After washing he came in and put his rifle on the bracket over the door and greeted Vivian with a kiss. "Mmmmm, something smells good. Venison stew?"

"Yes, dear, venison stew. It'll be on the table in just a minute."

That evening they ate their dinner of venison stew, and fresh bread covered with homemade butter without much conversation. There wasn't much news to discuss since neither of them had seen another human being all day. She asked if he'd done well. He allowed that he'd done alright. He had seen a grey fox that morning and wondered if it was the one that had bedeviled the neighbor's chickens last week. After supper Vivian cleared the table and washed the dishes and Lincoln lit his pipe and read a chapter or two from the good book. Soon it was time for bed. To-morrow they would do it all over again.

That next week went by without much variety from the norm. They went to town on Sunday and attended the little Protestant church that sat across from the school house. Lincoln continued to work his claim every day and Vivian tended to the household chores and to the needs of her husband. Sadly, Vivian lived with a knot in her stomach most days. She never knew what would set Lincoln off. She never knew if this was the day he would begin to feel sorry for himself and start drinking again.

Vivian had vowed to herself that she would try to make life as pleasant as she could for Lincoln. "Maybe if I make everything especially nice he won't go back to the bottle," she thought. She made a pie on Monday. He never got pie on Monday. "What a nice surprise," he said. On Wednesday she went out and gathered some of the last wildflowers of the season and arranged them in a vase and placed that as a center piece on the table. Lincoln commented that they made their little cabin look very cheery.

Saturday night was the best night of the week, though. Lincoln had spent the day doing chores around their cabin, working hard as usual. He mended the chicken wire on their coop and replaced a couple of shingles on the house. He fed their stock and finished pulling the plants from their vegetable garden. It seemed there were a hundred things to do. When he came in for the evening he discovered that his wife had taken her Saturday bath earlier and was dressed in her Sunday dress. Her hair was brushed and smelled like lilac. Then he looked at the table and saw that she had baked a chicken pot pie, one of his favorites. It had a lovely crust that was filled with chicken, gravy and some more of the vegetables she had canned late that summer. She'd even added a touch of rosemary from the little bush that grew outside of the cabin.

"What's the occasion?" he asked.

"I just wanted to do something especially nice for you. That's all. I want you to know how much I appreciate your hard work," she replied.

He paused for just a moment and said, "Well, thank you, dear. It's nice to be appreciated."

After supper was finished and the dishes were cleared, Vivian asked Lincoln to help her get the washtub filled with water. It was his turn for the Saturday bath. He helped by hauling in buckets of water from the well outside while she poured in water she'd heated on the stove to warm it up. After the tub was filled and seemed to be the right temperature, Lincoln undressed and stepped in. He lowered himself down slowly so as to get used to the warm water. He reached for the soap and a wash cloth which Vivian had placed on a chair next to the tub.

Vivian had stepped into the little bedroom in the corner of the cabin and called back to Lincoln, "I'll be right there to help scrub your back."

"Um, okay," he said in reply.

In just a few minutes Vivian was back beside the washtub. When Lincoln looked up at her he was surprised to see that she had taken off her dress and let her hair down. There she was dressed only in her drawers and her chemise. She knelt down next to the tub and took the soap and wash cloth from her speechless husband.

He could smell the lilac water she'd put on, when she leaned close to begin washing his back. He felt a little light headed with her so close, so nearly naked and smelling so sweet. But then she quit washing his back and started washing his front. "We've never done anything like that before," he thought. Then she leaned in and began to kiss him. First, the kisses were soft and tender and then they became more passionate. In just a moment they both stood and Lincoln stepped out of the tub. They embraced and kissed even more passionately. Somehow, almost magically, they were in the bed making love. It was the most passionate love making they had ever experienced and it was sweet.

The next day was Sunday. They rose as usual, did what chores needed to be done and had a quiet breakfast together. Whenever their eyes met, they would both smile a very silly smile, a smile that said, "Last night was really nice", but neither one said a word about it. Lincoln hitched up the buckboard and they rode into town. The church was filled as usual, but that day neither Lincoln nor Vivian could have told you one hymn they sang or one verse of scripture the pastor read. Their minds and hearts were simply filled with the joy of their love for one another. It was almost like the feeling they had when they were newlyweds. All the way home Vivian's mind was filled with thoughts about how things were going to be different, no, not different, better, much, much better.

That next week started off like any other week. Lincoln and Vivian went about their work, he at his claim and she at home. Everything was nice. He was attentive to her and she worked to please him. Wednesday evening Vivian served another venison stew with biscuits, homemade butter and apple jelly. Lincoln liked the apple jelly. After dinner, Lincoln looked at Vivian and said, "I'm going to have to go into town tomorrow. Gotta pick up some supplies."

"Oh," Vivian said. "Would you like me to go along?"

"No need to, dear," Lincoln said as he lit his pipe. "I need some large spikes, some timbers and a few other little things for the claim. It won't take me long. I'll be home in time for supper."

Vivian looked at Lincoln, studying his face. "Well, alright then." She hadn't felt the knot in her stomach for almost a week and a half, but there it was again. Should she be worried? "No, no need to worry. I'm sure of it," she thought to herself and she busied herself with the supper dishes so she wouldn't have time to worry.

Thursday evening Vivian prepared a venison roast with potatoes and carrots. Her fresh bread filled the house with a lovely aroma. The sun went down earlier in the fall and winter and he always tried to be home by sundown, but Lincoln was late for dinner. Five-thirty came and went and so did six o'clock. Dinner was going to be cold. Vivian stood at the window looking, wondering, no worrying, about what kept Lincoln. Then she could see a figure riding up the trail to the house. Was that Lincoln? If it was there was trouble because that figure couldn't sit up straight in the buckboard. He kept swaying from side to side. As he drew closer she could see that it was Lincoln, but she could also see that he had been drinking. The knot in her stomach got even tighter.

Lincoln climbed down from the buckboard and stumbled. He had to hold on to the wagon while he got his legs under him. He left the horses hitched up while he came in. The door opened with a crash and Lincoln burst into the cabin. It took him a long moment to get his bearings and close the door. When he saw Vivian standing by the door he took off his hat, bowed and said, "Madame."

Vivian had to work to keep her composure. She looked at her drunken knight in rumpled armor and said, "Lincoln, you're later than I expected. Is everything alright?"

Lincoln threw his hat into the room as he straightened up, "Of course everything's alright, dear. What could possibly be wrong?"

"I don't know, Lincoln. I'm just asking," she replied. "Your supper has gotten cold. Would you like me to warm it up for you?"

Lincoln swore then looked at his wife and said, "How did my supper get cold? You know I work hard and all I ask for is a hot meal when I come home. No! Don't warm it up. I'll just eat it cold." With that Lincoln stumbled to the table and sat down at its head. He picked up a knife and fork and said, "Well, where is this cold supper?"

Vivian hurried to slice some of the venison roast and dish up some of the potatoes and carrots. She set them on the table in front of him and brought him a cup of coffee. Lincoln took a bite of the venison and then of the vegetables. He swore again and then violently pushed the plate off of the table and onto the floor. Angrily he swore again and said, "I'll put the horses up. When I come back I'm going to bed without a proper meal. Thank you very much!"

Vivian couldn't stand it any longer. She stood in front of Lincoln and asked, "Lincoln, what has happened? Why are you so angry? Why have you been drinking? I don't understand."

Lincoln stood up as straight as he could, pulled at the bottom of his vest and straightened it. "If you must know I learned that Mex, Juan Valencia, hit a rich vein of gold this past month. And do you know what tops it off? His strike is only ten miles from my measly claim. Ten miles! Why would the good Lord allow a Mex like Valencia to strike it rich, while a white man like me struggles to keep a roof over his family's heads? Why?"

"Where did you hear such news, Lincoln," Vivian asked, not really knowing what else to say.

"I heard it from some of the men down at the general store, if you must know," Lincoln said with a scowl. "Several of the men were talking about it. They say it's one of the best claims in the whole territory! Seriously, how many beans can one Mex eat?! Why does he need one of the best claims in the territory? Where's my mother lode? Don't we deserve to get rich?" he asked while pounding on his chest and pointing back and forth between himself and his wife.

Vivian knew it was useless to try to discuss this logically when Lincoln had too much to drink so she moved out of his way and let him tend to the horses.

That night Lincoln fell into bed and passed out. The next morning Vivian was up at the crack of dawn as usual fixing Lincoln his breakfast and simply trying to stay out of his way. He ate his eggs, bacon and biscuits and washed them all down with two cups of coffee without so much as a "Good morning" to his wife. She packed his lunch bucket for him and he went off to work his "measly" claim like he always did.

That night Lincoln came home drunker and angrier than the night before. He swore a blue streak and nothing satisfied him. The knot in Vivian's stomach grew tighter and tighter as the evening went on. She continued to fix Lincoln's supper, but he ate very little of it and snarled every minute or two. She knew the best thing she could do was stay out of his way.

Lincoln stumbled through a few evening chores then sat down on the front porch of the cabin to smoke his pipe. Before long he had lain down and fallen asleep. Vivian found him there sleeping off his drunk and went into the cabin to fetch a blanket to put over him.

Saturday morning was as awkward as any married couple had experienced. Lincoln was still half lit up from the night before. He had nothing to say to his wife and she didn't know what to say to him. She cooked breakfast like she always did, but he only drank a cup of coffee then went back outside. Vivian watched through the front window as Lincoln saddled his horse and left. It looked like he was going to town again. Vivian knew he would come back drunk and trouble would be his companion.

She spent the day cleaning the cabin from top to bottom. Whatever was going to happen that evening was going to happen in a clean home. Vivian wasn't hungry for a noon meal, but she did prepare her usual supper for herself and Lincoln. She thought about putting on her Sunday dress, but decided things might get messy when Lincoln got home and there was no use getting her best dress soiled or torn.

The supper hour came and went. Lincoln did not come home in time to eat. Vivian did eat, however. She sat at the table by herself. The table was lit with a candle and her meal of roast venison, boiled potatoes, and green beans canned from the garden was consumed in silence, but Vivian had decided if this was how it was going to be, she would make the most of it. She put the leftovers in the cool pantry she had sitting against the north wall of the cabin, washed the dishes and put them away. She lit the kerosene lamp and sat down to read while she waited for Lincoln to find his way home. Two hours later he did find his way home, or more likely his horse found his way home as Lincoln was too drunk to have found his way on his own.

Vivian heard Lincoln coming up the trail long before she could see him. He was swearing up a storm. He was yelling about that "blamed spic" getting rich and he was asking where his gold strike was. He was angry and he was sloppy drunk. Vivian knew this was a dangerous combination. She screwed up her courage and waited for him to come into the cabin.

After Lincoln fell off his horse and managed to stand up, he began yelling for his wife. "Where's Mrs. Barrett? Vivian Barrett, where are you? Why aren't you out here to greet your loving husband?" Vivian was glad they lived a long way from their nearest neighbors. She would be mortified to think anyone could hear how Lincoln was carrying on.

Suddenly the door flew open and Lincoln stumbled into the cabin. Vivian was standing in the middle of the room with her hands folded on her abdomen. Her face showed no emotion as she faced the man she had married and had suffered so much from. "Oh, there you are, Mrs. Barrett. Where is my supper?" Lincoln yelled.

"Lincoln, supper has come and gone. If you really want something to eat, you'll find your supper in the cool pantry yonder. You are drunk!" Vivian said. She had found her voice. She wasn't going to be bullied or beaten again, not without fighting back, at least.

Vivian's words hit Lincoln like a slap in the face. For one quick moment he was shocked. Then he began to move toward her. His movements were slow, but deliberate and his eyes were fixed on her. Lincoln began to speak to her again, "Yes, I'm drunk! What are you going to do about it, you whore?" he asked.

Those words could not have shocked Vivian more. "Whore? Who are you calling a whore? I've never been unfaithful to you!" Vivian said.

"The way you made love to me the other night. Why you came on to me like a whore. Everyone knows men are supposed to initiate love making. You smelled like and acted like a whore that night. You, I'm calling you a whore," Lincoln said as he continued to walk across the cabin toward his wife.

Vivian stood there with her mouth open. She simply could not believe what she was hearing. She was stunned for just a second, then she forced herself to come out of it. She shook her head and thought to herself, "You know what you have to do tonight, Vivian Barrett. If you don't he will kill you."

In a flash Lincoln was within an arm's length of his wife. He swung his right hand and slapped her so hard that she fell to the floor. She scrambled to get up before he could hit or kick her. Then she literally ran right up to him. She was so close to him he couldn't swing his fists at her. In that instant she reached into the pocket on her apron and drew something out with her right hand. It was a Remington Double Derringer. Lincoln couldn't see what she was doing so the feel of the cold steel under his chin and the sound of the hammer cocking was a complete surprise to him. Vivian did not hesitate; she pulled the trigger and the .41 caliber bullet went up into Lincoln's skull. In the next split second she could see that Lincoln realized what had happened. His eyes were wide open and he looked down at her in disbelief. Then his eyes closed and he fell to the floor like a lifeless sack of potatoes.

Vivian looked at her husband's lifeless body and said, "I'm not a whore, Lincoln Barrett. Not yours. Not anyone else's." Then she shouted as if that would help a dead man hear her, "I'm not a whore!" The next sound in the room was the hammer of her derringer being cocked again and one more shot was fired. This time the shot was into his cold, stoney heart.

The next few minutes were spent in quiet contemplation. Vivian had pulled a chair out from the table and sat down. These thoughts were not new to her. She had been planning for some time what she would do if and when she had to kill her husband. She rehearsed the plan in her mind and refined them down to the last detail. Then she began to execute the plan.

One of the hardest things she would have to do was to drag her husband's lifeless body down to the root cellar. She put her hands under his shoulders and pulled. It probably took her a half an hour to get him out of the cabin and around to the side where the steps to the cellar were. Fortunately she had plenty of time and was able to stop for a rest when needed. Once she got him down into the cellar she laid him out straight and crossed his arms over his chest. She thought that was how a funeral director would do it. The idea of setting him up in the chair in the cellar had crossed her mind, but after dragging him down there she decided he was simply not worth that much trouble. He would be fine down there just the way he was. His body would last for quite a while since the cool weather of fall was upon them.

Vivian set out to execute the rest of the plan. She knew she had blood on her face and hands so took a hot Saturday night bath. At first she couldn't decide what to do with her blood stained dress, but decided that since it was her every day, work around the house and garden dress, she would simply get rid of it by putting it in the fire place.

She went to bed that night wishing she had not had to kill Lincoln, but knowing that if she had not, she would likely be the person stretched out in the cellar. She nodded off to sleep knowing that tomorrow was a new day.

The next day Vivian hitched up the horse to the buckboard and went to church like she always did. When folks inquired about Lincoln she would simply say, "Oh, he's not feeling well at all and told me to come to church by myself today."

One of the members of the congregation was a man she only knew as Red who ran the stagecoach station in Prescott. Red was a portly little man. His vest was barely able to cover his round little stomach and his shirt needed a good laundering. He didn't shave often and his teeth, well, the teeth he had left were tobacco stained and his breath had that stale coffee and tobacco odor. He got the nickname "Red" when he was young. His hair and beard had been red in color. Even though he had very little hair left and none of it was red any longer, the nickname remained. Vivian approached him and inquired about the next stage to Phoenix. He scratched his head like he had a hard time remembering, but then said, "Well, Mrs. Barrett, there's one stage that comes every day, but it runs through the Black Canyon and is pretty rough. The stage that comes up from Wickenburg uses a much better road, but it only comes up Monday, Wednesday, and Friday. It'll arrive 'bout noon and leave again 'bout 1:30. Why do you ask?"

"I was hoping to go to Phoenix to get a train to St. Louis to see my sister. I'm told she's not well and needs some help," Vivian explained.

"Well, ma'am, you'll have to take the stage all the way to Maricopa then. The railroad runs to Maricopa, but hasn't made its way to Phoenix yet," Lefty said.

"Oh," Vivian said. She spent a second pondering the information Red had given her. Then she said as much to herself as to him, "I don't believe I can be ready by tomorrow. I'll have to leave on Wednesday." Remembering Red was standing there, she turned to him and said, "Thank you for that information. I guess I'll see you on Wednesday then."

Red tipped his hat to Mrs. Barrett as she turned to walk away, "Good day to you, Mrs. Barrett."

Vivian turned back to him and said, "It is, it is a good day isn't it?" She walked straight to her buckboard with a little smile on her face. It'd been a while since she had smiled. It felt good.

Monday was spent cleaning the cabin and cleaning her clothes. Tuesday she tended to the livestock and packed her suitcase. She wanted everything to be "just so" when she left. Someday someone was going to find out what had happened there and she didn't want anyone to be able to say she hadn't been a good wife and housekeeper.

Wednesday morning couldn't come soon enough. Vivian fixed her breakfast and cleaned the dishes. She hitched the horse up to the buckboard again and put her suitcase in the back. Before she left she went down to the cellar for the first time since Saturday night. There he was, looking like he was taking a leisurely nap on the floor. Vivian looked at Lincoln's corpse and said, "Well, this is good-bye, Lincoln. I tried to be a good wife to you, but you were a monster. Liquor was your downfall. You would have killed me if I'd let you, but I wasn't about to let you. You weren't happy with the life we had together. What we had wasn't enough for you. I don't know if you are in heaven or hell today, Lincoln, but I do know that you won't hurt me or anyone else ever again. Good-bye."

With that Vivian left the cellar once and for all. She closed the door and never looked back. She enjoyed the buckboard ride into town. It was a quiet, cool, fall day in the prettiest part of the Territory. She would miss these woods, but she was glad to be free and on her way to a new life.

She reached town about 11:00 and went straight to the livery. She asked the boy working there to care for her horse. "My husband will come get him and the buckboard later in the week when he is feeling better," she said. Then she went to the Stagecoach Station and paid her fare for Maricopa. The diner was her next stop. She had a light dinner and then went back to the Stagecoach Station to wait for the stage to be ready to leave. At 1:30 the driver announced that they were ready to leave. Vivian's suitcase had been put in the boot and she was given a hand up into the coach. Vivian got a seat facing forward. She never wanted to look back.

The folks at the livery got worried when Lincoln hadn't come for his horse and buckboard after a week, but they were sure he would come any day. When a second and then a third week passed, they decided the bill was getting too big to ignore. They went to the Sheriff and expressed their concern that something might be wrong with Lincoln Barrett so the next day the he road out to the Barrett place to see if there was a problem. When he arrived he noticed the gate to the chicken coop was open and the chickens were all over the yard pecking for bugs. He knocked on the door of the cabin, but no one answered. Slowly he opened the door while calling out, "Lincoln? Mrs. Barrett? Anyone home?" but no one answered. What he saw was no real surprise. The cabin was as neat as a pin. Everything was clean and in its place. The only thing that seemed odd was that it looked like no one had been there in a while. There was a fine layer of dust on the furniture and the dishes. Odd. The Sheriff made his way outside and began to go around the cabin. There was an odd odor that got stronger the closer he got to the cellar door so he went down into the cellar. As soon as he opened that door the odor hit him in the face like a slap from his mother when he used fowl language. Then he saw him. Lincoln Barrett was lying on the floor with his arms crossed on his chest. It was obvious he was dead and that his body was the source of the odor. He used his neckerchief to cover his nose and mouth while he examined the body. There he found two bullet wounds; one under his chin and one in his chest. He wondered where Vivian was. Was she alright? Upon closer examination of the cabin, he discovered Vivian's wardrobe was empty. She couldn't have killed Lincoln, could she?

Chapter 5: Victoria Finds Hope

Victoria Foreman heard the sound of a man's voice that cool, spring morning in 1883. She was dressed in a blue wool dress with a grey cape over it to ward off the morning chill and a hat covered her light brown hair. The further she walked the louder the voice got. "What is going on?" she wondered to herself. There was no doubt that she was hearing the voice of a man calling out to people. Was it a politician trying to garner votes? It wasn't election season. Could this be a street preacher? The fervor in the speaker's voice almost sounded like that of a street preacher. Her curiosity was peaked until she rounded the corner and saw a wagon sitting on the other side of the street and a man calling out to the people who were on their way to work in the downtown district of Santa Fe. The wagon was covered with images and words advertising a "miracle cure all."

Victoria stopped dead in her tracks when she realized what the words said and what the man was hawking. "Are you serious?" she said softly to herself. "Really? Snake oil? Now I've seen everything," she said as she stared at the man on the soap box.

The snake oil salesman appeared to be in his thirties. She hated to admit it, but he was a handsome man. A full head of dark, curly hair framed his tanned face. His blue eyes seemed to sparkle as he tried to get the attention of those who passed him in the street. "But what in the world was he wearing?" she wondered to herself. He looked quite the dandy in that suit of clothes he had on. Victoria thought he looked much too much like the river boat gamblers she saw on the docks of St. Louis when she was a girl. He and they wore silk shirts and tailored suits. The ensemble included a silk necktie with a diamond studded tie pin and his boots were so shiny she was certain that he could see his reflection in them. "I'm sure he likes looking into them, too," she thought to herself.

As she stood there looking, the dandy started his spiel, "Ladies and gents, this morning I'm beginning my ministry here in the beautiful city of Santa Fe. Oh, I'm no reverend, but mine is a ministry just the same. The priests and parsons minister to the soul, but I'm here to minister to your body. Yes, I am making available to you, the good folks of Santa Fe, this miracle working elixir. I had the good fortune to meet a gentleman from the mysterious orient a few years ago and that gentleman shared with me the secret healing powers of snake oil. That's right, folks, the oil extracted from the snakes we have all around us, if processed properly, has the ability to cure nearly everything that ails modern man. That gentleman was over ninety years old when I met him and he wanted to pass down the secret process to someone he trusted before he breathed his last. I was that trusted someone and today I'm here to offer you this healing elixir."

At that moment the gentleman picked up a bottle from the table display he had sitting to his right and pointed to it. When he looked back to his audience he noticed Victoria standing across the street and their eyes met. For one brief second they looked into one another's eyes. Then Victoria rolled her eyes so far back in her head that only white was showing. Immediately she looked away from the well dressed huckster. She turned to walk away so quickly that her dress made a "swooshing" sound. It seemed so loud that she looked around to see if anyone noticed. Since no one seemed to notice, she continued walking toward the bank where she worked. The snake oil salesman followed her with his eyes as she walked away then turned his attention back to his audience and the task of selling his "healing elixir."

There was no time to think about the man she'd seen that morning, she had work to do. When she arrived at the door of "The Bank of Santa Fe", she took out her key, unlocked the door and stepped in. Turning back, she locked the door behind her and put the key back into her purse where it would reside the rest of the day.

Victoria was only a clerk in that bank, but she was often the first one in and the last one out each day. She took pride in her work and didn't want to give anyone a reason to question why she was there. Very few women had jobs like hers and she knew it. Everyday she knew she would have to work harder than any man in the bank in order to keep her job, but she also knew that no matter how hard she worked, she would not be able to advance like the men she worked with.

She breathed a short prayer as she opened her file drawer and withdrew several files that needed her attention. She breathed the same prayer every morning as she began working, "Lord, help me to do the very best I can today. Amen." One file was for the loan a local rancher had applied for. Another was for a money transfer a local merchant needed to make. One after another she dotted "i's" and crossed "t's". Columns of figures had to be checked for accuracy. Each one had to be checked and rechecked. She couldn't afford even one mistake if she wanted to keep her job.

One by one the other employees began to file into the bank. Then at 8:30 sharp the manager stepped into the bank and over to Victoria's desk. "Do you have those accounts ready for me, Mrs. Foreman?" he asked.

"Yes, sir, they're right here and ready for your signature," she said as she handed him the files she'd been finishing for him.

He took the files and looked at them for a quick moment and said, "Good. Thank you very much." Then he turned and walked away before Victoria could reply or engage in further conversation.

The bank manager, Randall Clarke, was all business all the time. He didn't socialize with his employees and he didn't call them by their first names. His suit was always pressed as were his shirts when he came in every morning. Compared to the snake oil salesman she had seen that morning, his complexion was absolutely pale and his hands were as soft as her grandmother's. Still, he was always polite to her. He had learned that he could trust her work and he made her feel like he valued her as an employee.

A minute before 9:00 Mr. Clarke stepped out of his office with his pocket watch in hand. He looked at one of the accountants, Mr. Taylor, and watched as Mr. Taylor walked to the front door, pulled up the shades and unlocked the doors for the customers to come in. Mr. Taylor was a slight man. He had worn a suit when he came in that morning, but had taken off his coat and put his black sleeve protectors over the sleeves of his shirt. He was ready for a long day of working on the books. No one was waiting to come in that morning, but heaven help Mr. Taylor if that door wasn't unlocked precisely at 9:00.

People did come and go that morning. There was the usual bank business to be conducted. Some were making deposits and others were making withdrawals. One of the local merchants came in with the receipts from yesterday's sales. He too wore sleeve protectors, but he also wore a shop keeper's apron to keep the front of his clothes clean while he waited on customers at his store. A cowhand came in covered with dust. Obviously he'd just ridden in from the ranch where he worked. He was in town to pick up supplies for his boss and stopped at the bank while he waited for his order to be filled. He had two silver dollars to deposit in his account. He told the cashier that he was that much closer to getting his own spread one day. It was all so very routine.

Things took a turn as the morning wore on, though. Three men came into the bank and, even though she didn't know it at the time, their presence would impact Victoria's life dramatically.

About 10:30 two men walked into the bank. One was tall and thin, perhaps six feet tall. He wore a derby hat and a dark brown coat. His clothes and hat were covered in dust just the like cowhand who had been in earlier. By the looks of him, he hadn't been close to a razor for a couple of weeks. The man with him was much shorter. He wore a flat crowned hat with a narrow brim and had a black colored coat on. He too wore a layer of road dust. He had a long mustache and several days of stubble on his face. Victoria looked the men over and made a mental note that a bulge under each of their coats indicated that both were wearing guns.

Both men stepped into the bank and stopped a few feet inside the door. They both scanned the room as though they were taking notes concerning the layout of the room and location of the employees. Victoria watched them with interest. Suddenly the shorter man's eyes caught hers. He looked directly at her and tipped his hat. He stepped aside and waited while his partner stepped up to the window and conducted some business with the cashier. Victoria couldn't see or hear what that business was, but it was over in a minute. As soon as it was, the two men exited. Victoria watched through the front window as the men walked across the street and stood looking at the bank for several more minutes. The tall man rolled a cigarette, lit it and smoked it in a leisurely manner while he watched the comings and goings of the bank. Victoria made mental notes of everything she was seeing.

A little later, right at eleven o'clock, another man came into the bank. Neither he nor Victoria would realize it at the time, but his entrance would prove to be life changing for both of them. This was the snake oil salesman Victoria had seen earlier that morning. There he was in all his splendor. His suit of clothes, his silk shirt and tie, his brilliantly shined boots and his derby hat. But now that he was closer, she noticed something else. She had seen his tanned face earlier, but now she realized his face was more than tanned. It was weathered. This was a man who had spent many more years working outdoors than he had selling snake oil to the gullible. The sun and wind had cut lines in his face. When she looked at his hands, she could see the same weathered look. When she saw him earlier, she was annoyed. She was annoyed that a huckster was in Santa Fe fleecing the residents who were looking for a little relief from whatever malady they suffered from. Now that she could see the dichotomy of this man who dressed like a river boat gambler, but showed evidence of being a hard working man, she had her curiosity aroused. Had he been a ranch hand? A farmer perhaps? Maybe a carpenter or brick layer? It didn't matter. She probably would never know, she thought.

He, too, stepped into the bank and glanced around. He noticed Victoria sitting at her desk and began to walk straight for her. He took his hat off and addressed her, "Good morning, miss."

"It's missus," Victoria said curtly.

"Excuse me?" the gentleman asked.

"You called me 'miss'. I'm not a 'miss' I'm a missus. Mrs. Foreman to be exact. How may I help you?"

"I apologize, Mrs. Foreman. My name is Hudson Campbell, but you can call me Hud if you like." He replied.

"Thank you, Mr. Campbell," Victoria said. "Again, how may I help you?"

"Ma'am, if I didn't know better, I'd think I'd done something to annoy you. Have I done something to annoy you, ma'am?" Hudson asked.

Victoria paused for just a second. She felt her face flush just a bit, so she took a deep breath and replied, "I'm sorry. How may I help you Mr. Campbell?"

"Well, ma'am, I'm new in town. I'm going to be working here and in this area for a while so I'd like to open an account," he replied. "If that's alright with you, of course," he continued.

Victoria took another breath before she replied, then she said, "Of course, Mr. Campbell. Please have a seat. We'll be glad to open an account for you. Here's a card to fill out. How much would you be depositing with us today?"

"A thousand dollars, ma'am," he said as he took the card in hand. "Do you have a pen I can use?"

"Yes, sir. Here you go," Victoria said as she dipped the pen in the ink well and handed it to him. "Your snake oil business must be doing well, if you have that much money to deposit today," she continued.

At that, Hudson Campbell paused and looked up at Victoria again. "Oh, you are the woman I saw this morning aren't you?" he asked. "I thought I recognized that lovely blue dress of yours," he said before she could reply.

Victoria felt her face flush again. "Yes, sir, that was me this morning," she said as she turned to look back at the files on her desk. "We can open that account as soon as you fill out the card, Mr. Campbell."

Hudson Campbell filled out the new account card and handed the pen and card back to Victoria. She walked him up to the cashier and said, "Mr. Michaels, this is Mr. Campbell. He'll be opening a new account with us today." At that, she left Mr. Campbell and began walking back to her desk.

"Thank you, Mrs. Foreman. I appreciate your help," Campbell said.

Victoria turned her head back slightly and nodded in response. "Why does this man make me so uncomfortable," she wondered to herself as she got back to the files on her desk.

Three days later it was finally Friday and Victoria was ready to have the weekend off. She enjoyed her job, but dealing with the public day in and day out simply wore her out. Even though meals were included at her boarding house, Victoria enjoyed going to dinner at one of the local restaurants every Friday evening and this would be no exception. Going to the St. Louis House Restaurant on Friday evenings was one of the few luxuries Victoria allowed herself. The owners were a couple who came from her native St. Louis, Missouri and the food they served reminded her so much of home. She didn't dare tell anyone that's why she went there, but she enjoyed it none-the-less.

That afternoon she finished her work at the bank. She put everything away and went back to her room at the boarding house to get refreshed and change her clothes. She dined alone every week, but always felt better after washing and putting on clean clothes. The stresses and worries of the week could be left behind and she could enjoy a nice meal in a bright, cheery restaurant. The waitresses had gotten to know her and placed her order as soon as they saw her walk in. She always had the same thing: roast beef and potatoes with gravy, seasonal vegetables, dinner rolls, whatever the pie was that night and a cup of coffee with her pie. Her mother would fix a meal like that almost every Sunday. Victoria felt the fifty cents they charged was worth it for a taste of home and a time to remember her mother and father and the wonderful home she grew up in.

Victoria thought this evening would be like every other Friday evening she had dined at the Saint Louis House, but she was wrong. After she was seated, but before her meal was served, he walked in. "What was he doing there? This was a nice restaurant, not the kind a snake oil salesman would find inviting!" she thought to herself. "What was his name? Campbell? Was it Campbell? Yes, that was it and his first name was…Hudson. Yes, he wanted me to call him Hud, didn't he?" She hoped Mr. Hudson Campbell Snake Oil Salesman wouldn't see her. And then he did. As he entered the restaurant and looked around the room, he noticed Victoria sitting there by herself. Then he did the unthinkable, he began to walk straight toward her.

Hudson Campbell walked right up to Victoria's table, removed his hat and greeted her, "Good evening, ma'am. Mrs. Foreman isn't it? How are you this evening?"

"Mr. Campbell? What a surprise to see you here," Victoria replied.

"Surprised? Why would you be surprised to see me here, ma'am?" he asked.

Victoria felt her face flushing yet again. "What is it about this man that makes me feel so uncomfortable?" she thought to herself. She looked at him and said, "I guess I never thought about this restaurant as being the type of place a snake oil salesman would frequent, Mr. Campbell. That's all."

"Ma'am, I'm getting the feeling you don't like me," Campbell said.

Trying to change the subject, Victoria said, "Well, it's nice to see you again, sir. I hope you have a nice dinner." At that she tried to look away, but Campbell wasn't going to be dismissed that easily.

"Will Mr. Foreman be joining you for supper, ma'am?" he inquired as he looked around the room.

Again, Victoria's face was flushing. "Well, if you must know, Mr. Foreman is dead. I'm a widow, Mr. Campbell."

"Ma'am, I'm sorry to hear that. I apologize for bringing up such a sensitive subject," he said. "Please excuse me. I won't be bothering you any longer. Have a nice evening, ma'am." At that he turned to leave to find a table of his own.

Victoria felt foolish being so rude to the man. He'd been nothing but a gentleman to her. So she said, "Mr. Campbell, would you like to join me this evening?"

Campbell stopped and turned around, as he looked straight into her eyes, he asked, "Are you sure ma'am? I don't want to be a bother."

"No bother, sir. I'd enjoy the company for a change. Please join me," she said in a soft and kind voice. It was a voice he hadn't heard her speak in before.

"If you're sure. I'd be glad to join you. Thanks," he said. Before pulling out his chair to sit down, Campbell placed his hat on the empty chair to his right and unbuttoned his coat. When he sat down, his coat opened slightly and Victoria noticed that Hudson Campbell had a small revolver in a shoulder holster. She didn't say anything, but she made a mental note of its presence.

A waitress came to the table and asked what Campbell wanted to eat. He looked at Victoria and asked, "Have you ordered?"

"Yes. I have the same thing every Friday night. The girls just put in my order when they see me coming," she said as she looked at the waitress and smiled.

"Well, miss, I'll have whatever Mrs. Foreman is having then. If it's good enough for her, it's good enough for me," he said as he closed the menu and handed it back to the waitress.

"It's fifty cents. Is that okay?" the waitress asked.

"Fifty cents?" Campbell asked trying to act shocked. He smiled at the waitress and said, "Well, I think that'll be alright."

Campbell looked at Victoria and smiled an impish little smile and said, "Fifty cents? You're kind of a high roller, aren't you?"

Victoria looked back at him and said very matter of factly, "It's my only vice and I think I'm worth it."

"Yes, ma'am. I reckon you are. I didn't mean anything by it. Please excuse my poor attempt at humor," Campbell said.

Changing the subject, Victoria asked, "How long have you been fleecing people with your snake oil?"

Campbell was taken aback by the question and it showed. "You don't mince words do you, ma'am? I don't really fleece the folks. The snake oil might have some medicinal value, but mostly it makes them feel better. To be honest, the bottle is mostly moonshine liquor with a little snake oil added. If a fella drinks a bottle of my elixir, he'll feel better for a while and who knows, he might even get better."

"Okay," Victoria said. "But how long have you been 'not fleecing' folks with your liquor?"

"To be honest, I have only been doing the snake oil business for a couple of years. It's pretty lucrative and it keeps me out of any real trouble," Campbell said as he admired the plate of food that had been placed in front of him.

Victoria placed her napkin in her lap and picked up her fork and knife as she asked, "And what did you do before that, Mr. Campbell?"

Campbell looked at her and asked, "Are you ever going to call me by my first name?" Victoria just looked at him so he continued, "Before the war I rode for the Pony Express. I was young and it was a lot of fun. Actually met Bill Cody back then. He was one of our riders, you know," Campbell explained.

"Did you serve in the war?" Victoria asked.

Campbell put his knife and fork down and replied, "Yes, ma'am. I fought on the side of the Union. After the war I went to Texas and cowboyed for a while. When they reorganized the Texas Rangers I hired on with them." With that he went back to his meal.

It was Victoria's turn to put down her knife and fork, "Why did you leave the Rangers to sell moonshine-snake oil?"

Campbell got deadly serious and looked at Victoria and asked, "Do you really want to know?"

"Yes. I really would like to know. Please, tell me."

"Ma'am, to be honest, I enjoyed the camaraderie with the other rangers and I enjoyed working outdoors, riding my horse and all that, but after the war and all, I really didn't enjoy hunting men down and sometimes having to kill them," Campbell said in a soft and very serious voice. He went on to say, "I'm not opposed to defending myself or folks I care about. I just can't hunt men anymore."

Just then Victoria's head snapped to her right. She saw two men walk in to the restaurant. It was the two men who had come into the bank the other day. They had the same layer of road dust on the hats and clothes and the same unshaven faces. Her eyes narrowed as she studied every detail of their appearance. Campbell couldn't help but notice that her attention was suddenly drawn away from their conversation and to something else. Slowly he turned his head and, he too, saw the two men. He couldn't take his eyes off of them anymore than Victoria could. He looked them up and down. He studied their every feature. He too noticed the bulges under their coats and he immediately knew they were carrying guns.

"Do you know those men, ma'am?" he asked.

Victoria slowly turned her attention back to her dinner companion. It took her a second to answer, but she finally said, "No, I don't know them, but they did come into the bank three days ago. It was the same day you came in. Probably half an hour or so before you did. Why?"

"Oh," Campbell said as he turned to watch the two being seated at a table across the room from them.

"Oh? What does that mean?" Victoria demanded.

"Well, I know who those men are. As far as I know, they are not wanted in New Mexico, but they were in Texas," Campbell said.

"How do you know that, Mr. Campbell?" Victoria asked.

Campbell leaned in toward Victoria. Speaking in a low voice, he said, "The Rangers have something they call 'The Ranger's Bible.' It contains information on people who are wanted in the state and those two hombre's were in it. The tall one's name is Seth Becker and the other man is James Doyle, also known as Shorty Doyle for obvious reasons."

Victoria leaned in and asked, "Do I dare ask what they are wanted for?"

"You can ask, but you won't like the answer," Campbell replied. He went on to say, "They are wanted for a number of things including cattle rustling, horse stealing, assault, murder and bank robbery."

Victoria put her hand to her chest and said, "Oh." She looked up into Campbell's eyes and said, "Oh, do you think they're planning to rob our bank?"

Campbell looked at her and asked, "What did they do when they came in the other morning?"

"To be honest, they acted like they were memorizing the layout of the bank and where each and every employee was. After they conducted some short business they went across the street and watched the bank for several more minutes," Victoria said. Then she asked again, this time a little more impatiently, "Are they going to rob our bank?"

Campbell had been taking a sip of water. He set the glass down before answering Victoria, "Normally, they come into a town, spend a day or two watching the bank and then they rob it. They've robbed three banks in Texas, that I know of. It would also appear they are not opposed to shooting folks, if they think it's necessary."

Victoria thought for a moment, then she asked, "They've been here more than two days. Why do you think they haven't robbed us yet?"

Campbell didn't want to answer that question, but he knew Mrs. Foreman well enough by now to know she wouldn't be satisfied with anything but the whole truth as he knew it. "Sometimes they have had a gang that worked with them. On smaller jobs, they work alone. I wish I could tell you who's going to show up on this job. If I had to guess though, I'd say they are waiting for other members of their gang to get here."

Victoria's brow was wrinkled as she asked, "What shall we do, Mr. Campbell?"

"Well, ma'am, there are at least two things I can do. I'll go to the town Marshall tonight and tell him what I know. Tomorrow morning I'll go to your manager's home and tell him to beware of these two snakes. Can you give me his address?"

This time Victoria asked, "Yes, I can give you Mr. Clarke's address, but again, what can I do?"

"You? Ma'am, I want to suggest that you take the a couple of days off. I'm sure these men mean to rob your bank Monday or Tuesday. Please take a couple of days off, just until this all blows over."

Victoria looked Mr. Campbell in the eye and said, "No, I won't be taking any time off. For one thing, I can't afford to take any time off. But for another, I won't be bullied by the likes of those two. I haven't run from a fight in the past. I won't run from this one, either." As she said that, she pulled the butt of her Smith and Wesson Model 3 revolver from her purse. Frankly, she was tired of men trying to bully her or tell her what to do to.

Campbell didn't know what she'd been through in the past, but he was certain that this lady meant business and arguing with her was useless.

Hudson Campbell and Victoria Foreman finished their dinner in silence. They ate their pie and drank their coffee, but every minute or two they would turn to look at Becker and Doyle. All the while Becker and Doyle seemed oblivious to the fact that anyone even knew they were in the room.

That night, Campbell went to the town Marshall's office, introduced himself as a former Texas Ranger and told him everything he knew about Becker and Doyle and what he believed their plan was. The Marshall seemed more than a little irritated that an outsider, and a former Texas Ranger at that, was trying to tell him how to run his town. He told Campbell he'd look into it, but Campbell got the impression he wouldn't.

The next morning he went to Mr. Clarke's home and laid out the scenario to him. Mr. Clarke thanked him for his time, but he, too, seemed to dismiss the whole idea that his bank was in trouble. They'd never been robbed before and he didn't think this was a credible threat. He'd heard of famous Texas Rangers like John Armstrong and Chick Bowdrie[1], but he'd never heard of Hudson Campbell. He'd heard of dozens of famous outlaws, too, but he'd never heard of these two Texas ne'er-do-wells Campbell was warning him about.

Campbell was frustrated. Neither the Marshall nor the bank manager would take this threat seriously. "What can I do," he thought to himself. "I'm not a lawman anymore and I don't want to get in the middle of a gunfight that's none of my business."

That afternoon Campbell set up his snake oil wagon in the downtown district of Santa Fe. After all, he had a living to make and if those folks didn't care their bank was going to be robbed, why should he?

---

1 Chick Bowdrie is one of my favorite characters from the writing of Louis L'Amour. I include his name as a tribute to a great American story teller.

Saturday found Victoria Foreman going about her normal business. She washed her clothes and hung them to dry. She mended what needed mending, cleaned her room and spent a little time reading. Truth be told, though, she was having a hard time concentrating on her chores.

When Sunday morning came, Hudson Campbell was no where to be seen and Victoria Foreman was in her usual seat in the Protestant church in Santa Fe. She knew all of the hymns that were sung and sang them by rote. She was aware that the pastor delivered a sermon, but, she was having a difficult time concentrating on anything he said that day. The rest of the day was spent quietly reading the Good Book in her room. She had been raised to "honor the Sabbath" as a day of rest and that was what she did.

Monday morning found Victoria dressing for work. Today she would wear her dark grey suit with a white blouse underneath it. Her hair was brushed and she would put on a flat crowned hat that had a turned up brim. It, too, was grey, but a much lighter grey than her dress. The band around the hat was black velvet and it was adorned with several attractive bird feathers. After breakfast she checked her purse and seemed satisfied she had everything she needed. There was a knot in the pit of her stomach. She had to wonder if this was the day her bank would be robbed. What would she do if it was?

It was another cool spring morning and Victoria walked briskly to get to the bank by her usual 8:00. She paused when she reached the point where she had first seen Hudson Campbell and his snake oil wagon. He wasn't there, but she couldn't help but wonder where he was.

She scanned up and down the street as she approached the bank. Would Becker and Doyle be watching the bank? Would they come rushing in when she opened the door? The only person on the street was a lone cowhand who appeared to be sleeping on the bench in front of the store that was directly across from the bank. His range clothes didn't appear to be dirty, but they were worn. This man had obviously fixed a lot of fence and bulldogged more than a few calves wearing those clothes. He had his head down and his hat was pulled low. He was as still as a store mannequin. He didn't look like either Becker or Doyle, so Victoria unlocked the door and went in as she always did. When she got to her desk, she took off her grey cape and hat and hung them on the oak coat tree near her desk. She opened her desk drawer and placed her handbag in the drawer with the opening facing her. She closed the drawer and opened it quickly several times. Each time she looked at the handbag and reached in to touch it. No one else was in the bank, but if anyone had seen her doing this, they would have wondered what in the world she was up to. Before she closed the drawer for the last time she bowed her head to breathe a prayer. This prayer was different than the one she usually prayed at the beginning of every work day. Today her prayer was, "Lord, I pray that I will not need to harm anyone today. But if trouble comes give me the courage to act and make my aim true. Amen."

That morning Victoria was quite busy helping the usual customers who came in on a Monday morning. Merchants who had been open on Saturday had deposits to make and the two saloon owners who had accounts with them were depositing their "ill gotten gains" from the weekend, as well. Sometime around 10 or 10:30 Victoria looked out the window and noticed that the cowhand who had been sleeping across the street was gone. She thought she saw Becker and Doyle walk by on the boardwalk across the street, but she couldn't be sure it was them. Mr. Clarke came out of his office and just looked around several times that morning. Victoria had to wonder if he was nervous about the possibility of being robbed. He certainly hadn't said anything to any of the employees about the prospect of being robbed, but still his behavior was not normal.

The morning came and went. Victoria and her fellow employees had lunch and had gone back to work, still nothing. Maybe this was a false alarm. Oh, she hoped it was just that, a false alarm.

The afternoon had warmed up considerably. Traffic on the street outside the bank seemed to be busy. Freight wagons hauling goods, the 2:00 stage coach and a dozen or more men on horses had gone past her window. The dust those travelers raised was covering everything that didn't move. Still, no Becker and Doyle.

Just before 3:00 Becker and Doyle were sitting on their horses behind the store across from the bank. Both took their Colts out of their holsters and slipped a sixth shell in the normally empty chamber. This was something one would do only if he expected to get into a gun fight. After re-holstering his gun, Seth Becker sat up straight in his saddle and took out his pocket watch. He checked the time and nodded to his partner. Shorty Doyle re-holstered his gun and said, "Let's do this." And the two urged their horses forward. They road up to the bank and swung down from their horses. They seemed to be joining two other men who were there standing next to their horses. Three of the men, Becker, Doyle and one of the men they met, handed the reins to the fourth, pulled their neckerchiefs up over their noses and began to walk towards the bank door. As they did, each drew a gun. Becker and Doyle both drew Colt revolvers from under their coats. The third man pulled a short barreled shotgun from under his overcoat.

At that moment, a man launched himself from between two of the buildings on the other side of the street. It was the cowhand who appeared to have been sleeping in front of the store across the street earlier in the day. It became obvious this was Hudson Campbell now that his hat was not pulled down over his face. While he was running toward the bank, Campbell pulled his coat back and drew his own Colt revolver. His face was set. He was going to do whatever it took to stop this bank robbery and he would certainly do whatever it took to keep Mrs. Foreman safe.

The man holding the horses had his back to the street and didn't notice Campbell until it was too late. Campbell ran up behind him and let the seven and half inch barrel crash down on the outlaw's skull. The crack of the barrel on that skull was so loud that people walking down the street stopped to see what had happened.

Inside the bank, Victoria heard a muffled thud coming from outside and looked just in time to see a man outside falling. At that moment three things happened.

Hudson Campbell ducked under the hitching post in front of the bank and took a step up onto the boardwalk. Three outlaws threw open the door of the bank. And Victoria Foreman drew a nickel plated Smith and Wesson revolver from her purse. She quickly slid the .44 caliber revolver into her lap and out of sight.

The man carrying the shotgun turned and shut the bank door and began to turn the lock. When Campbell saw the door shut he pointed his gun in the direction of the man on the other side, pulled back the hammer and fired. The glass in the door was shattered and the shotgun wielding outlaw was thrown back when the .45 caliber slug entered his body. His body landed five feet away from the door. The look that was frozen on his face forever was that of shock.

The customers and employees in the bank turned towards the sound of the shot and froze in place. All except Victoria Foreman. Victoria cocked the hammer of her revolver and kept it in her lap. Shorty Doyle, the man who had tipped his hat to her the week before looked her straight in the eye and said, "You, miss, come here!"

"No! You come and get me," Victoria snarled.

As Shorty took a step towards Victoria, Campbell kicked the door of the bank open and Seth Becker turned and fired in the direction of the noise. Shorty turned his head to see what his partner was shooting at just long enough for Victoria to pull her revolver from under her desk. Gripping her gun with both hands, she pointed it directly at Shorty's belly and fired. The .44 caliber bullet hit Shorty and spun him around. He was dead when he hit the floor.

Becker and Victoria could see that Campbell had taken a bullet in the shoulder. Both assumed he was dead. Victoria had one advantage over Becker. He'd never seen a woman wielding a gun and shooting like that before. His brain took a second to process what was happening in front of him. During that split second Victoria and Hudson Campbell cocked the hammers on their guns, pointed them at Becker and fired. They could not have timed their shots that closely together if they'd planned it. There was only one shot heard, but it seemed extra loud folks would say later. Two bullets, one from a .44 caliber Smith and Wesson and the other from a .45 caliber Colt, hit their target at the same time and the outlaw career of Seth Becker was ended.

Campbell collapsed just inside the door of the bank, his left shoulder bleeding profusely. Victoria kept her revolver in her hand as she got up from her desk and ran to him. Kneeling down next to him she touched his face with her left hand and called to him, "Mr. Campbell? Mr. Campbell?" she shouted. There was no response. Then she asked with a lower and more tender voice, "Hudson, are you all right?"

As though hearing his first name had roused him, he opened his eyes and looked up at Victoria and asked, "So, is this what it takes to get you to call me by my first name?" Victoria looked him in the eye and smiled.

Patrick Donovan
AKA The Prescott Parson

Chapter 6:
Parson's Night Out

The Parson was out late, past 9:00, but he and some of his church members had been praying together at Widow Mills' home and time just seemed to fly. They'd been praying for their town and asking God to show them how to bring the gospel to the people who needed it the most. But that caused him to have to walk home well past the time that decent folk were out. His boots sounded loud on the wooden sidewalk in front of the closed businesses in Prescott and he smiled as he thought about how folks said the town rolled the sidewalk up at 7:00 every night. The town didn't do that, but the sidewalks didn't get much use that late either.

Unfortunately, the Parson had to walk past the Last Chance Saloon, the worst den of iniquity in the little town he called home. As he approached he could smell the beer and cigar smoke and hear all the revelry coming from inside. Loud laughter, the clicking of the roulette wheel, swearing and music all came together and sounded like a symphony of the devil to him.

He didn't look in when he passed by the open door of the saloon. Frankly, he didn't want to know who was in there and what they were doing. He hated that place because he'd seen so many lives and families ruined by drink, gambling, and whores. Oh how he wished that place would close forever. He clutched his Bible just a little tighter and walked past, eyes straight ahead.

Just past the saloon there was an alley that separated it and the Maxwell Hotel next door. As the Parson was getting close to the alley he could hear some rustling sounds. The closer he got the louder the noise got, but then he heard something else. He heard what sounded like someone getting slapped or punched and then there was a cry of pain. The Parson stopped at the entry of the alley and called out, "Who's there and what's going on?"

"Keep moving," came the reply. "Nothing that concerns you." This was a man's voice. The words were harsh and loud, but with the slur of too much whiskey behind them.

Then there was a second voice, a woman's voice, it sounded weak and desperate, "Please, please, won't you help me?" The voice was almost a whisper.

"Shut up, you," the man's voice said. "And you, whoever you are, mind your own business and move on."

The Parson wasn't one to take orders from someone up to no good. He stepped into the alley and as he did he squinted to try to see what was going on and who was there. He also began to unbutton his long, black coat exposing the grip of his Colt Peacemaker. As soon as his coat was unbuttoned, he transferred his Bible from his right hand to his left. He wanted to be ready for trouble if it came. The closer he got to the voices the better he could see two figures in the light that came from a back window of the saloon. One was a cowboy in his range clothes, sweat stained and dirty. He was a young man. He hadn't had a close relationship with a razor for quite a while and his teeth were stained from the tobacco he chewed. The other was one of the soiled doves from the Last Chance. As he got closer he could see that the woman was really just a girl. She couldn't have been more than fourteen or fifteen years old. She was just a wisp of a girl with stringy brown hair. Her face was painted like all of the other women who worked at the saloon and she wore the garish clothing of a whore, but she was just a girl. How did she end up in a place like this with a man like that?

The girl's dress was torn and her face was red and beginning to swell from the beating this man was giving her. The Parson hated what went on in the saloon and he wished all the whores would leave Prescott forever, but this just wasn't right.

"Stop beating that girl!" the Parson shouted.

"Or what?" the cowboy asked as he turned to see that the man addressing him was Patrick Donovan, known to everyone in town as the Prescott Parson. "What are you going to do, Parson? Read the Bible to me? Pray over me? And what do you care what I do to this whore? Are you sticking up for whores now, Parson?" At that the cowboy tried to kiss the girl while she tried to squirm out of his arms.

"I'm not sticking up for whores, boy. But I will stick up for someone's daughter or sister. You need to let that girl go before it's too late."

"Too late for what?" the cowboy asked as he let go of the girl and began to clench his fists for a fight.

"Too late for this," and with that the Parson drew his Colt from under his coat. With one smooth motion his gun went up in the air and came down on the young man's skull. It seemed like the sound of the barrel slamming down on the cowboy's head could be heard all over town. The young man's hat flew from his head as his knees buckled, his eyes rolled back in his head, and he fell into the dirt in the alley. He would have a powerful headache when he woke up the next morning.

The Parson re-holstered his gun and turned to the girl. He reached out his hand to her and asked if she was alright. She allowed that she would be. Then the Parson said, "I don't know what to do with you, little girl. This life you've chosen is an abomination to the Lord. What do I do?"

The girl looked up to the Parson, one eye was swelling shut and blood was dripping from her lower lip where it was cut. "I didn't choose this life, Parson. After my Ma and Pa were killed there was no one to take care of me. I could either starve to death or work here. I didn't have no choice in the matter. You can just keep walking, if you're going to preach me a sermon. That's just about the last thing I need right now."

The Parson had never heard that side of the story before. It cut him to the quick. His tone softened as he said, "Little girl, I have a church member down the street here. Her name is Widow Mills. Maybe she'll take you in until we can figure out what to do with you. Are you willing to go to her house with me?"

"Yes, sir. Besides, I think I just lost my job at the saloon, what with you knocking out a paying customer and all."

With that, an odd couple, a frontier preacher and a soiled dove with a long black coat draped over her shoulders, started down the street. Suddenly, the Parson felt the Holy Spirit put his finger on his heart as he remembered the group's prayer that night, "Lord, show us how to take the gospel to those who really need it."

Chapter 7:
The Parson Fights Off the Wolves

It was a beautiful fall Saturday in Prescott. The temperature was no more than seventy degrees and a light breeze was blowing. The trees in the area didn't change colors like the ones in Pennsylvania where the Parson grew up, but seeing their leaves turn brown and then turn loose reminded him of home anyway. The Parson had just finished his weekly Bible study at Second Chance House and stepped out of the door and onto the front porch. He put his hat on with his left hand while his right hand held his Bible. Today's Bible study had been particularly helpful to the young women who made Second Chance House their home because it was on John 8 and the woman who was caught in the very act of adultery. The Parson had been teaching through the book of John and this was just the next chapter, but it was so helpful for these young women who were being rescued from the life of prostitution. These soiled doves could see that Jesus loved, accepted and forgave those who had been caught up in a life of sin. Several of them wept at the thought. All of them prayed prayers of thanksgiving at the close of the study.

Patrick Donovan, Brother Patrick to his flock aka The Prescott Parson to the folks in town, couldn't help but smile as he stood there on the porch that day. He breathed a prayer of thanksgiving and was about to walk down the street to the boarding house he called home when someone called his name. "Parson, excuse me, Parson. May we have a word?"

Patrick looked across the street and there stood four men. They were all wearing suits with dress shirts and ties, but none of them looked like they belonged in those suits. These were rough men. The "gentleman" speaking to Patrick had a large mustache under his crooked nose. It was obvious his nose had been broken at least once. Was it broken in a fight? It's possible it was broken some other way, but Patrick thought he might be the kind of man who gets into a brawl every now and then just for sport. Two of the others had full faced beards and the fourth simply hadn't had a shave in a week or so. It was obvious by the bulges under their suit coats that all of them were heeled.

Patrick continued to look the men up and down as he replied, "How may I help you, gentlemen?"

"There's someone here who wants to have a word," Broken Nose said. And at that the two men in the middle of the pack stepped aside and a very large woman stepped out of the shadows and into the sunlight. Everyone in town knew Big Bertha Kirbo[2]. She was a big woman. Almost six feet tall and she filled a doorway when she stepped into one. Today she was wearing a dark grey dress with a black hat on her greying hair. She had a small cigar in her mouth and a beaded purse in her left hand. Bertha ran the brothel upstairs in the Last Chance Saloon and had made a small fortune off of the girls in that brothel. She definitely didn't appreciate anyone who cut into her profits.

She took the cigar from her mouth and said, "Parson."

Patrick tipped his hat, "Ma'am."

Bertha looked around and said, "Beautiful day, isn't it, Parson?"

"Yes, Ma'am, it is," Patrick replied, "but my guess is you didn't come out here to discuss the weather did you, Miss Kirbo?"

"Right to the point. I like that, Parson. No, I didn't come out to discuss the weather. I came out here to talk to you because you have five of my girls in that there house and I want them back," she said in a matter of fact way.

"Ma'am," Patrick said, "with all respect, the only young women in this here house are women who want to leave the life they had working for you."

Miss Kirbo took a step forward with her right foot and pointed at the Parson with the index finger of her right hand as she began to speak again, "Listen here, Parson, one of them girls was one of my best earners. She was making good money for herself and, frankly, for me, too. The other girls worked for me and a couple of them owed me some money." She threw the butt of a cigar down on the street and said, "I want my girls back. Am I making myself clear?"

The four men with Miss Kirbo all took a step forward as if they had been given the cue to move. Bertha put both arms out to stop them and said, "Now, boys, we aren't looking for a fight with the Parson here. We'll give him a little time to think about this situation. I'm sure he'll make a really wise decision and encourage the girls to come back to work." Then she looked at the Parson and said, "Hows about I give you until Monday at supper time to bring them girls to me, Parson? If the girls are back by then, we'll forget this little problem and consider it over. Okay?"

The Parson didn't like Bertha's tone and he didn't like the fact that she brought four thugs with her. He considered drawing his coat back in order to show his Colt, but thought better of it. He was outgunned and he didn't want to escalate the situation. At the same time, he wanted to let Bertha know where he stood. "Ma'am," he said, "I won't try to stop any of the young women, if they decide to return to you. I will try to talk them out of it, but I won't stop them if they make up their mind to do that. They are free to come and go as they please. But, ma'am, I will not bring

---

2 Big Bertha Kirbo was actually a madam from the Old West. This account of her is pure fiction.

them to you. Not on Monday or any other day. And, ma'am, you need to know that I will do whatever it takes to protect them. Am I making myself clear, Miss Kirbo?"

Bertha took another cigar from her purse, bit off the end and spit it out onto the street. She snapped her fingers at the man to her left. When he saw that she wanted her cigar lit, he had to fumble in his pockets to find a match. Then he hurriedly lit her cigar. She wasn't smiling as she took a big drag on her cigar and blew the smoke out. She squinted her eyes until they were mere slits and spoke through her clenched teeth, "We'll see, Parson. We'll see." With that, she turned and began walking away. Her "entourage" was a little slow on the uptake so she looked back and snapped, "We're done here, you idiots. Come on." With that the four thugs hurried to catch up to Bertha as she stomped off. Their eyes darted back and forth between the Parson and their boss lady. They weren't sure which one to fear the most.

Patrick watched Miss Kirbo and her four trained monkeys until they turned the corner to head back to the saloon. Then he made his way back to his room at the boarding house. He had a lot to think about and pray on. Before long he realized the sermon he'd prepared wasn't going to be adequate for the next morning's service. He would have to start from scratch. Brother McPeters, the pastor he'd trained with before moving to Prescott, had trained him to prepare his sermons before Saturday night, but he always told him to follow the Spirit's leading. "If the Lord tells you to change your sermon at the last minute, you'd better change it," he would say. Patrick believed Brother McPatrick would approve of this last minute change. His lamp didn't go out until well past one o'clock that morning. But when it did, he was excited because he felt the hand of God on that message like he rarely felt it. He slept soundly until his usual six o'clock wake up. The next hour was spent in Bible reading, prayer and a review of the notes he made in the early morning. After breakfast and a shave he dressed in his Sunday best, gathered up his Bible and notes and began walking to the school house where his little congregation would meet for worship that morning.

When the Parson was dressing for church on Sunday morning, he always felt like he was dressing for battle. He thought through the various pieces of armor the Apostle Paul named when he talked about the "whole armor of God."[3] With each piece of clothing he breathed a short prayer that corresponded with each piece of the spiritual armor he counted in the spiritual battle he was a part of. When he put on his shirt, he thought about the breastplate of righteousness. His pants and belt reminded him of the belt of truth. His boots reminded him that his feet were shod with the gospel of peace. No one could topple him because he stood firm in the knowledge that Christ was his Lord and Savior. He didn't have a shield, but always remembered that his faith protected him from the flaming arrows of Satan. He carried both his hat and his Bible to the front door of the house. He was confident

---

3 Ephesians 6:14–19.

in the Bible and knew it to be the weapon that would defeat the enemy. When he put his hat on, he always thanked God for the helmet of salvation through Christ. There were folks who didn't understand why he kept his Colt on his belt when he was preaching, but he knew that Jesus told his disciples to get a sword right before they went out to the Garden of Gethsemane[4]. He would use any tool necessary to protect the sheep in his care.

That Sunday morning, the Parson greeted everyone who came to the school house turned church. Widow Miller was often the first to arrive and she didn't disappoint that morning. Allan and Eunice came with the five young women from Second Chance House and took their places at the front of the makeshift church. The Parson wouldn't let them sit in the back. He wanted everyone to know that they were as much a part of God's flock as anyone there. A few people quit coming when the soiled doves started attending, but Patrick wished them well and prayed for them as the Lord brought them to mind. All in all, twenty-five souls gathered to sing the Lord's praises and to hear a word from the Lord through his servant, Brother Patrick.

After the congregation had sung "Tis So Sweet To Trust in Jesus", Patrick thanked Mrs. Fielding for her excellent organ playing and thanked the congregation for the spirit with which they sang. Then he began his message by asking the congregation to open their Bibles to John's Gospel chapter ten. "Please stand with me in honor of the reading of God's word," he said. "I begin my reading at verse eleven, reading through verse fifteen." As the congregation all found their place in the Bible and stood, Patrick read with the most passion they had ever heard him read from the Bible:

"I am the good shepherd: the good shepherd giveth his life for the sheep. But he that is an hireling, and not the shepherd, whose own the sheep are not, seeth the wolf coming, and leaveth the sheep, and fleeth: and the wolf catcheth them, and scattereth the sheep. The hireling fleeth, because he is an hireling, and careth not for the sheep. I am the good shepherd, and know my sheep, and am known of mine. As the Father knoweth me, even so know I the Father: and I lay down my life for the sheep."

Brother Patrick shared the conversation he had with Big Bertha Kirbo the day before. When he did the young women from The House began to look nervously at one another, but when they looked to their house parents, the Johansons, they saw that their gaze was fixed on Brother Patrick. They weren't distressed at all. They seemed to be at peace. That helped to calm the girls.

Patrick went on to say, "This passage from John ten is about Jesus who is the good shepherd, you and I need to know that, but you and I also need to know that God has called me to be his under-shepherd of this flock. As such, I have a respon-

---

4 Luke 22:36

sibility to care for and feed you, the sheep of his flock. A year ago, God called us to have a ministry to help young women who were trapped in a life of prostitution find freedom and a new life." He pointed to the Johansons and their charges and said, "As the under-shepherd, I have a responsibility to protect the sheep God has given us." He paused for several seconds, cleared his throat, grabbed each side of his little pulpit with his hands, leaned forward and said, "I will do everything in the strength God gives me to protect all of you including the young women from Second Chance House. If I must lay down my life, I will. Jesus said the hireling flees when he sees the wolf coming. I am no hireling. God called me to this place and to these people and I will fight to protect each and everyone of you. I hope you will be praying like you have never prayed before. Tomorrow night there may be a show down."

At that, Brother Jones, one of the two deacons in the church stood and said, "We need to pray for our pastor. Please, I'm asking that all of the men come to pray for Brother Patrick." At that the eight men in the congregation that morning stepped to the front of the little school house and laid hands on Brother Patrick. They began to pray with power and authority for God to lead and protect their beloved pastor. The women of the church all gathered in the back along with the children and they prayed. Their prayers were quieter than their husbands, but they were no less passionate.

After several minutes of prayer, Mrs. Fielding made were way back to the organ. Her son, Johnny, began pumping the bellows on the organ and she began to play and sing the first verse of "Tis So Sweet To Trust in Jesus" again. The whole congregation joined in and the service concluded. The men all patted Brother Patrick on the back and told him he was in their prayers. One or two even said, "I'm behind you Brother Patrick." At that, the congregation all dispersed to their homes and their Sunday dinner.

Patrick was invited to join the Johansons and the young ladies of Second Chance House for Sunday dinner, which he was glad to do. Sister Eunice had prepared roast chicken with potatoes and some of the vegetables she'd canned from the garden. Of course fresh bread and butter were on the table, too. After Allan said grace the group ate quietly. Everyone was thinking about the confrontation Patrick had the day before with Big Bertha and the message Patrick had brought that morning. "What did it all mean?" they wondered.

After taking a bite of potato, Allan cleared his throat, turned to Patrick and asked, "Do you have a plan, brother?"

Patrick wiped his mouth with his napkin, placed it back in his lap and said, "I've been thinking and praying on that, Brother Allan, and yes, I think I do have a plan. Several years ago I was driving a freight wagon up in Nevada and came across some

Basque people. Mostly they were shepherds and I learned some things about taking care of sheep from them. It seems that they use guard dogs to help the shepherds guard the flocks. When coyotes or wolves, or bears and mountain lions, as far as that goes, try to attack the sheep the dogs alert the shepherds and try to fend off the predators. Brother Allan, I can't cover this whole house so I'm going to be asking some of the men of the church to help me. They're going to be my guard dogs."

"Who do you have in mind?" Sister Eunice asked nervously. "What'll they have to do?"

Patrick looked at Eunice and then he turned to Allan. He reached out and put his hand on Allan's shoulder as he replied, "Well, I'm going to begin with Brother Allan. Allan, I need your help. You're here all of the time and know the layout of the house better than anyone. Will you help me guard the house? It's going to mean staying alert and being ready to fight, if need be."

Allan put his knife and fork down and looked at the women around the table. One by one he looked into their faces. First his sweet wife and then each of the young women who had come into that house to find a new life. Then he turned to his pastor and said, "I've never been a fighting man, Brother Patrick, but I'm no coward either. I'll do anything it takes to protect these lovely women." He thought for a short minute and said, "But, I don't have a gun. I haven't even shot a gun since I was a lad on the farm." After another moment of thought he sat up straight and continued, "I used to be pretty good at putting rabbits on the table, though."

Everyone seemed to be a little surprised to know that Allan had ever fired a gun. He was a quiet, gentle man who seemed to get along with everyone. But when they took time to think about it, they realized that every boy raised on a farm had used a gun at some point. He'd protected the flocks and herds from predators or simply put meat on the table like Allan. They realized it was only natural for Allan to have used a shotgun at some point when he was younger.

Patrick smiled at his older "brother" and said, "I'm hoping none of us will have to use firearms, brother, but I have my L.C. Smith twelve gauge up in my room and a couple of boxes of shells. It'll kick like a mule, but will definitely get the job done. I'll bring it over this afternoon, if that's all right."

Fifteen year old Mary Ann, the youngest of the doves in the house, couldn't hold back and anxiously asked, "What about us? Can't we help? After all, this fuss is really about us, isn't it?"

Eunice tried to shush Mary Ann, but Patrick said, "No, Sister Eunice, it's all right." Then he turned to Mary Ann and said, "Little Sister, I know you want to help, but best let us men take care of this problem."

Emily was the next to speak up. At the age of twenty-two, she was the oldest of the doves and had been in the life since she was fourteen. The hard years had taken their toll on her. Her eyes almost always looked sad and her shoulders always seemed hunched from carrying the weight of the world on them. Her brown hair already had streaks of grey showing, too. "Brother Patrick, if they get past you and your "guard dogs", we need to be able to defend ourselves. Please, give us a way to defend ourselves. Please," she pleaded.

Patrick knew she was right, but wondered how to arm them. "Do any of you have experience with firearms?" he asked.

The doves all looked at one another and shook their heads, "No."

Then Eunice spoke up, "Well, sir, I've got a kitchen full of frying pans. I don't reckon any of those men would fair to well if he got clobbered in the noggin by an angry woman with a frying pan." She looked straight at Patrick and asked, "Well, would he?"

No one was more surprised by Eunice's little speech than her husband. Allan cleared his throat again and said, "Well, I for one would not want to meet any of these ladies in a dark alley if she had a cast iron frying pan in her hands. I especially wouldn't want to cross my dear wife Eunice if she had one. Brother Patrick, I vote we give all of these girls a frying pan to defend themselves with." At that, all of the ladies gave a hearty, "Amen!"

"Well, I guess the motion carries," Patrick said. "Then here's the plan: Eunice, you and the ladies pair up. Each of you will get a frying pan or pot to use."

"How about a rolling pin? Could some of us use rolling pins?" Mary Ann asked.

Patrick had to chuckle to himself, "Yes, you can use rolling pins if you prefer."

One of the ladies interrupted Patrick and asked, "What about butcher knives or cleavers?"

Patrick sighed as he asked, "Have any of y'all ever had to stab a man?"

The ladies all shook their heads "no".

"Stabbing a man is way yonder different than hitting him in the head with a rolling pin. I think you all ought to stick with pans and rolling pins," Patrick said. Then he continued, "Now as I was saying, you all will be paired up and each of you will have your kitchen weapon of choice. Spread out into the bedrooms upstairs. Pray like you've never prayed before and be ready if those wolves get past us. Be ready like your lives depend on it, because they might."

That afternoon the Parson made his way to two other homes to enlist men to join him as his guard dogs. Deacon Charles Jones, who had called the little congregation to prayer that morning was the first to hear the pastor's plan. Much to his wife's dismay, he agreed to help. Then the Parson walked over to the Henry George home and enlisted Brother Henry's help. Henry's older son wanted to join the troop, but his father told him that at the age of ten, he was just a little too young. Patrick knew these men had served in the Army and had been in a few skirmishes. He knew they could handle themselves and they both had firearms of their own and would be ready when the time came.

At three o'clock on Monday afternoon, the guard dogs began to gather as per the Shepherd's instructions. Charles and Henry had their work clothes on with their Colts on their hips and their Winchesters in hand. Brother Patrick had arrived earlier and provided the twelve gauge for Brother Allan to use while he himself retained his Colt and his Winchester. Everyone gathered in the sitting room of Second Chance for instructions and prayer. Brother Patrick began, "Thank you all for being here today. It is certainly my prayer that we don't need any of these weapons and that Miss Kirbo and her lackeys think better of their threat to come and take the ladies by force. But if they do decide to carry out their threat we will be ready. Allan, you and I will be on the front porch ready to great our guests. Charles, you and Henry take position at the back corners of the house in case they come in the back way. Ladies, do you all have your weapons?"

The ladies all held up their pans and rolling pins as Eunice answered for them, "Yes, we do, Brother Patrick, and we're ready to use them if we have to." All of the ladies beamed with pride as she spoke. For the first time that Patrick could remember Emily's shoulders weren't hunched and her eyes were wide and sparkling with enthusiasm. "When she's smiling, she's a very handsome woman," Patrick thought to himself.

"Lord help any man who has to deal with you ladies," Patrick said with a smile. All of the ladies giggled when he did. "Okay, everyone, go to your assigned posts." At that the ladies went upstairs and the men went outside determined that no one would get past them.

Patrick and Allan sat in chairs at the opposite ends of the front porch, which stretched the full length of the house. Occasionally, some town folks would walk past the house and look at the two armed men sitting on the porch. Men and women would pass them wondering to one another or to themselves why those men were sitting on the porch with their guns ready for action. Some would pick up the pace when they saw them, but none were there to cause trouble.

Big Bertha was sitting at her usual table at the Last Chance as she lit a cigar and asked, "What time is it?"

One of her lackeys pulled a watch from his vest pocket and said, "It's six o'clock on the nose, ma'am."

Bertha snorted, "That's supper time to me and I don't see hide nor hair of any of them girls."

Across town at Second Chance House Eunice and Mary Ann were bringing coffee out to the shepherd and his guard dogs. "Any sign of them, Brother Patrick?" Eunice asked as she sat the cup on the porch rail.

"No, sister. No sign yet," he replied as he continued to sweep the street with his eyes.

"Do you reckon our prayers have been answered and they've decided to leave the ladies alone?" she asked.

Patrick looked up at Eunice and said, "Sister, I hope that's what it means, but right now I'm not going to let my guard down and you shouldn't either. I'll be here all night if need be."

Ewan Griffiths, owner of the Last Chance, walked up to Bertha's table to see how things were going. He was shorter and thinner than Bertha, standing at only five feet nine inches tall and weighing one hundred and ninety pounds. "What's the news?" he asked.

Bertha looked at his grey pinstriped suit and his silk shirt and tie and smiled. Her partner looked every bit the part of a Mississippi River Boat gambler, but she knew he was as tough as nails and and as ruthless a character as she was. "No news," she replied, "they didn't show."

Ewan picked up one of Bertha's cigars and lit it. After he blew the first puff of smoke out, he looked at the cigar, then at Bertha and asked, "So are you and the boys going over to get the girls now?"

Bertha looked at Ewan. There was a time she considered him a candidate for husband number four, but had decided that having three husbands mysteriously disappear was enough. She didn't need folks asking about the whereabouts of yet another husband. "No, we aren't going to go over there tonight. They'll be expecting us. I've got another plan to get my girls back," she said.

The old clock in the parlor of Second Chance struck eight o'clock and all of the men instinctively pulled their watches out and checked to see if they were all in synch. They were and nothing was happening. At half past eight Eunice and Mary Ann brought the men some supper, which they ate at their post. Nine o'clock came and went and so did ten. At eleven o'clock, Patrick gathered the men together. "I don't think they're coming, men. Charles, you and Henry ought to go home and get some sleep. I know you men have to go to work in the morning."

Henry piped up and asked, "Are you sure, Brother Patrick? I mean, I think we're both willing to stay if we are needed. Aren't we Charles?"

Charles shook his head, "Yes, sir. I believe you might need us, brother."

Patrick smiled as he said, "No, fellas, I believe the Lord has closed the lion's mouth tonight. I think Bertha knows she's whipped. Brother Allan and I will be here all night and the girls have all got their kitchen ware in case I'm wrong. You fellas go on and get a good night's sleep."

At that, Charles and Henry went home and Allan decided to go to bed. Patrick sat his chair in the corner of the front porch where he could lean back and catch a little shut eye. He was sure he would hear anyone coming up with the intent to cause trouble.

Patrick was sleeping soundly when one of Big Bertha's henchmen snuck up behind him. It was Bart, one of the men from Big Bertha's entourage. For a big man, he was amazingly quiet coming up behind Patrick with a club in his hand. Patrick never knew what hit him. The club came down with a great crack and Patrick fell out of his chair unconscious. He wouldn't wake up until later and when he did, he would have a splitting headache.

Bart gave out a little whistle, which signaled his confederates that the coast was clear. The four men met at the front door. These were the same men who had accompanied Big Bertha the day before. Leonard had a long scar down his right cheek. It looked like he'd lost a knife fight. Another was short and rather stout. Everyone simply called him Shorty. Lefty was the last one up the stairs. He was left handed and carried his revolver in a cross draw holster on his right hip. They had a plan and had every intention of carrying out that plan.

Leonard went to Allan and Eunice's bedroom, which was on the ground floor. His job would be to hold them, while the others rounded up the girls upstairs. He slipped into the room and quietly lit the lamp that was sitting on the bureau to the right of the door. Then he quickly drew his gun. It was an old Colt Navy revolver that he had carried since the war. It showed its years of use. The blueing was almost completely worn off, but he bragged he could shoot the eye out of a gnat at fifty paces with that old gun. Allan woke up when he heard the hammer being cocked. Leonard put his left index finger to his mustached mouth and shushed Allan. Eunice woke up when she heard the man shushing her husband. Her eyes were as big as saucers when she saw who was in their bedroom. She looked at this stranger and then looked at Allan. The two embraced and both began to whisper prayers for the Lord's help and deliverance.

The other three thugs made their way up the stairs to the girls' bedrooms. Bart and Lefty slipped into the first bedroom. There was a full moon that night, which gave just enough light that they could see who was in the room. The two girls who were sleeping in that room were the oldest and youngest residents of Second Chance House. The two men slipped up to Emily and Mary Ann. Each had his sidearm drawn. They looked at one another and nodded. When they did, they both cocked the hammers on their revolvers and at the same time put their left hands over the girls' mouths. The girls woke up with a start. They wanted to scream. They tried to scream, but they couldn't because of the hands over their mouths. They could barely see the men who were holding them, but they could definitely feel the cold steel of the revolvers pressing against their chests. Bart, the man who had clubbed the Parson, spoke in a whisper, "Girls, you all are coming with us. Do you understand?" The girls were silent. "Nod your heads, if you understand," he said harshly. The two girls nodded their heads as they looked across the dimly lit room at one another. "Good," he said. "We are going to let you up now. Do not scream and you'll be alright."

Mary Ann was so frightened that she was shaking, but Emily knew they had to do everything in their power to escape so she screamed, "H-e-l-p!"

When Emily screamed the big man swung his revolver and hit her in the side of the head. She was thrown back onto her bed. Blood spurted from her head onto the wall as she was knocked unconscious. The big man looked at little Mary Ann and said in a low, harsh voice, "Do you see what happens when you don't do as you're told?"

Mary Ann was so frightened she thought she might pass out, but she had the presence of mind to nod her head, "Yes."

The fourth man, Shorty, was about to open the next bedroom door when Emily let out her blood curdling scream for help. He stopped and turned towards the sound of the scream when two more girls came out of their bedroom. One was carrying a cast iron frying pan and the other was carrying a rolling pin. When they saw the intruder in the hall way, they immediately sprang into action swinging their weapons with all of their might. Deborah was a fireball of a redhead. She was only five feet tall, but she had both hands on the handle of her frying pan. She raised that pan in the air and cracked the thug in the back of his head while he was look-ing in the direction of the scream. The other girl, Leah, was taller and bigger than her roommate, when she saw the man go down in front of her, she began beating him with her rolling pin. At one point she was pretty sure she heard his leg break.

There was a great deal of commotion in the hall way, which drew the final res-ident of Second Chance out of her room. Candace was in her nightgown like the other girls. Her round face always looked like she's been out in the sun too long and tonight it was as red as branding iron just out of the fire. She was a little confused, but she had brought her frying pan with her, just in case. When she saw Deborah and Leah beating on the man in the hall way, she joined in by giving him a crack or two of her own.

Suddenly two men emerged from the first bedroom. One had Emily slung over his shoulder and the other was holding a gun to Mary Ann's head. Bart raised his gun and fired a shot into the ceiling. The blast of the gun and the flash from the barrel caused the girls to cringe and scream with fright. The two men pointed their guns at the ladies in the hallway. Bart yelled, "Stop! Stop right now! You all are coming with us so hush up and put them things down. We don't want to hurt none of y'all."

Little Deborah looked at those two men, squinted her eyes and snarled, "No, we are not. I'll die right here before I go anywhere with you sidewinders."

Lefty had his arm around Mary Ann's shoulders and pressed his gun into Mary Ann's head harder than before and said, "If you all don't come with us right now, I'll shoot this little girl." At that Mary Ann let out a whimper.

Candace looked like she was about to breath fire from her nostrils. She tightened her grip on the frying pan and said, "Mister, you'll have to kill all of us 'cause we ain't coming with you, no matter what."

The man holding Mary Ann said, "Fine. If that's how you want it, fine." With that said, he pointed his gun at Candace and fired. The girls all screamed and Candace went down as the forty-five slug tore through her leg.

There was a shout from the Johanson's bedroom, "What are you all doing up there? Come on, let's get out of here."

The two men tightened their grips on the women they were holding and Bart said, "Come on, let's get out of here before everyone in town is on us." Dogs were barking around the neighborhood and lamps were being lit as people were awakened by the gunfire. The two pointed their guns at the women who were holding Candace and began to back down the hallway and down the staircase.

"What about him?" Lefty asked as he pointed his gun towards Shorty. "Are we just going to leave him there?"

"He's on his own. Besides, they might have killed him already. We need to go!" Bart replied. Then Bart looked at the women and said, "If we see any of y'all stick your heads out the front door, we will blow it plum off! Do I make myself clear?"

The women all had their heads down when they nodded, "Yes" in response to Bart's question.

After the three men left the house with Emily and Mary Ann, Allan and Eunice came upstairs to see how the women were. Allan, holding the shotgun Patrick had loaned him, sent Deborah to fetch the doctor and the town Marshall. Leah was to stay with Candace as he and Eunice checked on Brother Patrick. They found him unconscious, lying in a heap on the front porch. They both ran to him, but it was Eunice who knelt down to pat his cheeks and speak softly to him. Allan stood with his back to them while he kept watch, in case the three thugs decided to come back.

Patrick was revived after just a minute of Eunice's gentle touches, but he had a goose egg on the back of his head and a throbbing headache to go with it. He tried to stand, but couldn't at first. "The ladies?" he asked weakly, "How are the ladies?"

Eunice's eyes dropped as she spoke, "Emily and Mary Ann were taken and Candace was shot in the leg. Leah is tending to Candace and Deborah has gone to fetch the doctor and the Marshall. The only good news is that the girls got one of the men. He's upstairs and the girls knocked him clean out. They worked him over pretty good," Eunice said with a hint of a smile on her face.

The doc checked the Parson's head, dug the bullet out of Candace's leg and set Shorty's broken leg. Patrick and Allan were outraged when the Marshall was about to let Shorty go. "That man broke into our house and attempted to kidnap these women," Allan declared.

The Marshall shrugged his shoulders and said, "But, Mr. Johanson, they're whores. No one really cares."

Patrick's blood was boiling. He wanted to scream, but the throbbing in his head forced him to speak in a whisper, "Are you serious? These women have left that life. They're trying to get their lives straightened out and serve the Lord. Don't you understand, they are someone's sisters and daughters, Marshall? God loves them as much as he does anyone."

"What exactly do you want me to do, Parson?" the Marshall asked.

"What do I want you to do?" Patrick asked. "I want you to do your job. I want you to arrest this skunk and go get those women who were kidnapped. That's what I want you to do."

The Marshall looked at Patrick and said, "Parson, no jury is going to convict this fella of anything, so it would be a waste of my time to arrest him and try him for kidnapping. If you want them whores back, you'll have to go after them yourself." At that he turned to leave the house.

Patrick was wobbly when he stood up, but once he got his feet under him he reached out and grabbed the Marshall by the shoulder. He winced in pain as he spoke, "If you won't arrest him, at least leave him here so we can question him and find out where they have taken the ladies."

The Marshall turned back to face Patrick as he spoke, "No, sir, I can't do that. This man has already been assaulted. He's bruised all over and has a broken leg. I'm afraid these women will kill him, if I leave him here. No, I'll take him with me and deliver him back to the Last Chance." At that he turned to Shorty and said, "Come on, pard. I'll take you back to the Saloon and buy you a beer."

Later that afternoon word had spread throughout Prescott about the late night raid on Second Chance House. Members of the Baptist Church started coming by to talk with Patrick and the Johansons. Some of the church members were aghast that their pastor would be involved in activity like this. They questioned if a pastor should be fighting with men and taking up for "those kinds of women". Patrick's response to those questions was simple: God had called him to be a shepherd and a shepherd protects his flock. If anyone hinted they might leave the church because of this situation, he simply said they would be missed and he would be praying for them. Others were supportive and pledged to pray for their pastor and the safe return of the ladies. A few men offered to help Patrick if he was going to take any action.

Just before supper time, Charles Jones and Henry George, the guard dogs from the night before knocked on the door of Second Chance. They were there to help Patrick develop a plan. Allan joined the other three in the parlor. They spent several minutes praying together then Charles asked Patrick, "How are you doing, Brother?"

Patrick put his hand on the back of his head and said, "Well, thanks to Sister Eunice getting some ice to put on my head, my goose egg is going down and the head ache is getting better. I believe I'll be well enough to go find our sisters by tomorrow morning."

"I hate to wait that long," Henry said.

Allan turned to Henry and said, "I do to, but I think we need Brother Patrick to be with us if we are going to be successful. I can't imagine facing those wolves without our shepherd."

The other men nodded in agreement and Charles asked, "Are there any others who can join this pack of guard dogs?"

"The three McDougall brothers came by earlier and pledged their help," Patrick said.

"Those three would be a tremendous help," Allan said. "They're all miners and tough as nails. I believe we could count on them in a scrape."

Patrick smiled at the men around the room and said, "That'll make seven of us. A good number according to the Bible. Let's make some plans"

That afternoon the shepherd and his guard dogs put their heads together and developed a plan of attack for the next day. Patrick sent Henry and Charles out to inform the McDougalls and then home to get some sleep.

The next morning Patrick and his guard dogs all met at Second Chance House at nine o'clock. They and the ladies who lived there gathered in the parlor to go over their plans one more time and then to spend a season in prayer. Brother Patrick reminded them all of the story of David and Goliath. "We need to remember that young David was smaller and, as far as anyone knew, had inferior weapons, but God had a plan to save his people through this young, ruddy boy. We are not going to fight for ourselves. We are going to rescue our sisters in Christ. I believe God will give us the victory today, but that doesn't mean that none of us will be harmed. This is a dangerous mission. No one will think less of you, if you want to turn back now." He stopped to look at each of the men, but no one was taking him up on his offer.

"We're with you, brother. We're with you all the way," Allan said as he looked around the circle of men in that room.

Each man in turn looked at Patrick and said, "Yes, sir, we are with you."

"Then each of you know your job, let's go," Patrick said as he picked up his Winchester and started for the door. Each man had his weapon at the ready. Patrick, Charles and Henry all had revolvers on their hips and Winchesters in their hands. Patrick levered a round into the chamber and lowered the hammer to quarter cock and the others followed suit. Allan had the twelve gauge Patrick had loaned him and the McDougall brothers, Donald, Dennis and Jeffrey, all had pick handles. People passing them on the street could see that trouble was brewing and a small crowd began to form as people were following them. One man grabbed a young boy and told him to run and fetch the Marshall. By the time they reached the Last Chance, they had attracted a crowd of twenty on lookers.

When Patrick got to the Last Chance, he looked in and there they were, the King and Queen of Sin. Miss Bertha Kirbo and Ewan Griffiths were sitting together at a table against the north wall of the saloon. They both had cups of steaming hot coffee in front of them as they talked business. Two of Griffiths' henchmen stood to the side of them. Each had a revolver on his hip and each stood ready to use that revolver to expedite any problems the boss might assign him to. There weren't many customers in the saloon yet. The card tables were largely empty and most of the soiled doves were sleeping in after a busy night.

Patrick pushed his way through the batwing doors followed by his guard dogs. Charles and Henry filed in together, then Allan and the McDougalls. Patrick kept his eyes fixed on Miss Bertha and Mr. Griffiths, but the other men kept their eyes moving around the room. Donald and Dennis McDougall even turned around to watch the door.

Ewan Griffiths was the first to speak, "Well, good morning, Parson. I wouldn't have taken you for a morning drinker, but, hey, to each his own, I say." Then he turned to the bartender and said, "Sammy, set up drinks for our guests. The Parson's drink will be on the house."

"Griffith, you know we aren't here for drinks," Patrick said very matter of factly. "We're here to take the ladies your men kidnapped home."

"Those are pretty strong words there, Parson," Griffiths replied. "Accusing a man of kidnapping is pretty serious stuff. As a matter of fact, many would consider them fighting words." Then he turned to Big Bertha and said, "Miss Bertha, do you know anything about some girls going missing from that house the Parson runs?"

Bertha picked up her coffee cup, blew on it, took a sip then turned to Griffiths, "No, sir, I do not." Then she turned to Patrick and asked, "Which girls have you lost there, Parson?"

Patrick tipped his hat before speaking again, "You know very well which girls I'm referring to, ma'am. I'm talking about Emily and Mary Ann. Four of the men in the employ of either you or Mr. Griffiths broke into the Second Chance House and abducted them. We just want to take them home."

As Patrick was finishing addressing Miss Bertha, the two henchmen standing to the side of Kirbo and Griffith's table took a step forward and put their hands on their revolvers. Patrick and the others stiffened and Patrick pulled the hammer on his Winchester to full cock.

Ewan Griffith put his hands out in order to stop his men from drawing their guns and said, "Now see, I told you those were fighting words. Let's be very careful here. We don't want to begin the day with bloodshed. The women you are looking for are not here. I can't help it if they didn't want to stay at your little house, Parson, but they are simply not here."

Patrick raised his Winchester to his shoulder and looked Griffiths in the eye, "We are not leaving without those ladies, Griffiths. If there's going to be gun play, you will be the first to taste lead."

Just then the Marshall came bursting into the saloon. "What's goin on here?" he shouted. "You men put your guns down. Parson, that means you, too!"

Patrick kept his Winchester pointed at Griffith's head while he spoke, "Marshall, I told you that two of the women from Second Chance House were kidnapped. Since you wouldn't do anything about it, we decided we would. We have come for the women and we aren't leaving without them."

The Marshall drew back his coat, drew his Smith and Wesson revolver, and pointed it at the back of Patrick's head and said, "Parson, if you don't put that rifle down, right now, I'm going to blow a hole in the back of your head big enough to drive a stage coach through. I can't miss at this distance and I'm not bluffing." As he finished speaking, everyone in the saloon could hear the Marshall cock the hammer of his revolver. No one was breathing for a moment.

Allan Johanson was the first to break the silence, "Brother Patrick, he's not joking. Let's back off for now and live to fight another day."

Patrick was seeing red and couldn't hear Allan's plea. He felt that, as the God called shepherd of the sheep, he would rather die trying to protect the sheep than live knowing he'd let the wolves get his sheep. His finger began to close in on the trigger of his rifle. At least he could kill the head wolf, he thought.

Suddenly, one of the soiled doves who was watching from upstairs shouted, "Parson! Parson, the girls you are looking for ain't here! Parson, did you hear me? Emily and Mary Ann ain't here!"

Allan called out to Patrick again, "Patrick, did you hear her? The women we are looking for aren't here." Patrick didn't seem to be hearing anything anyone was saying so Allan reached out and touched Patrick's shoulder and said again, "Patrick, did you hear her? The women we are looking for aren't here. We need to go and find out where they are."

Finally Patrick heard Allan and turned to look at him. "They aren't here?" he asked.

"No, Patrick, they aren't. Let's go and find out where they are so we can bring them home," Allan said pleadingly.

"Okay, Allan, we'll go," he said. Then he turned back to Big Bertha and Ewan and said, "We will find those ladies and we'll be back if they've been harmed in any way." At that Patrick and his guard dogs began to back out of the saloon.

When they got out onto the boardwalk they were met by one of the soiled doves who had snuck out the back of the saloon and run around to talk to them. She wasn't wearing anything but her undergarments and a sheer robe to cover herself. She spoke to Allan first and he brought her to Patrick. "Brother Patrick, this young woman says she knows where Emily and Mary Ann are and she'll tell us if we take her away from here."

Patrick turned to see a chubby girl who couldn't be more than sixteen years old. Her hair was curled and piled up on her head and her face was painted up like, well, like a whore. But he also noticed that her makeup was running down her cheeks from the flood of tears she had shed. Immediately he was able to calm down as he spoke to her, "What's your name, little sister?"

"They call me, Roxy, Parson," she said rather sheepishly.

"First of all, you can call me Brother Patrick and second of all, what's your Christian name?" Patrick was speaking as gently as a father would speak to a beloved daughter.

"My parents named me Roxanne, sir," she replied.

"Well, Roxanne, what do you know about the whereabouts of Emily and Mary Ann and what can we do to help you?" Patrick asked.

Roxanne looked around to see that the guard dogs had surrounded her, but she didn't feel closed in or threatened. She felt protected. "They've taken them girls to Griffith's house out in Miller Valley, Brother Patrick. I think they're planning to take them to one of Big Bertha's other houses in the next day or two," she replied.

"Thank you, Roxanne. Now how can we help you?" Patrick asked again.

Roxanne looked around again to see who was listening. Then she leaned in to Patrick and whispered, "Can you take me to that Second Chance House of yours? I don't want to live like this anymore." At that she began to weep again.

Brother Allan took off his coat and put it around Roxanne. Then he took her in his arms and began to speak tenderly to her, "It's going to be alright, little sister. You can come with us and we'll do everything we can to keep you safe and help you find a new life, a life away from Miss Bertha and this place."

Patrick looked at the men and said, "Let's take Roxanne back to the house. We can plan out our next move from there." The men surrounded Roxanne so no one could see that she was with them, then the group all walked back to the house together.

The ladies all shared some of their clothes with Roxanne and helped her get settled in. Then Patrick, the guard dogs and the ladies had their noon meal together. Roxanne told them what she knew about the situation at Griffith's house. After dinner the men retired to the parlor to make their plans. It was decided that the McDougall brothers would stay at Second Chance in case another attempt was made to kidnap the ladies who were there. Patrick and the other men would go to Griffith's house and rescue Emily and Mary Ann. Allan would drive the wagon so they would have a way to bring the ladies back and the others would ride their own horses.

The men stopped about fifty yards from the house and tied their horses to some trees a little off of the road. Everyone checked their firearms and those with pistols loaded the sixth cylinder, just in case. Quietly, they walked up to a pile of granite rocks that stood at the entrance to the lane that led to the house. No one was outside, but several horses were tied up in front of the house and smoke could be seen curling up from the chimney. Before they moved forward, Patrick took a look around. The sky was as pretty a blue as he'd ever seen. The air had a mix of the smell of pine trees and of smoke from the chimney. This was about as nice a day as one could ask for, but it was about to be shattered by violence and blood shed.

As the men moved forward, they had twenty or more yards to close before they reached the cabin. After just a minute Patrick noticed something shiny on the ground. He leaned down to pick it up and realized it was the necklace with a silver cross on it Emily had been given the day of her baptism. The ladies were here. He held the necklace up for the others to see and motioned for Charles and Allan to go to the back of the cabin. He and Henry would go in the front door. They had already agreed that when the men in the front kicked in the door and shouted, the men in the back would crash through the back door.

Henry and Patrick crept up to the front door and waited a long moment to give the others time to get to the back door. Then Patrick looked straight at Henry as he nodded his head three times. Immediately after the third nod he kicked in the door and shouted, "Everybody down. Get down on the floor or we will shoot." At that moment splinters of wood flew from the back door as it was kicked open. Charles and Allan came in with their firearms at the ready. Inside the house two men sat at a table playing cards. Ewan Griffiths was sitting on a couch next to Emily and a third thug was standing over Mary Ann. The three men with Griffiths were the ones who had kidnapped the women at the house. The only one missing was the man with the broken leg.

Patrick was seeing red again. His anger was boiling up inside of him and his hands were starting to tremble. He'd felt like this when he was deer hunting, but had never experienced "buck fever" at any other time. He could see that none of the men who were holding the women had laid down on the floor and that made him even angrier. A voice came out of Patrick that no one had ever heard before, "I said to get down on the floor and I meant it," he screamed.

Griffiths' three henchmen immediately dropped to the floor, but Griffiths actually stood up. His arms were crossed on his chest and his eyes were glued on Patrick who was breathing heavily. "Let's talk this over," Griffiths said calmly.

Patrick didn't swear as a habit, but there were times he had to restrain himself and this was one of those times. His voice lowered as he pulled the hammer back on his Winchester, "I'm not here to negotiate with you, Griffiths. I'm here to take these women home. If you or your men try to stop us, we will shoot. Do you understand me?"

Griffiths grinned just a little when he replied, "Yes, Parson, I understand you perfectly." What Patrick didn't realize was Griffiths' right hand was holding the grip of his revolver, which rested in a shoulder holster under his coat. He drew it, cocked the hammer and fired wildly towards Patrick and Henry. Both of them instinctively ducked and dove behind chairs that faced into the room. While they were diving for cover, Griffiths grabbed Emily with his right hand and jerked her up off of the couch. He pulled Emily in front of himself and pressed his Smith and Wesson revolver against her head. He used her as a human shield.

Patrick dropped his Winchester when he dove behind the chair, but was able to grab it and shoulder it again. With his carbine pointed straight at Griffiths' head, Patrick called out, "Let the lady go, Griffiths. This doesn't have to end in bloodshed."

Griffiths looked at Emily and then at Patrick, "I don't see any ladies here, Parson. All I see is some whores who need to get back to making me some money. You all back out of my house and I'll forget this little incident ever happened."

Lefty thought his boss had the upper hand and decided he would join him in taking control of the situation. He rolled onto his left side and went for the revolver he carried on his right hip. When he did, Henry pulled the trigger on his Winchester. There was an explosion of fire and smoke and the forty caliber slug found its mark. Lefty's body was thrown backwards. He crashed into a small table and overturned the lamp sitting on it. He wouldn't be bothering anyone again.

The women both screamed when Henry fired his gun and Griffiths swore out loud. Griffiths wasn't as calm as he had been. He realized this small town parson and his pack of guard dogs weren't going to go away quietly. In that moment Patrick stood up from behind the chair and kept his gun trained on Griffiths' head. He turned his focus to Emily whose eyes were focused on him and begging for help. His buck fever had subsided and he was calm when his hand came off of his carbine and motioned downward twice. Emily looked confused. She didn't understand what that motion meant at first. Quickly, while Griffiths was still distracted, Patrick motioned again and Emily nodded to show she understood his intent.

"Now!" Patrick shouted and at that Emily simply let her knees buckle under her. She fell straight down pulling herself out of Griffiths' grasp. Griffiths looked down to see what was going on then looked up at Patrick again. In that instant he realized what was happening and ducked to the left as he was turning his gun towards Patrick, but Patrick had the drop on him and fired first. This time it was Patrick's bullet that found its mark. The bullet didn't hit him in the head, but it did shatter Griffiths' right shoulder causing him to drop his gun.

The guard dogs all moved in and disarmed Griffiths' henchmen. Patrick picked up the boss man's revolver and tucked it into his waist. "Griffiths, we are taking you all to the Marshall and pressing kidnapping charges against you," he looked up at the others and continued, "against all of you." Then he turned to Emily and Mary Ann, "Sisters, are you all alright?"

The two women were holding each other tightly and weeping. Emily composed herself for a moment and replied, "Brother Patrick, we're alright now. Thank you, thank you for coming for us."

The next few minutes were spent making preparations to go back to town. The three living criminals were tied and placed on their own horses. Allan had brought blankets to wrap the women in and they were helped up into the wagon. The dead man was wrapped in a blanket from one of the bedrooms upstairs. As the men placed his body in the back of the wagon with the women, Allan apologized for making them ride with his body. Emily looked at the body and then at Allan, "It's alright, Brother Allan, he can't hurt us now."

The party looked like some sort of bizarre parade coming down Main Street to the jail. The Parson led the way, then the wagon filled with blanket clad women and a blanket wrapped body. Bringing up the rear of the parade were three men tied up on horses followed by three men with guns. The horses and wagon kicked up a little dust, but that didn't keep the town's folk from following to see what in the world was going on.

Someone had run ahead to tell the Marshall about the folks that were coming down Main Street. He stepped out of his office and onto the boardwalk just a minute before Patrick rode up. "What in blazes is going on here, Parson?" he demanded.

"Well, Marshall, it seems we've been out doing your job for you. Ewan Griffiths and his henchmen kidnapped these ladies. Since you wouldn't do anything to rescue them, we decided we had to. They're our sisters and we weren't going to stand by and let Griffiths force them back into a life of prostitution. There was a gun fight and the feller lying in the back of the wagon was shot and killed, in self-defense. Griffiths was also shot in self defense, but I'm sorry to say, he might just live. We are pressing charges against the lot of them." At that, Patrick began to dismount from his horse and step up onto the boardwalk.

As Patrick began to approach the Marshall someone was pushing their way through the crowd. It was Big Bertha Kirbo. She pushed men and women out of her way, threw a small cigar onto the ground and pulled a revolver out of her purse. People gasped, but no one acted and in that instant she cocked the hammer of her gun and fired. The bullet hit Patrick in his lower back. After what seemed like several minutes, but was in reality less than a second, Patrick's knees buckled. He tried to turn to see who had shot him in the back, but hit the boardwalk before he turned completely. Someone in the crowd grabbed Bertha's gun from her hand and two men restrained her. She didn't put up a fight, though. She simply stood there glaring at the Parson who was lying in a growing pool of blood.

The Marshall broke the silence as he called out, "Someone go fetch the doctor." Two men responded and ran off to the doctor's office.

Emily jumped down from the wagon and ran to Patrick. She took the blanket from her own shoulders and began to wrap Patrick in it. Dressed in the nightgown she was wearing when she was kidnapped, she sat next to him and gently stroked his forehead. Tears were rolling down her cheeks as she gently spoke to him, "You can't die. Do you hear me, Patrick? You are not allowed to die today." She choked as she said, "You can't leave me."

Patrick looked at her sweet face and was sorry to be causing her this sadness. He knew she'd seen plenty of sadness in her life. He grinned just a little as he spoke,

"Don't worry, I'm not going to die today. I won't leave you, not today, not ever."

At that moment two things happened. A spark shot between Patrick and Emily. Something neither had felt before. And the doctor arrived to care for his patient.

CHAPTER 8:
THE PARSON TAKES A WIFE

There were two big items of gossip in Prescott that week. They both related to the shooting of the Prescott Parson in front of the Marshall's office. The first was that Big Bertha Kirbo had escaped jail. Because there were so many witnesses to the shooting, the Marshall had no choice but to charge her with attempted murder, but somehow his jail couldn't hold her. The consensus seemed to be that she had bribed the deputy on duty the night she escaped. He wasn't fired or arrested and that shiny new pair of boots seemed awfully suspicious. Most seemed to agree that the Marshall himself had received a bribe for looking the other way, too.

The second item of gossip was was even juicer than the first. The Parson had been taken over to the Second Chance House to recover. He, a single man, was living in that house with "all them whores". The fact was that there was only one doctor in Prescott and there was no hospital to care for his needs.

After the Parson was carried to Second Chance, the doctor had the dining room table cleared and used it as an operating table. Allan Johanson held a lamp over the wound so the doc could see what he was doing. He removed the bullet from the Parson's back and did the best he could to repair the damage to his bowels. He was able to remove the thirty-six caliber slug, but it had punctured the bowels which worried the doc greatly.

After the surgery was over, the doc took Allan aside and said, "Allan, I've done all I can."

"He's going to be alright, isn't he, doctor," Allan pleaded.

As the doctor was putting his instruments back in his bag, he looked up and said, "He should make a full recovery, if sepsis doesn't set in, but if it does, well…let's pray that it doesn't."

The two older of the McDougall brothers, Donald and Dennis, were at the house waiting to see how Patrick was doing and making sure there wasn't another attack on the ladies who lived there. Brother Allan asked them to help carry Patrick up the stairs to one of the bedrooms. It was there that the residents of Second Chance would tend to his needs and hope for his recovery.

The day after the surgery, Patrick developed a fever and that fever only got worse for the next twenty-four hours. One of the residents of Second Chance was with Patrick every minute. They mopped his head and face with cool, wet cloths. They sang hymns to him and prayed several times a day, but he wasn't getting better. Emily Chadwick, the oldest of the rescued doves in the house, insisted on taking the night shift with Patrick. She changed his bandages, held his hand, mopped his face, and read scripture to him. She would sleep in a chair next to his bed, but she wouldn't leave him for even a moment all during the night.

On the third day after the surgery, the doctor came back to check on Patrick. He took Allan aside again and told him things were worse and he was certain sepsis had set in. There was little hope for recovery now.

After the doctor left, Allan called everyone into the parlor to share the doctor's prognosis. All of the women began to weep when they heard the news, but Allan refused to give up hope. "The doctor's done all he can, but I don't believe God is finished with Brother Patrick. We need to pray for a miracle. Please, let's pray like we've never prayed before."

At that, all of the residents of Second Chance House knelt and held hands as they prayed for their beloved pastor. All of them prayed, but it was Roxanne who expressed the prayer of the group best, "Lord," she said, "I ain't been here long, but if it wasn't for Brother Patrick and these folks, I would still be whorin'. I know I just got saved, but won't you hear the prayers of a girl who loves you more than anything in the world? Please, please, please give us a miracle. Please. Save Brother Patrick. Please." Everyone was weeping, but they choked back their tears to join Roxanne in a most hearty, "Amen!"

That afternoon the doctor came by to check on Patrick again. Sister Eunice was changing his bandage when the doc came into the room. The wound was as red and filled with puss as it had been the day before. When Brother Allan came into the room, the doctor said, "This is going to sound crazy, but during the night I remembered something I'd read years ago. It seems the Egyptians used a poultice of moldy bread on infections. Believe it or not, it worked. Well, at least it did sometimes."

Allan was very surprised to hear that moldy bread could be good for anything. "We don't have any moldy bread here," he said. "With all of these mouths to feed, the bread gets eaten up pretty quickly."

"I thought that might be the case, so I stopped at Swenson's bakery to see if they might have some laying around and they actually did," the doctor said as he was pulling a piece of moldy bread wrapped in a handkerchief from his coat pocket.

Allan held the bread in his hands and looked at the doctor as he asked, "Do you think it'll work?"

"To be honest," the doc replied, "it'll be a miracle if it does."

Allan smiled when he heard those words, "What are we waiting for? Let's try it."

Allan helped the doc make a poultice of the bread and secure it in place with fresh bandages. When they were finished, Allan asked the doc if he would join him in prayer. "Lord, you know we've prayed for a miracle. If it would be your will, would you give healing to our brother Patrick? I don't know if you can use a piece of moldy bread to heal him or not, but I'm reminded of the time Jesus healed a man's eyes with a little mud. So please, by your power and for your glory, heal Patrick. In Jesus' name. Amen."

The doctor wasn't a man of prayer and wasn't quite sure how to respond so he looked up and said, "Um, uh, amen."

That night, as Emily was tending to Patrick, the fever broke. He broke out in a sweat and his body immediately began to cool. Emily rushed downstairs to wake Allan and Eunice. The three of them could see a marked improvement in Patrick and began to thank the Lord for the miracle he was doing. About six thirty that morning, as the sunlight was coming through the bedroom window, Patrick opened his eyes. He looked up into Emily's face and gave her a weak, little grin. Emily's heart leaped within her when she saw that smile, even as weak as it was.

That day began a long road of recovery. Patrick could drink water and took a little broth. He couldn't get out of bed yet, but he could talk a little and enjoy the life God was restoring within him.

Every day Patrick made improvement. He began to eat solid food and walk up and down the hall. By the seventh day he asked for a wash basin, some soap and a razor. He washed himself, shaved, and combed his hair. He put on the clothes Sister Eunice had washed for him and waited for his afternoon visit with Emily. Emily found him sitting up in bed, clothed, smelling like Sunday morning. She'd been coming in every afternoon to read to him from the Bible. Inwardly, they both looked forward to that time together and knew that the Bible reading was a good excuse to be together, yet neither had said as much.

The day before, Emily had read the whole book of Daniel. They both admitted they found it to be a beautiful book, but neither fully understood all of the prophesies it contained. "Where would you like me to read today," Emily asked her patient.

Patrick looked at the loveliest nurse he'd ever seen and said, "Well, sis, we finished Daniel yesterday. Why don't you just continue on and read the next book, Hosea?"

As she began thumbing through her Bible in order to find Hosea, she said, "Hosea? I don't believe I've read that one yet."

"It's been a while for me," Patrick replied. "There'll be some names that are hard to pronounce, but otherwise it's a good book. It really shows God's love for unfaithful Israel."

Having found the book, Emily began reading, "The word of the LORD that came unto Hosea, the son of Beeri, in the days of Uzziah, Jotham, Ahaz, and Hezekiah, kings of Judah, and in the days of Jeroboam the son of Joash, king of Israel." Emily stumbled over most of the names in that verse, but Patrick patiently helped her. "You were right, there are some difficult names in this book," she said.

She picked up the reading at verse two, "The beginning of the word of the LORD by Hosea. And the LORD said to Hosea, Go, take unto thee a wife of whoredoms and children of whoredoms: for the land hath committed great whoredom, departing from the LORD."

Patrick put out his hand to touch Emily's arm, "Wait! Read that again, please?" he pleaded.

"The beginning of the word of the LORD by Hosea. And the LORD said to Hosea, Go, take unto thee a wife of whoredoms and children of whoredoms: for the land hath committed great whoredom, departing from the LORD," she read.

Patrick only heard eight words, "Go, take unto thee a wife of whoredoms". He'd read Hosea before and had even done some preaching from it, but those words were like an arrow from the Lord's quiver. They pierced him. It was like the Holy Spirit had put his finger on his heart. It was as if they weren't there before, but God had put them there for him to hear for the first time that day.

He put his hand out and touched Emily's arm again. "Emily, I think that's all for today. Please, would you mind if I spent some time alone today?"

Emily was confused. They had always enjoyed their time together. "Why would he ask me to leave?" she wondered to herself. She looked into his face, her eyes darting back and forth, searching for a clue to this sudden mood change. "Patrick, have I done something wrong?" she asked.

Patrick looked at her and could see by her expression that she was deeply worried. "Oh, no!" he said. "It's, well, it's just that something has occurred to me and I think I need to spend some time praying on it. Please, you have done nothing wrong and I'm sorry to have worried you. It's not you. It's not you at all. I just really need to spend some time alone. You understand, don't you?"

"To be honest, I don't understand, but I'll leave you alone so you can pray. May I come back later?" Her eyes were pleading with him as she spoke. She really didn't understand all of her feelings for Patrick, but she knew she wanted to spend time with him.

"Emily, I'll see you at supper time. Please, understand, you haven't done anything wrong. I just need to pray on something. I'll tell you more when I'm able." His voice was as gentle and calm as it could be and somehow she felt comforted by it.

Patrick got up and followed Emily to the door. She turned to look at him one more time as she left his room. She smiled at him. He smiled back, but at the same time was closing his door. She didn't know what to think or feel as she walked down the hall to the staircase. She stopped at the top of the stairs and looked back at the closed door to the room he was in. "What was happening?" she wondered to herself. She walked down the stairs and went straight to the kitchen to help Eunice prepare the evening meal.

As soon as Emily left and the door was closed, Patrick stepped over to the bed, picked his Bible up from the nightstand, and dropped to his knees to pray. Normally, he would have gone out into the woods by himself to spend this time with God, but since he was still recovering from the bullet wound and fever, he knew he didn't dare get on a horse and ride out by himself. As quietly as he could, he prayed and read scripture and prayed some more. The afternoon was consumed with prayer, Bible reading, and quiet reflection. By the time Allan called everyone to supper, Patrick Donovan felt certain he had discerned the Lord's will. If he was right, everything was going to change and nothing about that change was going to be easy.

When Patrick came down for supper, he sat at the opposite end of the table from Allan. He quietly greeted everyone and ate his meal in silence. Emily watched him. She watched the expression on his face. He hadn't really looked at her through the whole meal, but he didn't look upset. Actually, he looked like he was at perfect peace. She'd never seen anyone look like that before and had no way to understand what was going on.

At the end of the meal, Patrick folded his napkin and placed it on the table next to his plate and said, "Sister Eunice, that was a wonderful meal, as usual. Thank you." Then he turned his attention to Allan and said, "Brother Allan, could I meet with you," then turning his head so he was looking directly into Emily's eyes, "and Emily in the parlor, please?"

Allan and Emily looked at one another and then at Patrick. Then Allan replied, "Yes, of course."

Everyone at the table looked confused for a long moment, but Eunice broke the silence, "Ladies, let's clear the table while these three have a conversation." At that everyone got up from the table. The ladies began clearing the table while Patrick, Allan and Emily began walking toward the parlor. All eyes were on the three leaving the room. Eunice spoke again, "Ladies, let's attend to our own duties."

When they got to the parlor, Patrick closed the doors and asked Allan and Emily to have a seat. Allan had a little grin on his face, but Emily felt like she was going to jump out of her skin. "What was this about?" her mind screamed to itself.

Patrick looked at the two of them and knew he was being needlessly mysterious and he could see by the look on Emily's face that he was causing her no little amount of emotional pain. "Please forgive me for being so mysterious, but I've got something I need to share with you and I'll get right to the point," Patrick said. Two pairs of eyes were glued on him. Emily was holding her breath. She had a handkerchief in her right hand and was twisting it into a knot. She wasn't sure she could take any more of this.

"Brother Allan, I can't thank you and the ladies enough for the care you all have given me. I wouldn't be here if it wasn't for your prayers and your around the clock nursing."

Allan looked at Patrick and said, "Brother, you know we were glad to help."

"Yes, I do know that, but it's time for me to go back to my room at the boarding house."

Emily let out a little gasp and touched her handkerchief to her mouth.

Allan looked at her for a brief second then turned to Patrick, "Your being here is no trouble, brother. Are you sure you're strong enough to be on your own?"

"Thank you, Brother Allan. I do feel I'm strong enough to go back, but I won't be alone. Mrs. Cleveland is always at the house and she'll provide all of my meals. Now they won't be as good as Sister Eunice's meals, but they'll keep me from wasting away. Besides, I believe my being here any longer would not be appropriate."

Emily blurted out, "Why? Why wouldn't it be appropriate?"

Patrick looked at Emily, then he turned to address Allan again, "Brother Allan, you are the closest thing to a father or brother that Emily has. I'd like to ask your permission to call on Emily. You know, to court her." Then he turned to Emily and said, "If that's all right with you, of course."

Emily's hand dropped to her lap. She was in shock. She was so young when she entered a life of prostitution that no one had ever asked permission to come courting before. Frankly, she never dreamt that anyone ever would.

Allan looked at Emily and then Patrick. He cleared his throat and asked, "Patrick, have you thought about what you're asking? You know people are going to talk. This isn't going to be easy. Emily, please forgive me, I only want the two of you to think this through."

Patrick sat down next to Emily on the settee and took her hand. "I want both of you to know my feelings for Emily have been growing for sometime. These last few days have been wonderful, having her close, spending time with her. I didn't think anything could come of those feelings because of her past and my calling. But this afternoon when I heard the words God spoke to the prophet Hosea to take a wife of whoredom, well, it was like God was speaking directly to me. He seemed to be saying that if Hosea could marry a wife who was still a whore, I could love and marry a woman who used to be…well, used to be one."

Patrick turned to Emily and said, "You know I spent the afternoon praying and now you know what I was praying about. I wrestled with God and he showed me several scriptures. In John 4, Jesus loved and accepted the Samaritan woman who'd had five husbands and was living in sin with another man. Then in John 8, Jesus forgave and loved the woman who was caught in the very act of adultery. Emily, we all have a past. I've had lust in my heart and I've had hatred in my heart. Jesus says those thoughts are as sinful as adultery and murder. There are many other things, too. My temper has gotten me into a lot of trouble in the past and I'm afraid it will again sometime in the future. God has forgiven both of us and we are new creatures in Christ. Why couldn't we court?"

Emily's expression changed from one of shock to a grin. This was the best news she'd heard since she heard the good news of Jesus' love for her. She tried to compose herself. It didn't seem very lady like to be grinning like a Cheshire cat. She turned to Allan and simply asked, "Well, Brother Allan?"

Allan looked at the two young adults sitting there and smiled, "Patrick, you are right. It would not be appropriate for you to be staying here if you and Emily are going to be courting. If you are going to do this, it will be a proper courtship. You will have a chaperone at all times you are together and if there comes a point that you feel you want to wed, you will come to me first. Is that understood?" Allan felt quite proud of himself for being so firm.

Patrick looked at Emily and she nodded at him. He then replied, "Yes, sir, we wouldn't have it any other way."

The next several months were a mix of highs and lows for the young couple. Their courtship was going as planned. Patrick would come to the house and spend time with Emily. They would read scripture and other books together. At times they would go outdoors to play games like croquet or simply go for walks. Occasionally, Patrick would borrow or hire a carriage so they could go for a ride, but whether they were at the house or outdoors there was always a chaperone with them. Usually, it was one of the other rescued doves who lived at Second Chance House who accompanied them, but occasionally it was Sister Eunice herself.

Unfortunately, there were also times when things didn't go well. Prescott was a small town and everyone seemed to know everyone's business. The town gossips had a field day with the story that the Prescott Parson was courting a whore. Patrick had expected the town to talk. What hurt him the most was the fact that a few people left the church. They simply couldn't understand how the pastor could consider courting a woman who was a whore. "Oh, yes," they would say, "we know. She used to be a whore, but once a whore, well…you know."

Patrick knew he had to provide a home for Emily, if they were to ever marry. He found ten acres south of Prescott that had tall pines and rugged boulders on it. But it also had a clearing for a cabin and a some land he could clear to make a pasture for the cattle he hoped to have one day. He was able to work four or five days a week hauling freight to the little outposts around Yavapai County. On his days off he cut trees, worked on building a cabin, and prepared his sermons for Sunday morning. Every two or three weeks he would call on his beautiful Emily. They would sit in the parlor and talk, read together, or listen to one of the other residents of Second Chance sing and play the piano. But every evening, right at eight-thirty, Brother Allan would step into the parlor. He would pull out his pocket watch, look at it and then look at the young couple sitting there. He never said a word, but Patrick got the message. It was time to say good night and go home. Emily would walk him to the door, where the couple would hold hands and look longingly into one another's eyes. Allan only had to clear his throat to let them know they were lingering a little too long. One night, after they'd been courting for about six months, Allan forgot to stand at the door to watch the couple say good night and Emily noticed. She took advantage of the situation and stood up on the tip of her toes and gave Patrick a kiss on the cheek. His knees felt like they were going to melt like ice cream on a hot Arizona afternoon. He blushed and smiled and went out the door as quickly as he could. Out on the porch, Patrick put his hat on and let out a whoop that would make an Apache warrior proud. He hadn't looked back so he didn't know Emily was peeking through the curtains. She was smiling from ear to ear and her eyes were filled with tears of joy. Before she came to Second Chance House she had never allowed herself to believe she could find love and happiness like this. She turned her face towards heaven and breathed a simple prayer, "Thank you, Lord. Thank you."

After church one Sunday, Patrick had dinner with the residents of Second Chance House and after dinner he, Emily, and Candace, their chaperone for the day, took a buggy ride out to the cabin Patrick was building. Patrick had put down a good wooden floor and the four outer walls were up. Door ways and openings for windows were apparent. The trio got out of the buggy and inspected the inside of the cabin. Patrick proudly pointed out where the fireplace would be. Then he asked Emily where she thought the kitchen should go. Before she could answer, Patrick said, "And where do you think the bedroom should go?"

Emily blushed and turned her face towards Candace, "Patrick, why would you ask me such a question? After all, this is your cabin."

Patrick realized he'd embarrassed Emily and replied, "I'm sorry. I didn't mean to embarrass you, but I want your input. After all, after this is finished, I'm going to ask Brother Allan for your hand in marriage. I'm hoping this will be our home together."

Emily was motionless as she looked at Patrick for a full minute. She could feel her heart beating like a rabbit that was being chased by a coyote. She realized her mouth was open and closed it. Then she closed the distance between her and Patrick with two quick steps and threw her arms around his neck. She kissed him directly on the mouth before she knew what she was doing. For the first second, Patrick's arms were hanging at his side, but then he embraced her and enjoyed the long, passionate kiss.

Candace knew she was the chaperone, but wasn't really sure what she should do at that point so she cleared her throat and said, "Um, do you all want me to leave and give you some privacy?"

Patrick and Emily finished their kiss and turned to Candace while still hugging. It was Patrick who broke the awkward silence, "No, Miss Candace, we don't want you to leave. Please forgive our display of affection. We will certainly try to never embarrass you again." At that, he looked down into Emily's face and they both smiled.

The two ladies spent the next half hour listening to Patrick explain where he would put a corral and how he would clear a pasture for livestock. He even showed them where "the little house outback" would go, which caused them to blush again. Finally, they got into the carriage and made their way back to town bringing an end to a very lovely day.

A few weeks later, Patrick hired a young man from town to help him put up the rafters. Eighteen year old Justin was a good hand and eager to work. Patrick was glad he'd hired him. It was a Friday afternoon when they were finishing nailing the rafters in place. Suddenly they were aware of the sound of horses approaching. There was a little road that went past Patrick's property, but it didn't get much traffic. Both men wondered who could be coming their way. There hadn't been an Indian attack in that area for several years and highwaymen wouldn't have any reason to come looking for them, still Patrick realized he was unarmed. He had taken the saddle off of his horse and left it outside. His Winchester was still in the scabbard tied to the saddle and his Colt revolver was in it's holster on the floor of the cabin.

The two men were standing on the ceiling joists, looking to see who was approaching when Justin said, "I don't hear them horses anymore. Where do you reckon they've gone?"

Before Patrick could answer, a shot rang out and a bullet struck one of the rafters, sending splinters flying into the air. Then another shot rang out and a bullet just missed Patrick's head sending splinters into his face. The shock caused him to lose his balance and he fell from the joist to the floor of the cabin. Justin saw what happened, bent down and grabbed the joist with both hands. Then he swung down to the floor. He dropped down next to Patrick and asked if he was alright. Patrick was dazed at first, but looked up and told Justin that he thought he was okay. The two men scrambled to get closer to the log wall facing the road. Patrick stretched up and tried to look out one of the windows to see where the shots were coming from. Suddenly, two more shots rang out. Patrick could see the black smoke curling up from behind a pile of granite boulders and from behind a tree. Both seemed to be about twenty-five yards from the cabin. Patrick assumed the assailants were using rifles or carbines to be making shots from that distance.

Picking up his gun belt and revolver, Patrick looked at Justin and asked, "Are you heeled, son?"

"No, sir, I ain't. We've got firearms at home, but I don't have any with me today," he replied.

"Well, do you know how to shoot?"

Justin looked Patrick in the eye and said, "Oh, yes, sir, my pa taught me how to shoot when I was younger. I'm a fair shot."

Suddenly a voice came from outside, "Hey, Parson, Mr. Griffiths wanted us to come out and bring his greetings. You know he's out of jail now. He's real interested in how you and that whore Emily are doing. Why don't you come out and we can have us a pow wow."

"Ewan Griffiths," Patrick exclaimed. "That no good rat has sent these men out to kill me. Justin, I'm sorry to involve you in this. They're after me, but I'm sure they won't want to leave any witnesses."

Justin looked Patrick in the eye and said, "It's not your fault. What's our plan?"

"You take the Colt and my gun belt. There's twenty-four extra cartridges on it. I want you to shoot to keep their heads down while I run around the cabin to get my Winchester. Then I'll join in."

"Where are they?" Justin asked.

"Real quick, let's look out this window and I'll show you," Patrick replied.

The two men peeked out the window opening and Patrick pointed out a dead tree twenty-five yards away. "Do you see that dead tree?"

"Yes, sir, I do."

"One fella is behind the live tree just to the north of the dead one and the other is behind those boulders ten yards to the south."

Justin poked his head up one more time, looked quickly, and nodded to Patrick that he'd seen them. He ducked back down just ahead of more bullets hitting the window frame.

"Okay," Patrick said, "as soon as I go out the back window, you start shooting. Remember your job is just to keep their heads down."

"I'll do my best," Justin replied. As soon as Patrick starting moving, Justin loaded the sixth chamber of the Colt and got ready. Patrick looked back and gave Justin the "thumb's up" and went out the window. Justin did his part. He fired two rounds at the rocks and two at the tree, then he alternated firing one at the tree and one at the rocks. When he ducked down to reload the attackers opened up on the cabin again. Justin could only hope that Patrick had enough time to get his rifle.

Patrick did make it to his saddle and his rifle undetected. He grabbed the rifle and quickly rolled over behind a tree. In just a second, he could hear the barrage of bullets being fired at the cabin and could see them dig holes in his new log wall. "I hope Emily thinks those bullet holes add character," he thought to himself. Then he noticed one of the attackers come out from behind his tree while his partner kept shooting at and through the window in the cabin. This was a Mexican looking fella. Black hair, brown skin and an unshaven face. His sombrero had seen a lot of Arizona sun and a lot of summer rains. He had two bandoleers, half full of ammunition, around his chest, but his pistol was holstered. It looked like he had something in his hands. "What was that?" Patrick asked himself. Then he saw the answer. The man had a stick of dynamite in one hand and a match in the other. He was going to blow the cabin.

The Mex began running toward the cabin and stopped about ten yards from it. He bent down to strike the match and light the fuse. Patrick acted quickly. He levered a round into the chamber while he was throwing the gun up to his shoulder, took quick aim and fired. The match was lit, but never made it to the fuse. That two-hundred grain lead bullet went screaming down range and struck the Mex in the left side of his chest. He dropped where he stood, his devilish plan was thwarted.

The man behind the rocks turned his attention to Patrick and began peppering the tree with bullets. Bits of lead and splinters from the tree were flying every where and Patrick kept his head down to keep from getting shot. But while the attention was on Patrick, Justin snuck out of the cabin and past the dead man to his former hiding place. There he could clearly see the man shooting at Patrick. He was a white man, crouched down behind the rocks. He was dressed in dirty work clothes. They were so dirty, you could barely tell that his pants and boots were supposed to be black. He wore an old grey shirt with a dirty black vest over it. His mustache completely covered his mouth and his head was uncovered. He'd thrown his hat down when the gun fight started and it lay on the ground a few feet from him. Justin rested his right hand holding the Colt on a low limb of the tree and took as careful aim as he could. He remembered the things his father had taught him: take a deep breath and let it out, then squeeze the trigger. The Colt roared, a ball of flame escaped from the barrel, and a cloud of smoke obscured Justin's view. He couldn't see if he hit his mark or not, but down range that hunk of hot lead hit the assassin's rifle. The fore end shattered into a thousand pieces and the rifle flew from the man's hands. He swore loudly and looked over to see Justin behind the tree. After that moment of shock, he stood up and drew his revolver, but when he did, he gave Patrick a perfect target. Patrick had already levered another round into the chamber of his rifle and was ready to take his shot. When he did the bullet hit the would be assassin in his right side, shattering two ribs and lodging just under his lung. The assassin turned briefly to see where the bullet had come from and then dropped where he stood.

Patrick and Justin ran up to the man in the rocks. Both kept their guns at the ready. Patrick got there first and could see that the man was still breathing. He held the man's head in his lap and asked him, "What's your name? What's your name? Why did Ewan Griffiths send you?"

The man opened his eyes to look at the man who was speaking to him. He coughed up some blood and then spoke. His voice was barely above a whisper, but he said, "They call me Stoney. That's all, just Stoney."

It looked like he was about to slip away so Patrick shook him gently and asked again, "Why did Griffiths send you?"

Stoney opened his eyes again and said, "He sent us because you took his whores away. He never got over that." Those would be the last words Stoney would speak in this life. He breathed out one last rough, raspy breath and then was still. His eyes were still looking at Patrick, but there was no life in them. Patrick closed Stoney's eyes and laid him back on the ground.

When Patrick looked up at Justin, he could see that Justin's eyes were as big as saucers. "Never seen anyone die before, eh?"

It took Justin a few seconds to answer. He was still looking at the dead man when he said, "Not like that I ain't. What are we going to do now?"

"We're going to pack these hombres on their horses and take them into town. I've got some business to take care of, then we'll deliver them to the Marshall," Patrick said as he was standing up.

Justin fetched the dead men's horses and brought them over to the cabin while Patrick saddled his horse and reloaded his Winchester.

When the two men got to town they stopped at the livery stable and asked Patrick's friend Juan to hold onto the two horses with the dead men tied on top until he finished some business. Juan called Patrick "padre" because of his upbringing and agreed to hold on to the two. "Besides." he said "I don't think they can hurt anyone anymore." Then he did the sign of the cross.

The word in town was that Ewan Griffiths spent his days at his cabin in Miller Valley and didn't come to town until about supper time. So Patrick told Justin he was going to head his horse in that direction. Justin asked, "What do you want me to do?"

"I want you to go home and get cleaned up. If I live until tomorrow, I'm going to need you to come back out to the cabin so we can finish those rafters? This is something I've got to do myself. Comprende?"

"Yes, sir, I comprende," Justin said.

An hour later, Patrick rode up to Griffiths' cabin in Miller Valley. There weren't any horses tied up outside, but there was smoke making its way up out of the chimney. Patrick snuck up to the front window and peeked in. The only person he could see was Ewan Griffiths. "This might end up being a fair fight." Patrick thought.

Patrick had loaded the sixth chamber of his revolver and jacked a round into the chamber of his rifle. He had brought the Mexican's sombrero with him and stood at the door ready for action. He whispered a prayer for God's help and took a deep breath to calm his nerves. He threw the front door of the cabin open and tossed the sombrero in. "Your henchmen failed, Griffiths. It's time you and I finished this!" he called.

"Parson? Is that you, Parson? Well, congratulations. I'm glad you made it. Now I can kill you myself," Griffiths called out.

Patrick stood to the side of the cabin door, his rifle at the ready when he answered Griffiths, "Come on out, Griffiths. Let's finish this man to man." At that he pulled the hammer on his Winchester back to full cock.

"I'm not going to make it easy for you, you pompous, self-righteous, bag of wind," Griffiths shouted. Then suddenly two shots rang out and Patrick could hear the bullets whiz past him as they exited the cabin.

Patrick leaned into the doorway just enough to fire two rounds into the cabin, but then he knelt down. Griffiths fired two more rounds, which hit the door jam where Patrick had been. There was a moment of silence. Griffiths hoped the silence meant his bullets had found their intended target. He stepped out of the shadows he'd been hiding in, a revolver in each hand. He was leaning to see where Patrick was, but he couldn't see him. "Was he down? Was that why he couldn't see him?" He took another step out into the light of the open door. It was then that he could see the muzzle of Patrick's rifle. But it was lower than before. In an instant, before he could make a move, he saw flame belch out of that muzzle and he just began to hear the blast of the round going off when he felt something hot in his chest. He looked down and saw blood spurting out of his vest. Both of his revolvers fired, but they fired into the floor, then he felt a second bullet burn its way into his chest. He looked up and realized that Patrick Donovan had killed him. The Prescott Parson had bested him. He took two steps backwards and everything went black…forever.

The Marshall charged the Parson with the murder of the three men who died that day, but Justin's testimony and everyone's knowledge of Ewan Griffiths' hatred for Patrick led the jury to find him "not guilty" on all charges. Patrick was simply defending himself from a man bent on murdering him.

Six months later, the cabin was finished and partially furnished. Emily's sisters at Second Chance House had made curtains for the windows and a beautiful quilt for the bed. Sister Eunice gave Emily her mother's china, which she put into the hutch that Brother Allan had made along with a dining table and chairs. It wasn't a mansion to anyone else, but it was to Patrick and Emily.

The couple gathered in the meadow below the cabin along with their friends and Patrick's mentor in the faith, Brother Frederick McPeters, who was known to everyone simply as Brother Mac. Brother Mac officiated the ceremony. No one knew a "just cause" why the two shouldn't wed and almost everyone shed a tear when Patrick and Emily said their "I do's". At the end of the day, the Parson had taken a wife, a woman who was able to love a cabin shot full of bullet holes, a woman who knew her man would do anything necessary to keep her safe.

Sargent Tom Madson

Cochise County Sheriff's Department

Chapter 9: Dreams Come True

Stepping out of the Sheriff's office in Bisbee, AZ, Sargent Tom Madson looks every bit the great-great grandson of Swedish immigrants. He stands six feet tall and weighs one hundred and seventy pounds. Some would say if he let his blond hair grow longer he would look like Thor from the movies, but his hair is cut short and kept under a Stetson hat. His uniform consists of a long sleeved, white, button down dress shirt, starched and pressed Wrangler jeans, and a pair of custom made boots. Normally he wasn't one to splurge on luxuries, but those boots had already lasted him three years. His duty pistol isn't a single action Colt, but it is in forty-five caliber. Tom likes the forty-five and often tells folks their nine millimeter rounds might expand on impact, but his forty-fives are never going to shrink on impact. As much as he loves a good Colt, he prefers the thirteen plus one capacity of his Glock 21. Besides it's the only gun he's ever shot a perfect qualification score with. His belt and holster are custom made. There's a holster maker in Ashfork that makes his rigs for him. The rig has a basket weave stamped design and is dyed a light tan that almost matches his hat perfectly.

It's Friday and he's ready to spend the weekend backpacking in the Chiricahua's. After driving his department issued Tahoe to his small ranch outside of town, he changes his clothes. The white dress shirt becomes a long sleeved, well worn camo t-shirt. The starched Wranglers become an equally well worn pair of Levis and his custom boots become a pair of hiking boots. He locks his full sized Glock in a small safe on the night stand next to his bed and trades it for the smaller Glock model 30. It's still chambered in forty-five, but much lighter and considerably more concealable.

Tom had his pack ready to go the night before and took it out to his Rubicon, but before he left he needed to check on his horse and the two calves he was raising. He needed to fill both of the hay feeders and the water troughs before he left. His neighbor was going to check on them over the weekend, but Tom wanted to give them one last check before he left.

It was early afternoon when Tom jumped in his Jeep and drove off. He had a two hour drive before he would get to the Chiracahuas, but he didn't mind. It meant some quiet time with no radio chatter. He couldn't turn off his brain, which meant he would always have his head on a swivel and he would look at everyone he encountered like they were someone he would have to describe in a report later, but ultimately, he wasn't going to be responsible for everyone and everything that happened in his district for two and a half days.

He headed out of town on Highway 191 and drove north until he came to State Route 181 which turned east and would take him to Turkey Creek Road and from there into the Chiracahuas. No matter how many times he'd driven down this road, he had to turn his head and look at the sign that marked the turn off to Johnny Ringo's grave. He'd stopped and looked at it a couple of times and had read about Ringo's death. Some thought Ringo had committed suicide and others thought that either Wyatt Earp or Doc Holiday had killed Ringo. Ultimately, the good Lord knew and he wasn't telling. The fact remained that Johnny Ringo was a part of Territory history and plenty of fans of the old west had stopped over the years and asked the land owners if they could see the grave site.

Tom looked, but he didn't slow down. It was onward and upward into the mountains. He drove until the road ended. There was a small parking lot next to the trailhead. His was the only vehicle there that afternoon, but Tom knew that could change at anytime. As he got out of the Jeep, he took a deep breath and smiled. He could smell the fresh air. There was the scent of pine trees and the sounds of birds flitting from one place to another. He looked around and took in the sights. The forest service had erected a sign near the entrance to the trailhead giving the usual instructions on how to take care of a camp fire and the usual warnings about the wildlife in the area. Tom knew there were too many flat landers who thought they could take a selfie with the bears and mountain lions that might be in the area, which made these warnings only too necessary. He took out his pack and put it on. Finally, he patted himself down. He checked to make sure he had his cell phone, his keys and his sidearm. Check, check and check again his dad had taught him. Everything was in place.

Tom started down the trail, which was, in fact, and old wagon trail. Freight wagons had cut a road into the mountains to get supplies to the miners who worked the area. There were still places where you could find ruts cut into the rocks from the wagon wheels.

Whistling wasn't his thing and neither was humming. Tom walked in silence. He kept his head on a swivel watching for anything that moved. It was rare for a hiker to see a bear or a mountain lion, but he knew it could happen. He also knew it was more likely he would cross paths with a rattle snake or a skunk. He'd like to steer clear of both if possible. He might see a deer or a grey fox if he was alert enough. So he tried to stay alert.

As a lawman in southern Arizona, Tom was also painfully aware of those who crossed the border illegally. Many were simply trying to find a better life for their families and meant no harm, but too many were smuggling drugs and involved in human trafficking. He'd rather tangle with a rattler than one of those skunks.

The trail had been going due east and climbing steadily in elevation. As a result, he was moving from a high desert environment into more woodlands. Granite boulders were scattered about with shrubs and trees seemingly growing right out of them.

This time alone was something Tom valued. It gave him time to think about things other than sheriffing. For a little while, he could forget the drug traffickers and the pile ups on the highway. He didn't have to think about the morons who were beating their wives or trying to lure children into their cars. Yes, this was time he valued. That day he was thinking about the fact that his father was stationed at Fort Huachuca in the Army. The great grandson of Swedish immigrants, he was born and raised in Minnesota, fell in love with the desert Southwest, and moved his young family to Arizona after he got out of the Army. They had been farmers in Minnesota and became ranchers in Arizona. Instead of dairy cows he raised beef cows. Instead of bib overalls he wore jeans and cowboy boots and never looked back. Tom smiled to himself thinking how blessed he was that his father was stationed at Fort Huachuca.

The trail turned to the north, but Tom didn't want to go north. He wanted to explore the canyon just to the east of the old wagon trail. There was a cliff about fifteen or twenty yards away from the trail. Tom walked to the edge of that cliff and searched for a way down. There to his left was a deer trail that led to the canyon floor. He stopped for a drink from his canteen. Stowed it away and began the descent into the canyon. He wondered to himself what he might see down there.

Tom was pretty sure he was the first human to take this trail into the canyon. It was steep and more than a little treacherous. There were plenty of rocks to do a high step over. The deer had been picking their way down this trail for a long time so there wasn't much vegetation on the trail that was only six inches wide at times, but there were plenty of bushes reaching out to grab his pants and arms all along the way. The thought occurred to him that he was going to have to come back out at some point. He wondered if there might be a better way to climb out of the canyon.

After he'd been going down this trail for about half an hour, Tom stopped to take a short breather. He took off his pack and got out his canteen and binoculars. After taking a drink, he began glassing the hillside around him. There was a whole lot of the usual sage and juniper mixed among the granite boulders. He scanned the hillside to his left and then swung over to the right. Nothing out of the ordinary until he saw something that didn't fit. About fifty yards directly in front of him was something that was neither brush or boulder. It looked like some sort of machinery. Or was it a car? What ever it was, it was crushed up against a boulder with brush growing up around it. Tom put down his binoculars and looked at it then he put the binoculars up again to see it. He wondered what in the world that was. It was definitely man made and it was made of metal, but the rocks and brush hid it so well that he couldn't tell what it was.

Tom wanted to get over to the thing, whatever it was, to get a better look, but he knew it was getting late in the day and he needed to get to the canyon floor and make camp for the night. He did his best to note the exact location of the "object". He tried to triangulate its location based on the trail, notable boulders and sizable trees. Then he continued his descent.

After another half hour or so of hiking Tom was at the bottom of the canyon. Based on his topo map of the area, he knew there should be a creek nearby. So he headed north about half a mile and found the creek. As it was early spring, there was water flowing freely in the creek. He hiked back about a quarter of a mile to a flat spot where he could make his camp. There was a boulder the size of a Mini Cooper at the north end of his camp spot. He decided to put his sleeping bag next to the boulder and gathered wood for his fire for the evening.

After boiling some water and adding it to a pouch of dehydrated chili-mac and making a pot of coffee, Tom settled in for his evening meal and a time to just relax. His thoughts kept going back to that "thing" he saw on the hillside. What in the world could that be and how in the world did it get there?

Before hitting the sack for the night, Tom made his way down to the creek and pumped his canteen full. His water filter took a couple of minutes to pump his canteen full, but he was there to relax and was in no hurry. While he was pumping the water into his canteen he enjoyed listening to the sounds of the early evening. The sound of the creek water flowing by was soothing and the sound of the coyotes lighting up always amazed him. He hadn't seen any coyotes all day and to hear them howling so close is what he found so amazing. There had to be some within twenty-five yards of him. He never felt threatened by their howling. He knew they were just communicating with their family and friends.

That night, probably a little after mid-night, Tom began to have the most vivid dream of his life. He saw an old Ford Model A station wagon with wooden sides, only it didn't look old. It looked brand new. There were three people in the car. Two men in the front seat and a woman in the back seat. The car was racing down the road and was being chased by another car. The car chasing the Ford was also a Model A, but this one was a sedan with the word "police" painted on the side.

The two men in the front seat of the station wagon wore dark suits. Their hats had been taken off and thrown onto the back seat. The driver was intent on out-running or out maneuvering the cops who were in hot pursuit. The man in the passenger seat was looking back, watching the police car and yelling orders to the driver. Both were sweating and neither wore a smile. The woman in the back seat was wearing a blue dress with a white flower print and a white collar. Her white hat was askew on her head. One could see by her black hair and light brown complexion that she was either an Indian or Mexican, but her English was perfect when she yelled, "Lon, we've got to get out of here. They're gaining on us!"

The man in the passenger seat looked at her and responded, "Nina, Alf is doing the best he can. This crate won't go any faster!" Then he looked at the back seat and pointed to the Tommy Gun sitting there. "Hand me the Tommy Gun, Nina. I'll slow them guys down." At that Nina grabbed the Tommy Gun and handed it to Lon. Next to her, on the floor of the car, were bank bags from the National Bank in Bisbee and others from banks in both Benson and Tombstone. These folks had been busy the last two days.

Lon took the Tommy Gun and leaned out the window of the car opening fire on the police car behind them. He and Nina could see sparks as the bullets hit the right fender of the car. Then they saw the right head light shatter and the driver of the police car swerved to the left to get out of the line of fire.

Alf looked in the rear view mirror and yelled at Lon, "Give 'em some more! They ain't slowin' down!"

At that, Lon fired off two more bursts from the Tommy Gun. Those forty-five slugs were hitting the car, but most of them ricocheted off the hood or the fender. A couple of them shattered the windshield, though, which caused the driver to swerve again.

Lon got back into the car and said rather smugly, "That ought to slow them down." It didn't, though. Nina watched as the police driver got the car under control and continued the pursuit. Then Nina saw the officer in the passenger seat lean out the window of his patrol car with a Winchester rifle in his hands. He leaned out as far as he could, levered the gun and fired. The first bullet hit the back of the station wagon. He fired again and the back window shattered. He fired a third time and Nina screamed. Lon looked back only to see Nina turn to him with blood gushing from her chest. In the next second Nina slumped down into the back seat of the car. It was obvious that she had left this life.

Lon and Alf were in shock for just a moment. Somehow they had not considered that Nina could be killed in a chase like this. For just a second Lon was a tender man. He gently reached down to stroke Nina's hair. Then his face was filled with rage. "You sons'a…You're dead now!" and at that Lon put a new magazine in the Tommy Gun, leaned out the window and fired. He didn't quit until the magazine was empty. Lon had lobbed 20 rounds of forty-five ammo at those cops. He didn't know if he'd hit either of them, but he could see that he'd hit the radiator, probably several times. The car swerved and then stopped in a cloud mixed with dust and steam.

Lon couldn't relax. He'd lost his girlfriend Nina and was pretty sure more cops would be hunting for them, if not today, at least by tomorrow.

Lon looked at Alf and said, "Alf, you've got to get us out of here. Find us a place the cops won't find us." Alf still looked like he was in shock. Lon grabbed Alf's arm and shouted, "Alf, get a hold of yourself. We've got to get out of here!"

Alf composed himself enough to respond, "I know a place. It's in the Chiricahuas. They'll never find us there. We can lay low for a couple of days then get out of the country. Lon, I'm sorry about Nina."

"Yeah, she was a sweet kid. Just get us out of here," Lon said as he leaned forward and put his head in his hands.

They raced down the highway until they got to Turkey Creek Road. It was a dirt road and a lot of it was as rough as a wash board, so they couldn't go as fast as they had before. Still Alf had a pretty good cloud of dust behind him and the car fishtailed around several of the curves. By now the sun had gone down. Alf and Lon kept looking for headlights following them, but there weren't any.

When it looked like they were going to run out of road, Lon said, "I know an old wagon trail that we can take. It goes back to an old stone house. That's where we will lay up." At that, Alf turned the car up the old wagon trail.

Even though the trail was pretty rough, Alf pushed the Ford as fast as he could. He didn't want any cops catching up to them. Lon had his right hand on the dashboard as he continued to turn to look behind them. He hoped against hope they wouldn't see any headlights following them and they didn't.

Alf kept looking intently out the windshield. He leaned forward and squinted trying to make sure he stayed on the trail. The headlights were better than nothing, but their light was certainly less than ideal for this kind of nighttime driving. Alf remembered that the trail turned north at some point, but he'd never driven it at night and wasn't sure just when that turn would come.

Suddenly, an eight point mule deer was standing in the middle of the trail. The deer looked up, his eyes wide with fear. Alf panicked and swerved to the right missing the trails turn. His foot was to the floor on the accelerator and he didn't see the cliff until it was too late. Lon turned and saw the cliff the same moment that Alf did. They both shouted something you couldn't say in Sunday School as the car launched into the air. Both of them reached forward. Both of Alf's hands were on the steering wheel, his arms were locked straight. Lon's hands were on the dashboard and his arms were likewise locked straight as though he could brace himself against the impact that was coming. It seemed like it took forever, but they were probably only airborne for a full second or two. Then gravity took over and the front of the Ford dipped down and they landed in a pile of granite boulders. Lon was thrown through the windshield, his body landing on the rocks below and Alf was crushed when his face hit the steering wheel. Nina's lifeless body was thrown around the inside of the car. She landed on the floor boards of the front seat area, never to move again.

At that moment, Tom Madson sat straight up. He was breathing heavily like he'd just run a foot race and his face was covered in sweat. "What a dream," he thought to himself. "That was wild!" Tom grabbed the flashlight he'd staged next to his sleeping bag, crawled out and went off to a nearby bush and relieved himself. He sat back down on his sleeping bag, brushed off his feet and wiggled back in hoping he could go back to sleep.

About six o'clock in the morning Tom was wide awake. The dream he'd had that night still bothered him. He couldn't remember ever having such a detailed and vivid dream before. The details of the dream seemed so real. He remembered each person he'd seen. He remembered every word and relived every twist and turn as he relit his fire, made coffee and had breakfast. As was his habit, he took out his Bible and journal and had his quiet time. He knew God was everywhere all the time, but seemed to enjoy communing with the Father out in woods a little more than anywhere else. That morning, though, he struggled to concentrate as the dream kept running over and over in his mind. It was like a video recording that was on a loop and no one knew where the stop button was.

After he put out his breakfast fire and got his campsite squared away, Tom went back to the cliff he'd climbed down. He wanted to see what that object was he'd seen the day before. He couldn't see any part of whatever it was he'd seen earlier from the canyon floor. The rocks and brush were much too thick.

Tom knew the only way he was going to solve this mystery was to climb back up those rocks. Slowly he began picking his way up the slope. He could hear his mother say, "Thomas, you be careful. Nothing's worth getting killed over." So he was very careful as he made his way up. It wasn't hard climbing, but slow. Once in a while one of the bushes would reach out and grab his arm or the leg of his pants, but those little scratches were nothing to worry about. He'd certainly had worse as a boy growing up in the high desert of Arizona.

Suddenly, as he made his way between two large boulders, he saw it and it was the front of an old car. A car that had tangled with an immoveable boulder and lost the fight. It was still a good fifteen yards to his left and there were several decent sized boulders and any number of bushes between him and the car, but the object he'd seen the day before was definitely a car.

After nearly losing his balance once and getting his arm scratched again, he finally made it to the wreckage of the old car. He wasn't really an antique car buff, but his dad was and because his dad liked to drag him to car shows he recognized that this car was probably a Model A Ford. It was pretty obvious this car had gone over the cliff and crashed on the rocks. As he got closer to the wreck, this was feeling really familiar. Why? He'd never been here before and he'd never seen this wreck before. When he got up next to the wreck, he could see that it was a Model A station wagon. Then it hit him like a ton of bricks. This was exactly like the car in his dream last night. Suddenly the "tape" began to run in his mind again and he could see this car flying off the cliff and nose diving in the rocks. He could see a man flying through the windshield to his death on the rocks below. He could see another man smashing against the steering wheel and a woman's lifeless body flying over the front seat onto the floor. He had to move some brush out of the way in order to look into the wreck, but there was part of a skeleton smashed up against the steering wheel. The skull and upper torso were there. It starred out the window like it had been doing for many years. Some scraps of clothing were still clinging to the bones. They were faded and dirty, but looked like a man's suit coat. He looked over to the passenger side floor. Most of it was rotted away, but he could see other bones and other scraps of cloth. Most had undoubtedly fallen through the floor over the years, but there was no doubt that this was a second person. Could it be the woman? What was her name? Nina. It was Nina. When he looked into the back seat area, he could see that the wooden floor boards were rotted away, too, but he imagined that if he could look under the wreck he would find at least pieces of the bank bags he had seen in his dream.

This was the car from that dream he'd had. These were the remains of the bank robbers he'd seen. How was this even possible?

Tom took his cell phone out of his back pocket and took fifteen or twenty pictures of the wreckage and the remains. He took pictures of the area around the car, too. He wanted to be able to find this again.

Tom wanted to get back to town as quickly as possible, but he knew that trying to scramble out of these rocks and brush could get him hurt. Carefully, he picked his way back down to the canyon floor and walked back to his campsite as quickly as he could. It was ten-thirty in the morning now. Should he wait until after lunch to head back? No, why wait? He packed his gear back into his backpack and started out. He had a full canteen of water and a couple of protein bars he could eat. He was going back to town now because he knew he had to report what he'd found.

The trip out of the canyon and back to Bisbee took him about three hours. The whole time he was hiking and driving the "tape" of his dream kept playing in his mind. What in the world did any of this mean?

Tom waited until he got back to his office before contacting anyone. He knew it was the weekend and his lieutenant wouldn't be in. When he got there one of the newer deputies was manning the fort. He looked pretty miserable, but perked up when Sarge got there.

"Afternoon, Sarge, I'm surprised to see you here on a Saturday," the young deputy said.

"Not as surprised as I am," Tom said as he booted up his desktop computer. "I've just found something out in the woods that is an absolute mystery to me," he continued.

Deputy Frank Thompson was twenty-three years old and only months on the job. He'd done a four year hitch in the Air Force before going to the academy and was looking forward to a long career in law enforcement. He looked every bit the young, fit deputy in his standard deputy's uniform, khaki shirt and OD green pants. His black boots shined and his duty belt still squeaked when he moved. Real leather does that. Frank was taller than Tom. He stood every bit of six feet two inches in his stocking feet and was close to two hundred pounds of lean, youthful muscle. He kept his brown hair cut short. His haircut looked more like he'd served in the Marine Corps than the Air Force. It was tight and white.

Frank got up from the desk he'd been riding all morning and stepped over to the Sarge's desk. "Whatcha got, Sarge?" he asked.

"I found an old wreck out in the Chiricahuas this morning and I think it relates to a cold case," he said as he logged onto the department's website. "I need to see if I can find any information on a bank robbery back in the roaring twenties or early thirties."

"Do the computer records go back that far?" Frank asked.

"I doubt it," said Tom, "but it's a place to start." In fact, Tom discovered that the computer records don't go back that far. He scooted his chair back from the desk and pondered his next move. His brow was wrinkled and his right had stroked his unshaven chin as he blankly stared at his computer screen.

"Sarge, I can smell the smoke, you know, from thinking so hard," Frank said nervously. He didn't know the Sarge all that well and was hoping he could take a joke.

Tom looked up, paused for a second and smiled, "Yeah, I'm just trying to figure out what my next move would be." Suddenly, he snapped his fingers and said, "I know. I've got a friend down at the Observer. Maybe she can check some archives to find some information about this crime."

Tom picked up the phone and called his friend Fran Booth. Fran was a reporter for the Bisbee Observer and was the kind of person who loved this kind of research. She and Tom went to the same church and had known each other for several years. When she answered her phone, he described what he knew about the car he'd found and the approximate date of the supposed crime. Sarah was eager to take up the challenge. She said, "Our paper isn't that old, but I'll check to see if we have any archives that go back that far. If not, I can access the archives from the Daily Star over in Tucson. Give me a day or two and I'll see what I can find."

After he hung up the phone, Tom was tempted to call his lieutenant and report what he'd found, but then thought better of it. That car may have been sitting in that pile of rocks for ninety years. It wasn't going any where and the lieutenant didn't need to be bothered on the weekend.

Since he was back from his back packing trip early, Tom got up on Sunday and got ready to go to church. His Sunday "go-to-meeting" clothes weren't too different from his work clothes—the starched and pressed Wranglers, polished boots, and his Stetson hat were the same. The difference was that he didn't wear a white dress shirt, he wore a freshly pressed western shirt with pearl snaps. The one he wore that day was plain blue with blue snaps. He didn't wear his duty holster and belt, either, but since he was always on duty, he wore his Glock 30 under a sport coat. Anyone who was halfway observant could see the bulge under his coat, but Tom didn't care if they could or not. He picked up his Bible, got in his jeep and drove into town. The parking lot at the Evangelical Free Church was only half full when he got there so he got his favorite parking spot. It was a spot that he could pull through and, if he had to, it was a spot he could pull out of and onto the street quickly.

After greeting the pastor and several other church members, Tom saw Fran sitting in a row near the back of the church. "My kind of girl," he thought to himself as he slid into the empty seat next to her. She was a pretty girl. A few freckles on her nose and shoulder length brown hair. She had blues eyes and a gorgeous smile. Today, she was wearing her Wranglers and a western shirt. She had her pant legs tucked into her very girly looking red cowboy boots. Together the two of them looked like they could be modeling for a western wear catalog.

As Tom laid his hat on the seat next to him he said, "Morning, Miss Fran."

She turned and smiled as she said, "Morning to you, Sergeant." Tom had to admit to himself, and to no one else, that her smile made his heart skip a beat. "Say," she said, "I started looking for information on that case you called me about yesterday and I think I've found something."

Tom sat up a little straighter and said, "You did? What'd you find?"

"We can talk after church," she said as she pointed to the pastor who was stepping up to the pulpit to start the service.

Tom loved his church and loved his pastor, but that morning he struggled to worship. Normally he took notes on the pastor's sermon, but that day his mind kept running the tape of that dream he'd had out in the woods. He knew he would have to confess that distraction to the Lord.

After church Tom and Fran had lunch at their favorite Mexican food restaurant in town, La Casita. Their heads were together as they talked. Their voices were kept to a whisper, but the look on their faces was intense. Observers might assume that this was a young couple on a date, whispering sweet nothings to one another. In fact, Fran was sharing the information she'd found on the internet.

Fran was dipping a tortilla chip in the house salsa as she said, "I couldn't get this case off my mind yesterday so I began digging. As I suspected our files don't go back that far so I accessed the files from the Tucson paper. I looked for a string of bank robberies in Cochise County in the late twenties and the early thirties." Fran felt like she was bass fishing. She had presented the bait and set the hook and Tom was the bass she was reeling in.

"Well, what did you find?" Tom asked anxiously.

Fran smiled, not her usual sweet smile, this was a little bit of a devilish smile. She knew she had information that Tom wanted and contemplated stringing him along for a minute or two, but then decided against it. "I found one story that fits the scenario you described to me. It seems that in 1930 a three person gang robbed three banks in Cochise County in one day. They hit banks in Benson, Tombstone and then Bisbee and were chased by the police until the police car was disabled by bullets that hit their radiator. No one ever saw them again."

"That's them," Tom said excitedly. "Did they say who the robbers were?"

"Well, since they weren't caught, the police could only speculate, but they believed this gang was a couple who thought of themselves as the Bonnie and Clyde of the Southwest. Their names were Lon Hardy and Nina Chavez. It is believed that they joined forces with one of Lon's old friends, Alf Mayer."

Tom put his fork down as he said, "That's got to be them. I'm sure of it."

"Tom, what makes you so sure of it? What do you know about this case?" Fran asked.

Tom then told her about the most vivid dream he'd ever had in his life. He went on to describe climbing up the rock pile and finding the wrecked Ford. Then he described the bleached bones that were in the car. "That," he said, "is why I'm so interested in this cold case. I don't know why, but I think I've solved the mystery of what happened to that gang."

Tom and Fran finished their meal and got up to leave when Fran touched Tom's arm. She said, "Listen, if you plan to go out there and do some more investigation, I want to go along. This will make a great story."

Tom smiled when Fran touched his arm, then looked at her and said, "You've got it. You've been a great help and I agree, this will make a great story. I'll let you know what our next move will be."

That afternoon, Tom began to develop a plan for searching for and recovering evidence from the car wreck. He would need to talk to his lieutenant in the morning and they would need to involve the forest service in the project. The crime lab would need to be involved, too, he thought. After his chores and a light supper, Tom spent the evening watching a little television and reading. He went to bed right after the ten o'clock news.

The next morning Tom was up before dawn as usual. After breakfast he had his morning quiet time of Bible reading and prayer, fed his livestock and left for work. After the morning briefing Tom knocked on his lieutenant's door and stepped in. Lieutenant Frank Ballard was ten years older than Tom, forty years old to be exact. He was five feet ten inches tall and weighed about one hundred and sixty pounds. He, too, wore a button down, white dress shirt and starched and pressed Wrangler jeans. His boots, duty belt and holster were the same color of brown as the Stetson hat that was hanging on the coat tree in the corner of his office.

"L.T., I found something this weekend that will probably solve a ninety year old cold case," Tom said.

The lieutenant looked up from the pile of paper work that never seemed to end and said, "Well, Sarge, you've got my attention. Sit down and tell me about it."

At that Tom sat down and laid out the whole story. He told Frank about the hike into the canyon, the crazy dream and the discovery of the old Ford. By then Fran had sent over the article from the Tucson paper, so he showed the article to the lieutenant. Then he outlined his plan for calling the Forest Service and for taking a search party out to the canyon in the Chiracahuas. Frank listened intently and looked over the newspaper article and said, "Tom this is really interesting and, to be honest, I want to be a part of that search party. Let me run this up the chain of command and make sure we can do this on department time. If not, we'll have to organize the search on our own time."

Tom was happy with that response and thanked the lieutenant for his time. He got up and went out to get busy with the current cases they were working on.

By Friday morning the search had been approved and a search party had been organized. A representative of the Forest Service was there, two sheriff's deputies, two officers from the crime lab, Fran and her photographer from the paper were there, and Tom and his lieutenant.

A caravan of four vehicles left Bisbee about eight o'clock in the morning. Tom's Jeep led the way as they made their way into the Chiricahua Mountains and up the wagon trail. After they arrived at the cliff, the group met and developed their plan of attack. The first group to go down would be Tom, the two criminalists and the photographer. Tom would obviously show the way. The criminalists would gather evidence and the photographer would document the scene with photos. Later, if it was safe, the lieutenant and his deputies would make their way down to gather information and any other evidence they felt was relevant. Fran decided her story could be written from the photographs and interviews of those who went down.

The climb down was difficult and somewhat treacherous. The team had to scale down the pile of boulders that covered the slope. They had to work their way around the thick brush and one of the criminalists almost had heart failure when he thought he heard a rattler light up. It turned out to be the sound of a loose rock tumbling down the slope, but since he was already worried about snakes, it sounded like a snake.

The photographer took his pictures and the criminalists collected skeletal remains along with bits of clothing. Without going into the details of his wild dream, Tom directed the criminalists to search for bones a little further down the slope. He knew he had seen Lon fly through the windshield in his dream. Sure enough another skull and a few other bones were still about ten yards further down the slope. Time and critters had taken the rest of the remains away.

Later the lieutenant and his deputies went down and began to look for other evidence. Since the car was in a serious state of decay, much of the evidence had fallen under the car and the lieutenant was happy to direct one of the deputies to crawl under the wreckage to see what he could find. In fact he found more than they had hoped for. The rusted action from a Thompson submachine gun was pried out between two rocks and part of a canvas bank bag that had the words "National Bank" on it was recovered. Was there any money? Only a few scraps of currency were found. Most had decayed or been eaten by bugs and mice, but a few pieces were left and large enough to identify as being currency.

At the end of the day everyone was excited to have been a part of this treasure hunt. And a treasure hunt it was. Four large duffel bags of evidence were collected and cold case was solved.

The next week the Bisbee Observer's headline read, "Ninety Year Old Crime Solved." Below it the readers found two pictures, one was a picture of the wrecked Model A Ford and the other was a picture of Sargent Tom Madson, Lieutenant Frank Ballard and Sheriff Michael Miller who was holding what was left of the canvas National Bank bag. Fran's editor had asked that the Sheriff be included in the picture since he was running for reelection that year and the paper had endorsed his candidacy. The story included the fact that Tom Madson had discovered the wreck, but neglected to mention that he'd seen it in a dream the night before. Inside the paper there was a full page of photographs of the wreckage and the landscape around it.

The day after the article appeared, Fran stopped by the Sheriff's office to bring Tom a framed copy of the article. They only had a few minutes to talk that morning, but Fran smiled sweetly when she gave Tom the gift. Tom couldn't help watching her walk out of the office. She looked so cute in those Wranglers and he felt his heart skip a beat one more time.

CHAPTER 10:
THE AMBUSH

The Senator stepped out of the ranch house to consult with his eldest son who was the foreman of the family's one hundred and twenty year old cattle ranch. He stood on the wooden porch for just a minute to thank the Lord for allowing his family to continue to work the land as they had for generations. The retired Marine officer stood there wearing a pair of clean Levi's and a green golf shirt instead of his ranch clothes because today he was going to go back to being a politician. He had two meetings along the way to Tucson and then a flight back to D.C. The August break was just about over and he and his wife would have to get back in time to be about the nation's business.

He stepped down off of the porch and met his son Tod to talk about hauling water for the cattle. It had been an especially dry summer in Cochise County. There they stood, two Western men standing in front of the family home. The front portion of the house was over a hundred years old. It started life as a log cabin, but had been added on to over the years. Today, it was a five bedroom, three bath home with almost three thousand square feet of living space. Senator James McClanahan and his son were both six feet tall. Tod weighed about one hundred and seventy pounds while the Senator was about ten pounds heavier. Still, he was a fit man who could out work any hand on the place. He had abandoned the Marine Corps tight and white hair cut when he retired from the Corps, but he kept his brown hair cut fairly short and often covered with a cowboy hat. Today, he didn't have a lid.

The Senator carried a Glock 19 when he was home. As the chairman of the Senate Select Committee on Intelligence, he had made a lot of enemies. Enemies "foreign and domestic" hated how he had worked with both the CIA and FBI to crack down on those who would do harm to Americans and their allies and they had made many threats on the Senator's life. As a retired Marine Lieutenant Colonel, James was more than comfortable with the idea that he might have to protect himself and his family. His four deployments to the Middle East had given him plenty of combat training and experience. He was ready to act if he had to, but now he was having to travel, which meant he would have to relinquish his sidearm and put his complete trust in his security detail. He slipped his holster and gun off his belt and handed them to his son. "Put that in the safe for me, will you, son?" he asked.

"No problem, dad. It'll be there when you get back for Christmas," Tod said as he tucked the gun under his arm. He reached out his hand to shake hands with his dad and said, "Be safe. I love you and will see you when you get back."

The Senator took his son's hand, looked him in the eye and said, "I think a right smart of you too, son." They both smiled at the inside joke. Many years earlier, a senior adult woman had told James about the fact that she had never heard her father say the words "I love you" to her. The closest he'd ever come was one day when she was visiting the old man in the nursing home, as she was leaving she said, "Daddy, I love you" and he responded, "I think a right smart of you, too."

Just then two women stepped out of the ranch house and down the steps to join the Senator and his son. The older lady was the Senator's wife Sharon. She was a petite five foot three, but looked even smaller when she stood next to her husband. He was fifty-five and she was fifty-two. They met when he was a young Marine stationed at Camp Pendleton in Southern California. It was there that they fell in love and married. The other woman was Fran Booth, a reporter for the Bisbee Observer. The Senator had agreed to let her tag along on this trip in order to interview him and his wife for the local weekly newspaper. Both of the ladies were dressed casually as they anticipated spending several hours in the car.

The Senator's security detail consisted of six young men, all of whom had served in the American military and all of whom were armed and ready to defend their clients. Each man had a Glock sidearm and an MP5 submachine gun. They weren't wearing uniforms, but their civilian clothes didn't help them blend in either. Today they would travel in a caravan of three Chevrolet Tahoes. They weren't the stereotypical black SUV's as each was a different color, but the three of them traveling together would send a message none-the-less. Two men would ride in the front car and two accompanying the Senator, his wife and the reporter in the middle car and two in the third car. Each of the operators stood next to the car he would ride in. As the Senator and the two ladies approached their vehicle, one of the men opened the door and moved the middle seat forward so Fran could climb into the third row seat in the back. Then he assisted the Senator's wife as she got into the car and finally the Senator got in. All of the security operators got into their vehicles and started their engines. The Senator and his wife waved to Tod as the vehicles started out.

Friday morning, 8:00,

on a dirt road a mile north of Highway 90 in Cochise County

Seven men stood around the front of a Ford Explorer. They all looked at the map that was laid out on the hood and spoke to one another in Arabic. The men were of mixed nationalities. Two were from Iraq, two were from Pakistan and two were from Afghanistan. They had three things in common: they were all Muslim, they all spoke Arabic, and they all wanted to kill Senator James McClanahan. McClanahan's committee and his work with the intelligence community had led to the deaths of too many high level Jihadi leaders. These men wanted to see McClanahan and his family wiped off the face of the earth and were willing to risk their own lives to make that happen. Their plan was to ambush his caravan then to hurry to the family's ranch and kill as many of the family members as they could find. They believed Allah would give them success that day.

These men made up a Jihadi Cell that had been living in Southern Arizona for months. They had been scouting around the McClanahan Ranch and gathering intelligence about the Senator and his movements. They had managed to learn about the Senator's travel schedule for this day and realized they would either be able to kill the Senator and his family today or possibly miss their opportunity for months to come.

After discussing their plans, they hugged one another and repeated the words, "Allah akbar" to one another. They went to the two vehicles they would use in this ambush. Each man had an AK which was loaded with a thirty round magazine and their vests held two additional thirty round magazines. Three went to the Explorer and the other group went to their Toyota 4Runner. In each group one of the men picked up a Russian RPG and checked it over. These men meant business and considered it a holy business.

They drove out together, but split up when they got to their staging area. One of the men was designated as a look out. It was his job to spot the Senator's caravan and radio the others to put their plan into action. He would watch the road from the top of a ridge overlooking the highway. The others staged their vehicles just north of Highway 90. They knew the Senator was going to make his first stop in Ft. Huachuca and could launch their attack in some rough country west of Sierra Vista.

Friday morning, 8:00,
Cochise County Sheriff's Office, Bisbee

Sergeant Tom Madson had just completed his morning briefing with the deputies on duty when his lieutenant called him in to his office. "Tom, we've been notified that the Senator and his wife are leaving the ranch this morning to head back to Washington. He's got a six man security detail with him and they will escort the McClanahans to meetings in Ft. Huachuca and Benson, then on to the airport in Tucson where the Senator and his wife will board a plane for D.C."

"Yes, sir. Is there anything you need me to do, L.T.?" Tom asked.

"I'd like you to drive up the route they're taking and just give them some back up. We don't want anything happening to the Senator and his wife on our watch," the lieutenant replied.

Tom looked at the map on the lieutenant's office as he asked, "Do we know what route they're taking?"

Both men stepped over to the map and the lieutenant began tracing the route with his finger as he said, "Yes, we do. Of course they're taking Highway 80 north out of town until they get to 90. They'll turn west on 90 until they get to Ft. Huachuca. After that meeting they'll take 90 north to I-10 and, as you can imagine, they'll take I-10 west to Tucson. You don't need to cross the county line, but I want you to watch out for them until we know they've left our jurisdiction. Okay?"

"Yes, sir. I'll keep my eyes open," Tom said as he turned to leave. He walked out to the parking lot and got into his department issued Tahoe. He was confident he had everything he needed for the day because he checked his equipment before he left his ranch that morning. His emergency roadside equipment was in place as was his medical kit. He also knew that his personal AR was staged in the back of the Tahoe. His was a short barreled rifle in 300 blackout. The same firearm approved for the Sheriff's SWAT team. It was topped with an Aimpoint red dot sight. He knew it was dead on at fifty yards, which meant he was good out to at least two hundred yards. This was a gun he knew he could bet his life on. He'd never used it in a gunfight, but he knew from his hours of training it would do its job if he did his. His tactical vest was next to it with two spare AR magazines tucked safely away.

Tom cruised north on Highway 80 and spotted three SUV's that appeared to be traveling together. Even though they weren't the stereotypical black SUV's that government officials usually traveled in, he knew this was the Senator's entourage. The caravan was at least half a mile ahead of Tom, but he felt he could keep an eye on them from that distance without any trouble.

The caravan got to the turnoff to Highway 90 and with no oncoming traffic made the turn without having to stop. Tom wasn't as lucky. There were several cars traveling south on 80 when he got to the turnoff so he had to stop. Those cars were spaced out in such a way that it took Tom a full minute to make the turn. This added almost a full mile to the gap between his vehicle and the Senator's caravan.

The Jihadi outlook spotted the caravan as they approached the first mile marker and radioed his comrades about the Senator's approach. The plan was set in motion. There were no other cars ahead of the caravan so the Ford Explorer, which was staged four and a half miles from the junction of highways 80 and 90, pulled across the highway. The three men got out and took cover. The man with the RPG took cover behind the engine compartment of the Explorer. One of the other men took cover at the rear of the car while the third man ran to take cover behind a large bush on the south side of the highway. The lookout began running down the highway to join the second vehicle in the attack on the Senator as soon as the caravan was out of sight. He missed something, though. He missed seeing the Sheriff's SUV coming up behind the caravan.

The driver of the lead car in the caravan slammed on his breaks when he got to about fifty yards of the Jihadi's Explorer which was parked across the highway. The operator in the passenger's seat immediately got on the radio and began to yell, "Threat! Threat!" The Jihadi with the RPG stepped out from behind the SUV and fired his grenade at the lead car. The two operators could see the grenade flying toward them, but didn't have time to take any evasive action. In one second the grenade hit the Tahoe and exploded. The front of the Tahoe leaped into the air and the gas tank burst into a ball of fire. It was fully engulfed in flames when it landed. The only good news was that the burning SUV sat between the terrorists and the rest of the caravan. Something the attackers hadn't thought through.

The drivers in the other two vehicles in the caravan heard the "Threat!" call just a second before they saw the first vehicle explode. The Senator's vehicle quickly swerved to the left and stopped with the vehicle broadside across the east bound lane of the highway. The third vehicle also swerved and stopped broadside across the west bound lane. The operators in the Senator's car began to yell that everyone should exit out the driver's side of the car believing that the only threat was on the passengers' side. As everyone began to pile out of the cars the Toyota sped up to within twenty yards of the two remaining vehicles in the caravan. They too parked their car broadside and three terrorists piled out of their car. Two had their AKs at the ready and the third was getting the RPG out of the back seat. The lookout came running up and took a position on the north side of the highway in a clump of sage brush. He knew he was hidden, but he was not protected.

What no one had expected was the arrival of the Sheriff's SUV driven by Tom Madson. Tom was still about a mile behind the caravan when the lead car was hit by the RPG. He could hear the explosion and saw the ball of fire and column of smoke. He immediately radioed for back up and at least one ambulance to arrive at his location. He had been doing sixty-five as he followed the caravan, but when he saw the explosion he put his gas peddle to the floor until he was twenty-five yards from the second terrorist vehicle.

When Tom came to a stop he could see the terrorist with the RPG getting ready to take aim and fire on the Senator's position. Quickly, he unbuckled his seat belt and threw open the car door. He was already drawing his Glock as he exited. He didn't have time to aim but sent two rounds in the direction of the man with the RPG. His hope was to get him to duck and cease aiming at the Senator's car. The two rounds of forty-five lead hit the Toyota just to the right of the terrorist and succeeded in getting him to duck down and begin to look around to see where this new threat was coming from.

Tom left the car door open in order to keep the terrorists from seeing what he was doing. He ran to the back of his vehicle and opened the back hatch. He quickly donned his vest and pulled his rifle out of its case. He moved to the front door he'd left open. He looked up through the open window long enough to see that the man with the RPG was getting ready to aim again and fire. This was the biggest threat and needed to be dealt with immediately. This time he took careful aim with his rifle. Twenty-five yards was an easy shot, but he couldn't afford to miss. The red dot was high on the terrorist's back when Tom squeezed the trigger. With the adrenaline dump he'd experienced, he neither felt the recoil of the rifle nor did he hear the report, but he definitely saw the bullet make impact on its intended target. The terrorist screamed and was spun to his left just as he squeezed the trigger on the RPG. The grenade was launched, but shot out into the desert where it exploded in some granite boulders. Fortunately, the terrorist was wearing a tactical vest and not a bullet proof vest. His days of Jihad were over.

At this point the two terrorists from the Toyota were to Tom's right. Two were between Tom and their vehicle and the lookout was out in the brush. All of them were now looking to see where Tom was. In an instant they were peppering his Tahoe with rounds from their AK's. They hadn't seen him yet, but certainly knew where his vehicle was and they knew he was close. At the very least they hoped to keep his head down and at the most they hoped one of those rounds would find its target and knock this unexpected threat out of the fight.

Tom laid down on the pavement and looked under his vehicle. He could see a terrorist who was at the rear of the Toyota. He aimed his rifle under the Tahoe and fired two rounds. Both found their mark. The man was shot in the leg and fell to the ground. Tom fired once more hitting him in the chest. Another threat eliminated.

Meanwhile, the two terrorists who were at the other end of the caravan began to move forward. One was on the south side of the highway and the other was on the north side. The man who fired the RPG stayed with the vehicle and was busy reloading. The man who had been hiding on the side of the road moved out from behind his cover. When he did, one of the security operators saw him and fired a three round burst from his MP 5. Those three rounds hit their mark and the terrorist went down in a heap. His AK was thrown onto the desert floor and went silent. The terrorist who was at the other end of the Explorer was shooting as he moved away from his cover behind the car. One of the operators at the north end of the cars was shooting back, but neither man was hitting his target. That terrorist made his way behind a large boulder.

The operators from the third vehicle began to engage the remaining terrorists from the Toyota. Unfortunately the only cover between them and their attackers was the attackers' own vehicle. Both of them did a mag dump. One on the brush that hid the terrorist on the north side of the highway and the other on the Toyota itself. As if it had been choreographed by a broadway director both men dropped their empty magazines and reloaded with a fresh mag from their vests. Even though the man who shot at the brush wasn't giving careful aim, his bullets found their target and the lookout was taken out of the fight. The other man's mag dump managed to keep the terrorist's head down for a few seconds. He began to do his "duck walk" toward the Toyota, heel to toe, heel to toe, knees bent, heel to toe. He was ready to fire if he had a target, but for the moment, he didn't. The Jihadi began to slip towards the front of the vehicle knowing that hiding behind the engine compartment was the safest place to be. Tom and the operator saw the man's movement and both took aim. Tom was able to fire first and again the AR he carried was more than capable. Two pieces of thirty caliber lead went screaming out of his firearm and hit the jihadi in the left shoulder and the neck. He was down for the count.

At this point there were two terrorists on the north side of the road, one was hiding in the boulders and was engaging the security operator at the north end of the caravan with rounds. He was firing two and three round bursts at the security operator when suddenly one of those rounds found its mark and the operator was down. Tom ran up to the operators' vehicle. The three of them nodded to one another and ran five yards to the Senator's vehicle. The two security operators went directly to the Senator and his wife and checked on their welfare. Tom went straight to Fran to check on her.

"Are you okay?" Tom asked her.

"Yes, I'm alright, Tom. I'm so glad to see you," she said in a whisper. Then she looked him in the eye and said, "Tom give me a gun. You know I can shoot. Give me a gun so I can help." Tom and Fran had been with a church group that was out shooting one day. Fran's father always wanted her to be able to defend herself so he taught her to shoot. Of course, she wasn't as good a shot as Tom was, but she out shot most of the men who were at the outing. As a matter of fact, he knew she could out shoot most of his deputies. Tom reached for his sidearm and handed it to her. Their eyes locked for one brief second then Tom looked down at his belt and pulled a spare magazine and handed that to her, too. They both looked at the mag and they both held onto it for another second.

The Senator was a combat Marine and wasn't about to let others fight for him. He called to the operator who was closest to him and said, "Give me a gun. I'm a Marine. I know how to fight." At that the operator handed his Glock to the Senator. The Senator did a quick press check and then began looking for a target. For the moment there was none.

Tom looked at the three security operators and asked, "Do we know how many of them are left?"

The one man who had been with the Senator and his group from the beginning said, "As far as we can tell there are only two left. One is still up there with the vehicle and the other is behind those boulders on the north side of the highway." Just then, as if he heard his name called, the Jihadi who was situated behind the boulders sent a three round burst towards the car. Everyone ducked, but no one was hit.

The Senator reverted to his role as a Marine officer and began to give directions to the rest of the men. "Sergeant, you and Fred here need to take out the man behind the boulders. I want you all to go back to the other vehicle and see if you can get to a vantage point on the north side of the highway to take him out." Then he looked at the other two security men and said, "We are going to have to take out the other one. I'll run out to that clump of sage brush over there in order to draw his fire. You two take him out."

Sharon, the Senator's wife, said, "No. You can't leave me. Jim, I need you here with me."

Before the Senator could respond to his wife, one of the security men said, "She's right, Senator. We're here to protect you and your wife. You stay here while one of us draws his attention. You need to protect your wife if something goes wrong." Reluctantly, the Senator agreed.

Tom looked at Fran and said, "Honey, I need your help. I need you to lay down some suppressive fire on that pile of boulders. We need that clown to keep his head down while we get into position. Can you do that?"

Fran smiled to herself, "He called me honey," she thought. Then she looked at Tom and said, "Yes, I can do that."

"Listen," Tom said, "the magazine in the gun has eleven rounds and the other magazines has thirteen rounds. Watch us and empty the first magazine when we are moving. Then reload and save that last mag…you know, incase you need it later. Ok?"

"Got it, Sarge," Fran said confidently.

Just then the jihadi behind the Ford Explorer stepped out from behind the car with the RPG raised and ready to fire. Tom and two of the security team saw him at the same time and all yelled, "Everybody run!"

Instantly, Tom grabbed Fran by the arm, the Senator and his wife got up to run, and the security team all raised up to fire on the Jihadi. Before they could pull their own triggers, the Jihadi had fired his grenade. In the second it took for the grenade to find its target, three MP5s rang out and the Jihadi ended his struggle. Just as the bullets hit their target, the rocket propelled grenade hit the Senator's car and exploded. Everyone was thrown to the pavement and knocked unconscious. Those closest to the car were the Senator and his wife and the three remaining operators. Tom and Fran had gotten a few steps away from the car when it exploded and were a couple of yards away from the rest of the group.

As the car continued to burn and the Senator and his entourage lay unconscious on the hot pavement, the only surviving Jihadi began to emerge from behind the boulders. He crouched down to make himself as small of a target as possible and began to move toward the burning car. Instinctively, he dropped the magazine from his AK and inserted a fresh mag into the gun. He pushed it in and pulled to make sure it was seated properly. He raised his gun to his shoulder as he scanned to see if anyone was moving. He only had ten yards to close before getting to the Senator and the others, but he knew better than to rush. Slowly and carefully he made his way. Heel to toe, bent knees, heel to toe, he walked slowly toward the man he was sworn to kill.

Fran was the first to begin to regain consciousness. She looked around and found Tom lying next to her. His AR was several feet to his right and the Glock she had been given was just inches from her hand so she reached out and picked it up. Just then, above the sound of the car burning, she could hear the Jihadi's foot steps. He was making his way around the burning car. As far as she could tell, she was the only one who was conscious and the only one who could stop him from murdering everyone.

Out of the corner of her left eye she could see his feet moving toward the Senator and his wife. She watched him turn toward them and away from her. Immediately, she sat up and yelled, "Hey, you!" her gun pointed at his back. His head snapped to see who was calling to him. He turned to face the sound of her voice and as he did Fran squeezed the trigger of Tom's Glock sending a two hundred and twenty grain bullet into the man's chest. The gun bucked in her hands, but when the sights came back down, she sent another round his way. His body was spinning and the second round hit him in the side of his chest, which spun him again. His lifeless body hit the pavement next to the burning SUV.

It wasn't long before the scene was filled with Sheriff's SUVs, fire trucks, ambulances and FBI agents. Helicopters from various law enforcement agencies were overhead along with several from news agencies. Senator McClanahah and his wife Sharon were the first to be whisked away in an ambulance. Both were alive, but unconscious when the paramedics arrived. The two surviving members of the security detail were next to be removed. Again, both survived, but one sustained a broken arm and the other multiple cuts and abrasions. Finally, Tom and Fran were able to step up into an ambulance and were going to be transported back to the hospital in Bisbee. The two of them looked like they'd just been through a Friday night bar brawl. Their clothes were dirty, torn and bloody. Tom's hair was too short to be messed up, but he certainly didn't know where his Stetson was. Fran's hair, on the other hand, looked like she'd been in a "cat" fight and had her hair pulled. Tom had a pretty good case of road rash on the right side of his face and his right shoulder. He allowed that his dress shirt would have to go into the rag box when he got home. The sergeant really didn't want to go to the hospital, but department policy dictated that he be checked out and a sergeant certainly couldn't go against department policy. He and Fran would need to be checked to make sure they hadn't sustained a concussion.

As the two of them faced one another in the ambulance, Tom leaned forward and the two of them had their knees and foreheads touching. Tom said, "You saved all of our lives. You know that don't you?"

Fran gently put her hands on Tom's face and looked at him, "You called me honey, Sarge. You know that don't you?"

CHAPTER 11:
FIRST DATE

"If I was a dog, I'd be licking my wounds," thought Tom Madson. It was Monday morning and Tom had slept in until 7:00. He didn't have to go to work today because he was on both administrative and medical leave. He lay in bed thinking again about the terrorist attack on Senator James McClanahan just three days earlier. The faces of the men he'd killed kept flashing across his mind and the fact that his friend Fran Booth was there and could have been killed shook him to his very core. Tom played football in high school, but was never as sore and stiff the day after a game as he was this morning. His right shoulder and the right side of his face looked like someone had worked him over with a cheese grater. He'd had a little road rash when he was a kid and wiped out on his bicycle, but that didn't begin to compare to what he had after getting slammed against the highway when the Senator's car exploded. He didn't really want to get out of bed, but unfortunately, he had to haul himself out. His was a small ranch compared to his dad's cattle ranch. He only had two calves he was raising for beef and his one horse, but they needed to be fed and watered no matter how he felt. The one thing he had to look forward to that day was seeing Fran. He and she had interviews with the FBI at the Sheriff's office in town that afternoon. A smile crept onto his face when he thought about seeing her again.

That afternoon Tom Madson drove into town in his Jeep. He had on his usual starched and pressed Wranglers, his brown boots and a red long-sleeved shirt. But because of the road rash on the side of his head, Tom decided to forgo his Stetson. For once he left the house bare headed. He felt like everyone in town would be staring at him, but today this was how it would have to be. Even though he was on administrative leave, he still put his badge holder on his belt along with his Glock 30 and two extra magazines. Having just been involved in a terrorist attack, he felt he had to remain prepared for anything that might come along.

September weather in Bisbee was usually pretty and comfortable and this day didn't disappoint. The sky was blue and the temperature was only going supposed to get up to 78 degrees. Tom drove with the front windows down on his Jeep. The radio was off. He just liked riding in the quiet most of the time. It gave him time to think and his mind went to thoughts of Fran Booth. It seemed he couldn't stop thinking about her. Tom and Fran had been friends since she moved to town to take the job at the local newspaper. They actually met at church, but then got to work together when she was assigned stories Tom was involved with as a member of law enforcement. They had a lot in common and enjoyed one another's company, but recently Tom had been having more than just friendly feelings for Fran. He was thinking that it might be time to explore those feelings. Maybe he should ask her out, he thought. His mouth got dry thinking like that. "Horses," he thought. "I need to think about horses."

Thinking about horses didn't last long because Tom was only a few minutes from the Sheriff's office where the interviews would take place and waiting for him to arrive, standing by her car, was Fran. Her face lit up when she saw his Jeep pulling into the parking lot. She stood up straight and flashed a smile that would light any room up and her blue eyes seemed to sparkle. "I'm in trouble," Tom thought. "This girl may have stolen my heart."

Tom got out of his Jeep and began to walk over to Fran. Despite his injuries and sore muscles, he walked briskly and he had a sheepish grin on his battered face. When he got within arms length, Fran threw her arms around Tom's neck and gave him the biggest hug he could remember ever getting. He put his arms around her, too. He winced just a little because of the pain in his right arm and shoulder, but that wasn't going to stop him from letting her know he cared. After a long minute, they began to relax their hug and looked directly into one another's faces.

"Hi," Fran said.

"Hey," Tom replied. "How are you doing today? You feeling okay?"

Fran sighed and said, "Yeah, I'm okay. You?"

Tom swallowed hard and said, "I'm doing better now that I'm with you." At that, she hugged him again. When she relaxed her hug again, Tom said, "Listen, we've got these interviews to take care of, but could we talk afterwards?"

"Yes, of course," Fran said softly as she continued to look directly into Tom's eyes.

Just then the Lieutenant stuck his head out of the door and hollered, "Hey, you two, the FBI agents are waiting to interview you. Get on in here, would you?" Tom and Fran smiled at each other and turned to the Lieutenant. Tom replied, "We're coming, L.T."

Although Tom and Fran were escorted into separate interrogation rooms, these were definitely not interrogations. There was no question about the legality of both Tom and Fran's shootings of the Jihadi terrorists who attacked the McClanahan caravan. The goal of these interviews was simply to get their statements for the record and to warn them about talking to the press. Having been involved in killing Jihadis could put targets on Tom and Fran's backs so they needed to be careful.

Tom and Fran were interviewed separately, but the interviews were finished almost exactly the same time. The two FBI agents and the two interviewees stepped into the hall together. The agents shook their hands and thanked them for their courage under fire and their time. "We'll let you know if we need anymore information, but for now, we consider this matter closed," one of the agents said and that was that.

When Lt. Ballard saw that the interviews were over he stepped out of his office to speak to Tom and Fran. "You guys alright?" he asked.

Both of them nodded their heads as Tom spoke up, "Yeah, I think we're okay. Aren't we, Fran?"

"Yes," she said, "a little sore and very overwhelmed by all of the attention we're getting, but, yes, I'm alright." She smiled kind of a sheepish smile at the lieutenant and dropped her head a little. At this point she just wanted to get outside with Tom so they could "talk".

"Good," the lieutenant said as he turned his focus on Tom. "Sarge, you're on leave until the doc releases you. I don't want to see you around here until then. Got it?"

"L.T., you aren't going to get any argument from me. Doc says he wants to see me in two weeks. I'm sure he'll release me then, but I promise, you won't see me around here until then," Tom said.

"I'll see to it, sir," Fran said with a smile.

The look on both Tom and the lieutenant's faces was one that asked the question, "Really?" but neither no one said the word out loud. At that the couple continued to walk out the front door of the office and into the parking lot.

As soon as they stepped out of the door, Tom slipped his arm around Fran's waist. When he did Fran looked up, just a little surprised, but she definitely liked his arm around her waist. So much so that she slipped her arm around his waist and they walked out into the parking lot. "The park across the street seems to be pretty empty. Maybe we could sit over there for a few minutes and talk," Tom suggested.

Fran looked across the street at the little town park. It wasn't very big, maybe an acre of land, but it had freshly mown grass and the park benches were all shaded by the trees that were scattered about. She looked up at Tom with a smile and said, "I think that'll be perfect."

They kept their arms around each other's waists all the way across the street and into the park. The benches in the park were made of very durable and utilitarian concrete. They might not be made for comfort, but they should withstand the weather and use for years to come. Tom kept walking until they found a bench towards the back of the park, one that had several trees between it and the street.

"Is this okay," he asked.

Fran looked up at him again and said, "Yes, Tom, this'll be fine." as she began to sit down.

After he sat down, Tom reached up to brush Fran's brown hair off of her freckled face and said, "We've been friends for a long time now, but, Fran, something's changed."

Fran's eyes darted from Tom's eyes to his mouth, then she simply said, "Oh?"

Shyly Tom continued, "Yes, in the last few weeks I've realized I'm developing feelings for you and last Friday when I saw that you were with the Senator and his wife, my heart just sank. I was afraid something would happen to you and I would never get to tell you how I felt." Tom gave a big sigh after getting all of that out.

Reaching up to hold his face with both of her hands, Fran sighed and smiled, "I've had feelings for you for several months. I was just waiting to see if you felt the same way."

Tom's eyes scanned the area and seeing that no one was around he leaned in and gave her a gentle kiss. He looked at her and said, "I'm so glad to hear that. I'd like to ask you out for dinner one night this week. What do you think?"

Fran was still holding his face in her hands. She smiled as she asked, "You mean like a real date?"

Tom laughed as he said, "Yes, like a real date. What do you say?"

Fran's expression changed. Her face went from playful to serious as she looked at him and said, "Yes, Tom, I'd really like that. What do you have in mind?"

"Well, I'd like to have a couple of days to heal up a little more, so I was thinking maybe Friday night we could go to the Bisbee Steak House. It's the nicest place in town and, well, I can't think of any place better to take my girl," Tom replied.

"His girl!?" Fran thought to herself excitedly. "He called me his girl!" Then she calmly said, "I think that would be nice. Wait, I've got to cover an event at the VFW hall that afternoon. Could I meet you at the restaurant?"

"Sure," Tom replied, "would 6:00 be okay?"

"6:00 would be perfect," Fran said. Then she thought to herself that would give her plenty of time to get home and change for what she hoped would be the first of many dates with Tom.

As they stood to leave, Tom put his hands on Fran's hips and drew her to himself. He kissed her again. This kiss wasn't as gentle as before. It was such a passionate kiss that they both lost track of time and space. They shut out the world for a long moment. In that moment there were no terrorists attacking a senator's caravan. There were no drug dealers to arrest. There were no editors with deadline demands. There were just two young adults falling in love.

Tom and Fran walked hand in hand back to the parking lot at the Sheriff's office and Tom walked Fran to her car. After she had gotten into her car Tom leaned in and gave her one last kiss and said, "Friday night, I'll see you Friday night."

Fran looked up, her face a little flush, and said, "Yes, you will." and with that she drove off.

Friday afternoon Fran finished her assignment at the VFW hall. The veterans and their families had just finished a fund raiser for the Wounded Warrior Project and Fran had all the interviews and pictures she would need for her story so she headed home a little ahead of schedule. After a quick shower, she dressed for her "big date". It was a nice September evening in Bisbee. The temperature would drop into the low 70's after the sun went down so she decided on a dark blue cantina style skirt that went down past mid-calf and a white peasant blouse. "Shoes?" she wondered to herself. She debated between a pair of hand made leather sandals and her boots for just a minute. Ultimately she decided on her red cowgirl boots. That would make her outfit red, white and blue she thought. Her hair was pulled back behind her ears, which were adorned with a pair of silver earrings. They were shaped and stamped like ponchos and went with the necklace she had chosen. She picked up her brown leather purse and slipped her phone into it and then stopped to have another debate with herself. It had only been a week since she and Tom were fighting for their lives during the terrorist attack on Senator McClanahan's caravan. Should she take the little 38 special revolver her father had given her? Her purse actually had a special compartment on the side for just such a firearm. Suddenly, the face of the terrorist she had shot and killed came into her mind. This was an image she was sure she would never forget and the thought of having to use a gun against another human being was more than she could stand. No, she would not arm herself. This was going to be a fun night. It might even be a night that really began something special. She couldn't imagine she would need a gun on a date with Tom Madson. After all, Tom always had a gun, so she wouldn't need one.

A couple of miles outside of town, Sargent Tom Madson had just finished feeding and watering his horse and calves. He put some tools away in the barn and walked across the yard to the house. The weather that day was chamber of commerce perfect. The sun was bright, the blue sky had just the right number of fluffy white clouds in it and there was a gentle breeze blowing from the east. Tom stopped on his porch, closed his eyes and took it all in. He took a deep breath and enjoyed the clean country air. As he breathed out, he also breathed a prayer, "Thank you, Lord, for letting me live in a place like this." Opening his eyes he sat down on the deacon's bench on his porch to take off his work boots, which he sat next to the bench. He wiggled his toes in his white socks before standing up and going into the house.

After his shower, Tom began to dress for his "big date" with Fran. Tom had a number of girl friends over the years, but none were really serious. This felt different. Of course he was older now and at least a little more mature. But this felt like it was more about the girl than his maturity. This might be serious and he wanted to reflect that with the way he dressed for the evening. Tom's wardrobe didn't have a ton of variety. He really only had two choices, his better jeans and shirts that he would wear to work and church or the clothes he wore when he was working around the ranch or when he went camping. Tonight he would wear his newest pair of Wranglers, which were, of course, starched and pressed and one of his George Strait Wrangler shirts. His shirt tonight was long sleeved and navy blue and white plaid. His sock collection was one color, white. When you wear cowboy boots six or seven days a week, you don't need a bunch of fancy colored socks. But boots? Which boots should he wear? He had two pairs of boots he would wear to work or church, one was black and the other was brown. But there was another pair of boots sitting in the closet. On his twenty-first birthday, Tom's dad had taken him to El Paso to a custom boot maker and bought Tom a pair of custom made boots. He got to pick the toe shape, square, the color and type of the leather, brown ostrich hide, and the heel type, a stockman style heel. Those boot cost a little over $3000, but, because they were only worn for special occasions and were taken care of, they had already lasted nine years and looked as good as the day they were made. This was a special occasion, which called for his special boots. Tom never went any where without a gun and tonight wouldn't be any different. His Glock 30 went on his belt along with his double mag pouch on his left side, but because tonight he was going on a date, he wanted to carry concealed so he left the tail of his shirt untucked. Only the most observant person would know he was carrying and most folks don't pay enough attention to those around them to notice the slight bulge under his shirt. Tom's face and head had healed enough that his brown Stetson would be in place for the evening.

Fran arrived at the Steak House about twenty minutes early, but decided to go ahead and get a table. When she sat down, she made sure she was facing the door. More than once she had heard Tom say, "Wild Bill Hickok only sat with his back to the door once in his life." Knowing the story of Wild Bill's death, she knew that the day he sat with his back to the door was the day he was killed. She'd give the seat to Tom when he got there, but until then she would heed another of Tom's sayings, "Keep your head on a swivel." She would try to be very aware of what was going on around her.

After she was seated, she pulled her phone out of her purse and sent Tom a quick text, "Arrived early. I've got a table. Take your time, see you soon." She was tempted to put a heart emoji after the message, but decided that might be a bit much. Send. A minute later, three men walked into the restaurant. Their movement by the door caught Fran's attention, but it was their appearance and actions that kept her interest. They certainly didn't look like locals. They were dressed more like urban gang tweakers than Bisbee locals. Most of the locals dressed casually, but when they went to one of the nicer restaurants in town they would wear their nicer jeans and clean shirts. These three appeared to be in their late teens or early twenties at the oldest. They were all wearing baggy jeans with baggy button up shirts. Two were bare headed and the third was wearing a backwards baseball cap. Two were anglos and the third was a young hispanic man. One of the anglos was carrying a backpack that seemed to be empty. Fran's first impression was that they were tourists. No big deal, tourists loved Bisbee this time of year. The weather was nice and the old mining town had a lot of charm. People loved the craft and antique shops. But these three didn't seem like they would be interested in either craft or antique shops.

While she was taking a sip from her glass of water, Fran noticed that two of the young "urbanites" were walking toward the back of the restaurant while the third stayed by the front door. Fran thought, "That's interesting. He looks like he's standing guard." He had his arms crossed and seemed to be watching every movement in the dining room. The other two, the hispanic and other anglo, walked straight to the office door. Fran noticed that they didn't knock, they walked in and closed the door behind them. Fran kept drinking her water, but her attention shifted between the young man at the front door and the door to the manager's office.

Inside the office Freddie Valderama, manager of the Steak House, sat behind his desk, going over some paper work. He had just poured himself a glass of Dewars Scotch. He wasn't an extravagant man, but once in a while he felt like he could justify a glass of fine Scotch and a good cigar. Freddie was an Arizona native, born of Hispanic parents who were also Arizona natives. Forty-something, Freddie had curly black hair with hints of grey at the temples and was dressed in casual slacks and a clean white, short-sleeved dress shirt. The office was neat, but his desk was piled with food orders, employee schedules and other business papers. In one corner of the room there stood a large safe. It was black and looked like a gun safe with the word "Liberty" painted across the face of its door.

Freddie looked surprised when the two young men opened the door and walked in his office. "May I help you?" he asked.

The young man with the backwards ball cap closed the door and the other young man pulled a gun from under his shirt. The stainless steel revolver was pointed at Freddie's head when the young man spoke, "Yes, sir, you can. We want you to open that safe and give us the cash."

With his hands up in a surrender position, Freddie said, "Fellas, you've got to know that restaurants don't do a lot of cash business these days. Most folks pay with credit cards."

"We're not stupid!" the young Hispanic man said with a snarl. "We know this restaurant isn't your only business and that your other business is a cash business. Open the safe! Comprende?"

"Hombre, I do comprehend what you are saying, but you're wrong about the cash," Freddie said.

As the hammer was pulled back and clicked into the cocked position on his revolver, the young man said, "We know that you buy and sell gold and silver and that you keep the cash in that there safe." At that he waved the gun in the direction of the safe and said, "I don't want to use this on you, so move over to the safe and open the door."

Freddie kept his hands raised when he got up from his chair and went to the safe. He twisted the dial to the right a little and then to the left. Finally he twisted it just a little more to the right and turned the handle on the safe and it was open. Quickly, Freddie reached into the safe, pulled out his own revolver and fired a shot at the young man closest to him. He was point shooting and not aiming, but his bullet hit the young man in the side. At that the wounded man pulled the trigger on his revolver. The gun jumped in his hand and the bullet hit Freddie in the right side of his chest. Freddie was slammed against the back wall of the office. His eyes were closed and he wasn't moving.

The young Hispanic grabbed his side and looked at his partner, "Joel, get the cash and let's get out of here."

Joel's eyes were as wide as saucers, "What the…? What the…?" he stammered. "I thought no one was going to get hurt, Manny!"

Manny was doubled over at this point, but he looked up at Joel and said, "Listen, this is not how we planned it, but this is how it is. Get the money and let's get out of here."

At that Joel took his backpack over to the safe. Originally, this had been a gun safe, but Freddie had taken out the slots for rifles and replaced them with shelves to hold his gold and silver coins and the cash from his precious metals business. Joel had to step over Freddie's legs to get within reach of the money, but he quickly filled his backpack with the cash. He looked at Manny, who was struggling to remain standing, and asked, "What about the gold and silver coins in here?"

Manny groaned as he said, "We talked about that! It's too heavy. How much cash did you get?"

"Probably forty or fifty thousand," Joel said.

Manny thought to himself, "I don't want to die in this office." He looked up at Joel and said, "That's good enough. Let's go."

Meanwhile in he dining room, people screamed when they heard the two gunshots, but Fran turned her head to the right and looked at the man at the front door. When he heard the shots, he pulled his shirt up and drew a gun from his waist band. All that Fran could tell was that it was one of those black semi-automatic pistols that so many people carried these days. When some of the restaurant's patrons got up to run out, the man keeping guard at the front door began waving his gun around and nervously shouted, "Everyone down. Sit down and shut up!" People believed he meant business and did as they were told.

In the meantime, Fran picked up her phone and texted Tom, "Shots fired! Being robbed!" and then she turned her phone to vibrate and slipped it into one of the pockets in her skirt.

Most of the people had their heads down, a few had gotten under their tables, but Fran kept looking. Her journalism instincts kicked in. She was taking in every detail thinking this would be the front page story of next week's edition of the paper.

Manny and Joel emerged from the office. Manny's face was twisted with pain. He was holding his left side with his blood covered left hand and his revolver in his right hand. The look on Joel's face was one of sheer panic. He'd never seen men shot before. Fear was taking over. He didn't want to go to prison again and he certainly didn't want to die. Manny reached up and grabbed Joel's arm and said, "Dude, I think we need to take a hostage. This is going to get ugly and we're going to need some insurance."

Joel couldn't process what was going on. He began swinging his head from side to side unable to focus on anyone or anything. "Hostage?" he thought, "How? Who?"

Manny saw a family cowering in a booth near them and pointed at the young mother. "Her, grab her and let's get out of here!" he said.

The young woman looked at the men and screamed, "No! I have a family! Please! Please don't take me!"

Fran's table was only six or eight feet from the family in the booth. She could see the two children sitting with the woman. Terror filled their eyes so she decided she had to do something. "Hey! Hey! Over here! Take me. I'll go with you!" she shouted.

Joel and Manny both looked straight at Fran and Manny told Joel, "Grab her. Let's get out of here!"

Joel took two steps and reached out to grab Fran's arm. When he jerked her up, her table almost tipped over and her chair was pushed into the wall behind her. "Come on then. You're coming with us." Immediately, Fran began to question her decision to trade places with the young mother.

Across town Tom was on his way to the restaurant and his first date with Fran when the hands free cell phone system on his Jeep showed that he had a message from Fran. When he swiped on the message, the robot voice read, "Shots fired! Being robbed!" Tom couldn't believe his ears. He called out, "Repeat the message!" and the robot voice read the message again, "Shots fired! Being robbed!" then asked, "Do you want to reply?"

"No!" Tom said, "call 911!" When the 911 operator came on the line and asked what the emergency was, Tom said, "This is Sargent Madson of the Sheriff's Department. There's a report of shots fired and a robbery in progress at the Bisbee Steak House. Send officers immediately!" When the operator assured Tom that officers were being dispatched he hung up, shifted gears and floored his Jeep. All he could think about was the fact that Fran was in danger…again! He had to get to Fran!

Manny and Joel were moving slowly through the restaurant, Manny because of his gunshot wound and Joel because he had Fran in tow. But Manny was still thinking more clearly than either of his partners and called out to the third man at the front of the restaurant, "David, go get the car so we can get out of here." David's eyes were wild, he looked around unable to focus for a full second, but he was finally able to process Manny's words. He understood and turned to leave. Their Ford Explorer was parked in a handicapped spot in the restaurant's parking lot. It would only take a minute to get to it and pull it up to the front door. The three robbers and their hostage peeled out of the parking lot like a scalded dog. They needed to get out of there before the cops could arrive.

Manny's uncle had a cabin just outside of town. The three tweakers would often go there to party and do drugs. This is where they hatched the plan to rob Freddie Valderama the weekend before. It seemed like a fool proof plan when they were high. Manny was in the passenger's seat, clutching his side, bent over in pain. He looked over at David and said, "Get us to the cabin before the cops find us."

David kept looking straight ahead, but responded, "Dude, I'm going as fast as I can. We'll be there in five minutes."

The smell of burning rubber was still lingering in the air when Tom Madson and two other Sheriff's department patrol cars pulled up to the restaurant. Both of Tom's hands went to the his right side. They grabbed his shirt tale and pulled it out of the way as Tom drew his Glock. The other deputies all drew their side arms as the three of them entered the front door. They moved slowly and methodically at first, but when the customers started pouring out of the door, Tom told the deputies to get the customers out into the parking lot, but that they weren't to allow any of them to leave. "And call for back up," he said. "We're going to need all the help we can get."

Tom was scanning the crowd trying to find Fran. When he couldn't see her any where, he called out, "Fran, Fran Booth, are you here?" His question was met with silence, a silence that filled his heart with a sense of dread. As he moved on through the restaurant's dining room, Tom continued to scan the room. The room was large and decorated in western art. There were old west paintings that depicted cowboy and ranch life, the furnishings looked like they came right out of an old Arizona ranch house, but the room was empty of people. No robbers and no Fran!

Then he saw her purse. It was still sitting on a chair next to one of the tables. He picked it up and looked at the wallet inside it. The driver's license confirmed that it was Fran's purse. Tom knew Fran would never leave without her purse voluntarily. Again, he scanned the room and wondered where she could be. He kept the purse so he could return it to Fran and continued through the dining room. With Fran's purse in his left hand, he kept his Glock out in front of him as he walked. His eyes were constantly scanning the room. There was no movement around him. There was no one there.

Finally, Tom got to the office. The door was partially closed so Tom slowly pushed it open with the toe of his right boot. He stayed to the side as he scanned the room from left to right. Slowly he looked around the door and there he saw the manager lying on the floor in a pool of blood. Once he saw that there was no one else in the room he holstered his side arm and moved over to Freddie. Freddie lay on the floor next to the open safe. His eyes were closed, but Tom could see slight movement as Freddie breathed. He chest would rise ever so slightly as he inhaled and then lower again as he exhaled. Just then a deputy looked in the door. He had his sidearm drawn and was scanning the room the same way Tom had a moment ago. When Tom saw the young man, he said, "Call for an ambulance and for the crime scene techs. Freddie's been shot, but he's alive." Tom noticed the blood spray on the wall on the opposite side of the office. The deputy immediately got on his radio and made the call to dispatch. Tom looked at the deputy again and said, "Stay with him until they get here." Then he turned to leave the office.

"Sure thing, Sarge," the deputy said as he was kneeling down next to Freddie. He wanted to be close to him incase he regained consciousness.

Tom went back to Fran's purse. He checked its contents and noticed that something was missing. Her phone wasn't there. He looked around the table and didn't see a phone on either the table or the floor around the table. "Maybe she has her phone on her," he thought to himself. He put the purse back down and made his way back outside. As he looked at the crowd of restaurant customers and staff, he called out again, "Fran. Fran Booth. Fran, are you here?"

One of the waitresses answered, "Are you looking for Frannie? They took her."

Tom's head snapped in the direction of the voice, "What? Who said that?"

"I did," the young woman said. "I know Frannie and I saw one of the men who came out of the office grab her arm and take her with him."

Tom stepped over to the woman, "You saw them take her?"

"Yes, sir," she said.

"Did you see anything else? Could you give us a description of the men who took her?" Tom pleaded.

The woman was visibly shaken by the events of the evening. She put her hand to her forehead as she spoke, "There were three of them." Then she realized she knew something that might be important. She raised her face to look directly at Tom, "One of the men was wounded," she said excitedly. "He was holding his side and could barely walk. Is that helpful?"

Tom put his hand on her shoulder as he said, "Yes, it is. Thank you so much. Stay here, a deputy will be taking your statement in just a minute." At that Tom called one of the deputies over and said, "Take this young lady's statement right away and see if she can give you a description of the men involved." The deputy nodded and stepped right over to the waitress.

Before Tom stepped away from the crowd he asked in a loud voice, "Did anyone see what they were driving?"

An older man with grey hair and a beard raised his hand and said, "I did. I was sitting next to the window when they left and saw them get into an older Ford Explorer."

"Did you see what color it was?" Tom asked as he stepped toward the man.

The man thought for a second that seemed like an hour to Tom, then he said, "Yes, sir. It was red. Yes, it was definitely red."

"Thank you, sir," Tom said. "That's really helpful." Then he had another thought, "If Fran still has her phone, we might be able to track her." He called the crime lab and asked them to put a trace on Fran's phone. Within a minute, they called back and said the phone was located at a certain address just outside of town. Tom said, "I know that place. It's a cabin about a mile from my ranch." Tom told the criminalist to send back up to that location and to tell them that he was on his way.

Climbing into his Jeep, Tom reached for his portable police lights. He turned them on and placed them on the dashboard. As the lights began flashing red and blue, he quickly put the car into first gear and took off. He had to get to Fran. She had to be okay.

Tom knew all of the people who lived in his "neighborhood". "Who owned that cabin?" he wondered to himself. He remembered that this was a summer cabin. Some guy from Tucson owns it. "What was his name again?" he asked out loud. "Max? Was it Max? Max Gutierrez?" he thought. "Yes, Max Gutierrez!" Tom said out loud. Then he remembered seeing some younger men hanging out at the cabin on weekends. He remembered thinking they looked pretty sketchy. If those were the men who robbed the restaurant, he'd better get there before they hurt Fran.

In a few minutes, Tom was on the county road that led to his ranch and then on to the cabin Fran's phone had been traced to. He could see the emergency lights of two other Sheriff's cars coming up behind him and knew they needed to be careful as they approached the cabin. When he got within a quarter mile of the cabin, he pulled over to the side of the road. When the other two vehicles got within a hundred yards of him he flagged them down. He walked up to the two patrol vehicles and told the deputies to get out, they were going to walk up to the cabin.

The sky was ablaze with a red and orange sunset Arizona was famous for, but Tom and the other deputies didn't have time to admire it. They had to get to the cabin in time. Fran needed them. Fortunately the road was lined with mesquite trees, which helped to hide their approach. As they got to the cabin's driveway, Tom peaked around the last tree and noticed several cars near the cabin, but the closest was an older, red Ford Explorer. "This is the place, guys," Tom said in a whisper. "That SUV fits the description of the getaway car." Then he motioned for the men to follow him. All of them had their sidearms drawn and the adrenaline was pumping throughout their bodies. They knew things could turn ugly any second.

When they got next to the Explorer, Tom looked into the car. The front passenger's seat was soaked with blood. Tom pointed at the seat and whispered, "There's a lot of blood in that seat. One of the robbers was wounded. Looks like he's in real trouble." At that the other deputies looked into the car and nodded in agreement.

Tom looked at the two deputies and said, "Carter, I want you to sneak around the back. There's a door back there. If one of these rats decides to jump ship, you take him. Gonzales, I'm going to the side of the cabin. You go to the front door and call out for the men inside to come out. I'm going to try to make entry through a side window while you distract them with the demand that they surrender. Be careful that you aren't where they can shoot you, but be ready to kick in that door if you have to. If I give you a signal, you need to be ready to come in. You guys got that?"

Both of the deputies looked at the Sargent and nodded. All three went to take their posts. When Gonzales got to the front, he took cover behind a post on the front porch. He waited five seconds and figured the others were in place so he called out, "In the cabin, this is the Cochise County Sheriff's Department. You need to come out now."

Inside the cabin Manny was sitting in a chair at a small table. He was slumped over and unconscious. A pool of blood was forming under him. Joel, the man who had gone into the office with Manny, was frantically pacing back and forth. His heart was beating rapidly and he was hyperventilating. Despite David's objections, he'd been smoking meth since they got to the cabin. David was standing in the far back corner of the front room of the cabin close to where Fran was sitting.

When Deputy Gonzales called out, Joel and David looked at one another, while Fran smiled the slightest smile. She knew Tom would come for her. Joel was in an absolute panic as he looked to David for directions. "What are we going to do?" he asked frantically.

David looked at Joel and said, "We aren't going to panic. That's what we are not going to do. Remember we've got a hostage. She's going to get us out of here."

Gonzales called out again, "In the cabin, this is the Cochise County Sheriff's Department. You need to come out now. We don't want anyone to get hurt. Come out with your hands up. We know one of your friends is hurt. We can get him help."

At the back of the cabin, Deputy Carter holstered his firearm and pulled his baton. With a flick of the wrist it was fully extended. His hope was that if anyone came running out the back door, he could waylay him and not have to kill anyone.

Tom began working to open the side window, which fortunately for him, was not latched. That window opened into a bedroom, which, he believed, would lead to the front room where all of the robbers were.

David called from inside the cabin, "We've got a hostage. We want you to let us get to our car and drive away. We'll kill the girl if you don't."

"I can't make that deal on my own," Gonzales said. "Why don't you let the girl go as a sign of good faith. Then I'll call the Sheriff."

While Gonzales and David were talking back and forth, Tom began making his way to the bedroom door across the room. Suddenly, he stepped on a loose floor board that squeaked so loud Tom was sure it would wake the dead.

At that point Joel completely panicked and screamed, "I'm out of here, man!" He took off like a bat out of hell. He threw open the back door believing he would make his way to freedom. However, as soon as his foot hit the back step, he felt cold steel crash down on his skull. He saw what he would later describe as a bolt of lightning. Then all of the lights went out and he crumbled into a heap just outside of the cabin door. Deputy Carter moved quickly to handcuff his prisoner.

When David heard the floor in the next room squeak, he grabbed up Fran and pulled his gun. He then turned to the right to face the bedroom door, his gun pressed against Fran's neck. "Whoever's in that bedroom better come out slowly," he yelled. "I've got the girl and I will kill her." Tom kept his Glock in his right hand and reached for the doorknob with his left. Gently and slowly he opened the bedroom door. When the door was about halfway open, his left hand moved back to the gun as he re-acquired his fighting grip. He slowly stepped into the front room of the cabin. He was fifteen feet from the man who was holding Fran. He could see the man's gun pressed against Fran's neck. The look on Fran's face was not a look of panic by any means. She wanted to look relieved to see Tom, but she couldn't. Her brow was furrowed and she silently mouthed the word, "Help" when she saw Tom.

Tom scanned the room. He could see Manny slumped over the table at the far end of the room. The backpack filled with money was lying on the table next to

Manny's head. "Buddy, my deputies have both of the doors to this place covered. You aren't getting out of here. Put your gun down and end this," Tom said. Then he called to his deputies, "Gentlemen, let this fella know you're there. Deputy Gonzales, call out."

"I'm still here and I'm not going anywhere," Gonzales said.

"I'm here, too," Carter said. "And I've got your buddy in cuffs. He's taking a much needed siesta, pard. Come on out. Let's end this thing."

"No! That's not how this is going down," David said. "I'll tell you how this is going to end. You are going to drop your gun and back out of this room after you tell your deputies to leave the area. The girl and I are going out the front door and I'm driving off with her. Comprende?"

The tone in Tom's voice was deadly serious when he said, "I'm never dropping this gun. If you harm one hair on her head, you won't make it out of here alive. So far as I know, no one has died yet. But if the restaurant manager or your partner over there dies, you will face a murder charge. Surrender now and we can get help for your partner. Maybe, just maybe, we can spare you the murder rap."

David's face turned beet red as shoved the barrel of his pistol harder against Fran's neck. "No! I will not surrender! You drop that gun or I will shoot her," he screamed. Fran winced with pain. Her eyes were pleading with Tom to save her.

Immediately, Tom screamed, "Now!" and his two deputies jumped into action. Gonzales moved from behind the post on the front porch and kicked in the front door, but jumped back out of the doorway immediately and Carter began to make entry through the back door.

A chain of events was set in motion when the front door came crashing open.

David's face immediately turned to the door as he pointed his gun and fired through the open door. Fran raised her right foot and stomped on David's right instep. The heel of her boot sent pain shooting through her captor's foot. That pain caused his left hand to loosen its grip on her. Feeling her captor's grip loosen, Fran immediately dropped to the floor and Tom fired one shot hitting David in the temple. David's body was thrown backwards and it hit the chair he'd been siting in earlier. The chair fell backwards and David's lifeless body fell in a heap on top of it. His gun fell from his limp hand. The fight was over.

Fran was slumped over on the floor. Her hair looked like she'd just woke up from a fitful night's sleep. Her blouse was disheveled and had come untucked from her skirt and tears were starting to flow down her cheek, which was causing her makeup to run. But she was alive. Tom knelt down and scooped her up in his arms and held her close to his chest for a long while. Quietly he whispered to her, "Everything's going to be alright now. You're going to be okay."

Half an hour later the cabin was as busy as a bee hive. People were buzzing about everywhere. Deputies, paramedics, crime scene techs, the County Coroner, and the Sheriff himself, had all converged on the little summer cabin.

Off to the side, away from most of the activity, Tom Madson and Fran Booth sat on a little bench that had been placed under a tree in the cabin's front yard. The two were snuggled so close that there was definitely no room for the Holy Ghost between them. Fran's head was on Tom's shoulder and his arm was holding her tightly. The two sat silently for several minutes. Both starred off into space. Both knew this could have ended so differently.

Tom broke the silence when he turned to Fran and said, "You were incredibly brave in there."

"I was scarred to death, Tom," she replied.

"I have a confession to make, I was really scarred, too," Tom said softly. "I was so afraid something would happen to you and I don't know what I would have done if it had."

Fran pushed away from Tom, but not to get away from him, in order to face him. She reached up to touch his face with her hand and said, "You saved my life, Tom. I'll never forget what you did for me tonight."

A little uncomfortable with how serious things were getting, Tom smiled as he said, "I guess that makes us even since you saved me last time."

Fran laughed softly. Still touching his face, she playfully smiled at Tom as she replied, "Listen, this really doesn't count as a first date. You know that don't you?"

Bonus 1:

A Story by
Carolyn Danielen

Chapter 12:
Our September Visitor

Mama told me our house had once been a sight to see. Not just in Circleville, but, also, in the surrounding area. She said 2 years before I was born, Papa built the house. With a wistful look in her cornflower blue eyes, she sighed, "Such a beautiful house."

But, since Papa died of pneumonia 4 years ago, in the winter of 1893, and I became the man of the house, our house had fallen into disrepair.

As best I could, I did my chores, did the trapping, and helped Mama with my little sisters. But times were hard. Real hard.

In September of 1897, on my 11th birthday, I helped Mama wallpaper the interior walls of our house with newspapers, and other scraps of paper. We put them up with a paste we made from flour and water. Mama was hoping this would keep out some of the Utah winter that was heading our way.

A week or so after my birthday, a man knocked on our back door. The first thing I noticed was that he was carrying a Winchester rifle, and had a Colt Single Action Army revolver in a holster fastened around his hip. He looked weary and dusty. Speaking quietly, and politely, he asked, "Ma'am, do you have any food you can spare? I'm mighty hungry."

Mama replied, "Come on in. We ain't got no meat today, but you're welcome to the leftover pinto beans from dinner." As the man stepped inside, Mama said, "I've got some meal, so if you've got time I can make some cornbread."

"Sounds fine, ma'am, mighty fine. I got time," said the man, with a friendly smile. Then he asked, "Not much luck trappin' or shootin' rabbits these days, ma'am?"

"The traps have been empty all week, and the only gun we got don't work properly," said Mama, as she busied herself mixing the cornmeal and water.

As she spoke, I frowned, and thought, "The only gun we got is Papa's rusty old Remington revolver. So, yeah, not much luck shootin'."

After Mama put the cornbread in the oven, the man looked at me, and asked, "Got some water for my horse, boy? If so, I'd be much obliged."

Nodding my head, I ran out the back door, with the man following right behind me.

After I watered his horse, the man asked, "You a good shot with a rifle, boy?"

As I replied, "Pretty good, I s'pose" he handed me his rifle.

"See if you can hit that fence post over there, boy...the post way over there with the hawk sittin' on it...but, just the post, boy, not the hawk sittin' on the post." The man paused, and then added, "Always remember...hawks have a fierce reputation, but most of them are quiet and gentle."

After nodding, I took aim and shot. A bit off center, but I hit the post and not the hawk. When the rifle boomed, the hawk scolded me with a shrill, "Chwirk, chwirk", as he flew away.

"That is pretty good," said the man, with a chuckle.

Then he handed me five rocks and told me to throw them high and long. "One at a time, please," he said, as he took aim. Then, "Okay, boy...let 'em fly!"

Man, oh, man, he busted each of those rocks clean in half! He was an amazing shot!

After handing his rifle back to me, he gave me some lessons in aiming and shooting. He was very patient with me and his words were firm, but kind.

About twenty minutes later, when Mama called out that the food was ready, I handed the man his rifle and he followed me back into the house.

My family sat in silence...our eyes fixed on the man. We watched as he drank two cups of cold water and finished off all of the beans. I noticed he only ate two pieces of the cornbread. I smiled to myself, as I thought about how good that cornbread would taste for supper.

After the man finished eating, he pointed to one of the pieces of paper wallpapered on the kitchen wall. All of us looked over to see what he was pointing at. On the paper was a photograph of a man. I tried to read the writing under the photograph, but the paper was upside down and torn, so I couldn't. The only word I could make out was in large black letters...it said "WANTED".

Still pointing at the paper, the man asked, "Ma'am, what would you do if he showed up at your door?"

Still staring at the paper, my Mom replied, "Mister, you already know the answer to that...I'd feed him. Just like I'd feed any hungry soul who came to my door."

When the man cleared his throat loudly, all of us looked back at him. With a nod, he stood up and reached into one of the pockets on his pants. As he gave each of my little sisters some peppermint candy, he said, "Thank you, ma'am, I sure do appreciate your great kindness. I'll be going now."

Walking out the back door, the man waved for me to follow him.

Before he got on his horse, he handed me his rifle, and a box of ammunition that he took out of his saddlebag. With a smile, he said, "Boy, see if you can get your mama a rabbit or a possum for supper tonight."

I was shocked! Words escaped me! I just stood and watched the man as he got on his horse and road away.

When I walked back into the house, Mama was clearing the table. Under the old pie tin, that the man had been eating from, we found ten gold coins lying on the table. Mama didn't look the least bit surprised, but I was shocked! I'd never seen that much money in my whole life!

I showed her the rifle, and the ammunition, and told her what the man had said. She didn't look surprised by that either.

"Did you know him, Mama?" I asked, with great curiosity.

With a nod, Mama answered, "Haven't seen him in years, but that was Ann Parker's son, Robert."

Our September visitor was none other than Robert LeRoy Parker.

Oh…you might know him as Butch Cassidy…the outlaw. But I will always remember him as a gentleman who traded a rifle and ten gold coins for some watered down beans and two pieces cornbread.

Like the hawk on the fence post he had a fierce reputation, but he was quiet and gentle.

Bonus 2:

Cowboy Church Sermons[5] by
Prescott Parson AKA Rik Danielsen

---

5 These are sermons I was privileged to preach at the Cowboy Church of the Yavapai Range Wars hosted by the Arizona Yavapai Rangers, a Cowboy Action Shooting club in the Verde Valley of Arizona.

CHAPTER 13:
THE VERY DEFINITION OF SIN

ROMANS 3:23

What would you say is the most famous gunfight of the Old West? Would you agree that probably more people have heard about the Gunfight at the OK Corral than any other gunfight in the history of the Old West? Even though the gunfight didn't actually happen at the OK Corral, it is still very famous.

One of the questions about that gunfight was who fired the first shot? I've read articles and seen TV shows on the subject and different ones are named as the ones who fired the first shot. Here's one thing that is without dispute—Wyatt Earp emerged unscathed. Not one bullet hit or even nicked Wyatt that day. As a matter of fact, Wyatt Earp was never wounded in a gunfight. Never. His clothes were riddled with bullet holes at least once and I'm told that his saddle got shot, but Wyatt never knew what it was like to be shot by a bullet.

It's interesting that Wyatt was not in as many gunfights as people might imagine. There were times he settled a problem by cracking a cowboy's skull with the barrel of his Colt or stood off some trouble makers with a double barreled shotgun. However, when he was in a gunfight he knew how to handle his six shooter. But again, no one ever shot Wyatt.

Do you know what the very definition of sin is? It is "missing the mark". In both the Old Testament Hebrew and the New Testament Greek, the original words that are translated "sin" mean "to miss the mark".

Think about those people who tried to kill Wyatt Earp. They all missed the mark. Some of them came closer than others, but they still missed the mark. Shooting a hole in a man's coat, hat or saddle won't kill him or stop the fight.

Listen to what the Bible says:

For all have sinned, and come short of the glory of God.

(Romans 3:23)

How many of us does it say have sinned? All of us. Yesterday and today we've been shooting this Cowboy Action match. Some have been skilled or lucky enough to shoot a clean match so far, but all of us know what it's like to miss a target. That's the very definition of sin.

But the Bible isn't really talking about us missing targets in a Cowboy Action match. The Bible says we all fall short of God's glory. God is the very standard of perfection and none of us live up to it because we all inherited a spiritual gene called sin. By nature we are sinners and as a result we all sin.

Let me ask you to think about one other verse from the Bible:

For the wages of sin is death;
but the gift of God is eternal life through Jesus Christ our Lord.
(Romans 6:23)

We all know what wages are. It's what you earn when you do a job. If we choose to remain in our sin, the Bible says we will get what we've earned – eternal death. But we can choose to receive God's gift, the gift of eternal life through the person of Jesus Christ. Did you notice that the gift is free? You can't earn it; you can only receive it through repentance and faith.

Conclusion: Wyatt Earp went on to live a long life. He died just shy of his 81st birthday in Los Angeles, CA. He was the last surviving Earp brother and the last survivor of the shootout at the OK Corral. No one ever shot Wyatt. He died of natural causes, but the fact is he died.

I would not presume to know Wyatt's eternal destiny. I am not God and only God knows that about Wyatt. Here's what I do know based on the clear teaching of the Bible, for those who are Christ's followers, salvation, which includes eternal life is a gift from Almighty God.

CHAPTER 14:
THE TALE OF TWO COWBOYS

2 CORINTHIANS 5:17

Today I want to tell you the tale of two real cowboys. These men had some things in common, but their lives took very different directions.

The first is a man who was born James Brown Miller also known as Deacon Jim Miller or Killer Jim Miller. Jim was born in 1861 in Arkansas, but his family moved to Texas when he was very young.

Jim was outwardly a very clean cut church going man. He didn't smoke or drink. He dressed well and eventually married and raised a family. He also attended the Methodist Church on a regular basis. That's how he got the nick name "deacon".

Outwardly Jim was the epitome of an upstanding citizen, but he was what I would call a serial killer.

Some people believe that Jim murdered his own grandparents, but that was never proven. Here's what we do know, Jim Miller's brother-in-law was killed by a shotgun blast while he was sleeping in his bed. Jim hated his brother-in-law and was arrested for the murder, convicted and sentenced to life in prison. As was often the case in those days, Jim's lawyer was able to appeal the case and got him off on a technicality.

Jim's exploits as both a criminal and at times a law man are too numerous for us to recount today. We can say this, however, he became so proficient at killing folks that he decided to become a murderer for hire. At first he only charged $50 for a killing, but later was getting as much as $2000 for a murder. Imagine doing something you loved and getting paid for it.

At one time he worked for Sheriff Bud Frazer in Pecos, TX. It appeared that Miller and his friends were actually using his position to help them rustle cattle. At one point Miller murdered a Mexican prisoner because he was attempting to escape. It was learned however that the Mexican knew that Miller had stolen some mules and knew where they were hidden. Miller was fired.

He and Bud Frazer had a feud that included several gun fights and eventually Miller took his favorite firearm, a double barreled shotgun and killed Frazer. He was acquitted because Frazer had tried to kill him earlier. Evidently, that made it ok.

Ultimately, Miller was hired to kill retired US Deputy Marshall Gus Bobbitt. Miller and three co-conspirators were arrested and placed in the Ada, Oklahoma jail. The good folks of Ada were sick and tired of murderers getting off and took the men from the jail and hung them in a nearby barn. Before he died, Miller claimed the actual number of murders he had committed was 51. That number cannot be confirmed, but the fact is that he did kill a number of Mexicans along the border, which may have been how the number became so big.

Deacon Jim Miller, a church goer and a cold blooded murderer.

Let me tell you about the first real cowboy I ever knew. He was born Solly Robert McLeroy, but he went by Bob. Bob was born and raised in West Texas. His parents were the town atheists. In those days Texas had blue laws that made it illegal to work on Sunday, so his father worked on the back side of the ranch on Sunday so no one would see him. Bob's daddy told him that only a slicker would wear a short sleeved shirt, so Bob never wore a short sleeved shirt in his life.

In those days they drove their cows to the railroad through the poor part of town. When the little children came out to watch, Bob would pull his gun and shoot at their feet to make them dance. He told me the only thing he couldn't do was chew tobacco and drink whiskey at the same time.

Bob also told me he had planned to commit murder. He never told me what the man had done he was going to kill, but he was going to kill a man. He set a date for the murder, but God intervened.

Some one had shared the gospel with Bob and he started going to church. One Sunday night, exactly two weeks before he was planning to commit murder, Bob gave his life to Christ and Jesus took the murder out of his heart. Bob told me he was only a layman for thirty minutes because God called him to preach on his way home from the service where he got saved.

He only had a sixth grade education, but Wayland Baptist College admitted him to study for the ministry. He studied for one semester and got straight A's, but God called him to the mission field. Bob spent the rest of his life going to places where there weren't any Baptist churches. He would win the people and build the buildings. It was in one of those churches that Bob baptized me and became my pastor.

I could tell you many other things about Brother Bob, but suffice it to say he knew as much about the Bible as any PhD I ever met. He was the finest Christian man I've ever known.

What made the difference between Deacon Jim Miller and Brother Bob McLeroy? Here's what the Bible says:

Therefore if any man be in Christ, he is a new creature: old things are passed away; behold, all things are become new.

(2 Corinthtians 5:17)

What made the difference?

One man had a form of religion that didn't change his life. He was able to murder others with no apparent regrets.

The other man was raised without a knowledge of the Bible, but he had an encounter with the living Christ that changed him from a man with murder in his heart to a man who loved others and would do anything to spread the life changing gospel that had changed his life.

If you would like to know more about that gospel, I'd be glad to talk to you after the service.